# Everything I Wanted

ALSO BY ALESHA DYKEMA

STANDALONES

If She's Found

Everything I Wanted

# EVERYTHING I WANTED

ALESHA DYKEMA

JOFFE BOOKS

Revised edition 2025
Joffe Books, London
www.joffebooks.com

First published by Brandywine Publishing in USA in 2023

This paperback edition was first published
in Great Britain in 2025



Cover art by Nick Castle

ISBN: 978-1-80573-055-2

*For Brooks and Ryan*
*Everything I do is for you.*

# CHAPTER ONE

*"When I saw you, I fell in love. And you smiled because you knew."*
— *Arrigo Boito*

There isn't a soul I wouldn't sell, a person I wouldn't kill, or a dick I wouldn't suck to trade places with one of these women. With their perfectly aligned teeth and hair as smooth as the silk pillowcases they sleep on. I slide two plastic cups of coffee, dairy-free milk, and processed sugar across the countertop that is meant to be used as a surface but acts more as a barrier, separating the fortunate from the *un*.

Part of the reason I started working here was to be close to them. As though some of their status and good luck might transfer from their hand to mine in the exchange of their oat milk lattes.

"Thank you so much," says the brunette wearing a dress that likely cost more than my car.

I smile, keeping my teeth tucked behind my lips, and nod. "Have a great day."

The woman spins, moving toward the door, and sends a breeze of her shampoo over me. The lemony scent doesn't mix well with the smells of the café — coffee, baked goods, and rosemary. I watch her leave and wonder where she will go next. Maybe to work at the university a few miles away? Or the theater?

Café Rêvasser is an upscale coffee house with professional bakers, overly trained baristas, and a reputation for being the place to hang out if you're any kind of artist worth knowing and in downtown Indianapolis. It is the hub of the creatives in the Midwest who have been able to turn their passions into a lucrative career.

I only ever intended to work here until my own creative ventures got me to the other side of this counter. I foolishly believed that this place held a kind of magic that could be breathed in, absorbed like two-hundred-dollar moisturizer.

But it's been three years.

The only thing this place has ever given me is a subpar paycheck and an expanding waistline, thanks to a never-ending supply of world-class pastries. Not to mention a crushing realization that not everyone gets what they want.

My shift started two hours ago. I miss my night shifts. I must've pissed the manager off because he switched me to mornings a couple of months ago and never switched me back.

I take a sip of espresso while there is a lull in customers, trying to wake up. It's just about seven a.m., and there are already people occupying most of the tables in the café.

I watch two women in the far corner gathering up their things to leave. One woman wears a mid-length black dress with heels, her hair perfectly wavy. I wonder what time she has to wake up to look like that this early.

I imagine she's a literary agent meeting with a new author. She'll rush from here to another meeting on the other side of the city before going home to her doting husband in their two-story home in Meridian Hills. Of course, she could never afford the home on her own salary, but her husband will be an executive at a publishing house, making top dollar so she can pursue her passion.

I'm drawn out of my daydreaming by the feeling of eyes on me. Glancing over my shoulder, I see that I'm right.

Donna has caught me staring again, and she wears the same irritating expression she always does when I stare off. She follows my line of sight to the women packing up at the table in the corner.

I turn away, busying myself with restocking cups because I don't want to hear it. She tsks and sucks her teeth, the sound of which warms my blood with irritation. "Those folks aren't nothin' to worship, Laura."

Attempting to ignore her, I pull another stack of plastic cups from a plastic sleeve, cursing the idiotic do-gooders that think their war on plastic straws makes any kind of difference.

Donna doesn't take the hint and continues lecturing me. "They ain't perfect. Everyone's got their shit. Trust me."

I don't know what makes her think I would trust her with anything other than making a coffee, but I stand and face her with a tight-lipped smile. "I know, Donna. I was just spacing off."

She gives me a look like she knows I'm lying, but she doesn't know shit. She mistakes my interest in these people for worship. I don't worship them. I envy them.

Donna turns to the back counter, fetching her purse from a cabinet. "I'm gonna grab a smoke while there's no line. Holler if you need me."

I nod and watch her wide, lumpy frame totter toward the back door. Donna is a middle-aged woman with dirty blonde hair. And I don't mean dirty as in the color. I mean, if she took her ponytail out, her hair would likely keep its shape. Her clothes are always wrinkled, and the smell of cigarette smoke clings to her like the fabric of her uniform clings to flesh.

The door to the café opens and a group of women stream in. I stand at the register and wear the big fake smile that is just as much a part of my uniform as the ill-fitting brown apron they make me wear. Both of which I can't wait to take off. Four more hours.

I sense Donna back behind me, or rather, smell her. The slamming of the cabinet door confirms her presence. As I finish tapping the last of the orders into the computer screen, I turn around, attempting to help her prepare the orders. But she has a line of cups on the back counter and systematically pumps syrup, shovels ice, and pours non-dairy milk into their respective cups.

I suppose when you can make ten custom coffee orders in under a minute, they let you get away with neglecting basic hygiene.

When the women take their coffees and glide over to a table, Donna leans against the front counter, her back to the door. "What does everyone have against regular milk these days?"

I shrug. "Dairy intolerances."

She rolls her eyes and pushes off the counter. "People are pussies these days."

I cringe at her word choice. I hate that word. It's gross. Like her.

"I haven't seen that boyfriend of yours in a while. Tell him not to be a stranger."

"He started a new job," I say too quickly. "He won't be able to come by on morning shifts anymore."

"Well, that's a shame. He sure was nice to look at."

I sense my cheeks reddening, so I turn back to the register. The café door opens yet again, and I prepare myself to take another coffee order. My stomach does a little flip when I see the man walking toward me. He's tall. Dark hair. He wears a dark pair of jeans with a brown jacket. I feel my face flush like I often do when in close proximity to attractive people.

"Hi, what can I get for you?"

"Hello" — he glances down at my name tag — "Laura. I'll take a large dark roast. Black." He smiles, revealing perfect teeth. His voice is as deep and smooth as the coffee he's about to drink.

"Hot or iced?"

"Hot, please."

"Sure, no problem. $6.25."

He goes for his wallet in his back pocket, and I use the moment to admire his face. When he hands me his card, I sneak a look at the name while swiping it in the card reader. Theo Connor.

"Nevermore?" he says as I hand him back his card.

"Huh?" I look up to meet his eyes, but his eyes are focused on my shirt.

"Nevermore. It's a terrible guess, but it's my best one." He laughs.

My chest fills with heat. He's talking about the button on my apron that reads "What did they yell at Edgar Allan Poe as he walked into a tree?"

"Poe, a tree," I say. "Poetry."

He lets out a laugh, immediately getting the joke.

I smile. "It's a lame joke, but I saw it at the bookstore and had to get it."

His eyes cut to mine, and I look at the register. I can't quite pull in a breath. "It's funny," he says. "Cute."

"Thanks."

Donna leans into the counter, sliding his coffee across it. "Here you go, sir. Have a great day."

He nods at her. "You too, thank you. Have a good rest of your day, Laura." He turns and walks to the door, and I slowly exhale.

"Wow, he was a hottie, huh?" Donna nudges me and knocks me to the side. I grit my teeth, catching my balance.

"Yeah," I say.

"He had his eye on you. Should have asked for his number."

I roll my eyes. "I have a boyfriend, remember?"

She shrugs and walks away, presumably going out through the back door for another cigarette.

Theo Connor.

Just the sound of his name sends shivers down my spine. Who is he? Café Rêvasser is known for being an artist hotspot, but normal people wander in too. He didn't look like an artist. A novelist maybe. Or someone who works in the industry.

The urge to look him up online is a physical pull. My hands feel restless, itching for my phone in my back pocket. We're not supposed to leave the register unattended. I peek down the hall that leads to the back, but there's no sign of Donna.

I glance between the front door and down the hallway once more before deciding to bolt for the bathroom. Fuck it. This is her second smoke break in the last hour.

Slamming the door, I click the lock on the handle. I pull out my phone and sit on the toilet lid. I need to know more about Theo Connor.

## CHAPTER TWO

*"I was never really insane except on occasions when my heart was touched." — Edgar Allan Poe*

A cursory search of Theo Connor's name turns up only a few results. The first is a staff member page for Holloway University, the college I graduated from six long years ago. I moved to Indianapolis to attend because their writing program is unmatched. I fell in love with the city and never went back home. Not that I ever intended to anyway.

I scroll through the small thumbnails, and my pulse quickens when I finally see Theo's name and picture. He's listed as an English professor, and I know it's fate.

He certainly wasn't a professor when I was there. He must be newer.

I go back to the search results and click the next link. It takes me to a Facebook profile, but the picture looks nothing like him, so I go back again. The remaining results are websites and such that I need more time to sort through. I lock my phone and shove it back into my pocket as I exit the bathroom.

I stop in my tracks, a wave of heat rising from the pit of my stomach when I see the scene unfolding at the counter. A dozen annoyed-looking people stand in a broken line as Donna flies from one end of the drink station to the other making coffees, and Brice, my manager, sweaty with nostrils flaring, stands at the register taking orders and jabbing at the touchscreen.

I will myself into motion and hustle back behind the counter. "I can take over," I say, saving my defense for when the rush of customers has been taken care of.

He steps aside and lets me finish the order, disappearing to the back of the café. My stomach is in knots as I try to move through the orders as quickly and apologetically as I can. But I was gone for less than five minutes, and I can't help the rising feeling of annoyance with both the customers and my manager for being irritated by my brief bathroom break.

"Whew!" Donna says when the last of the waiting customers have retreated from the counter, caffeine in hand. "Gotta love the late morning rush."

"How long was Brice up here before I came back?"

"Probably a good seven, eight minutes." She leans against the counter and her hips widen with the pressure.

"I wasn't even gone for five minutes," I snap.

She makes a face. Shakes her head. "No. You were gone when I got back, and I was up here alone for a few minutes before he came in and the rush hit."

I sigh. Whatever. She takes a break every thirty minutes. I took one. The entire day. They can fuck off.

I start performing my end-of-shift duties to pass the rest of the time and distract myself from being angry. I clean pitchers and blenders, restock cups, and grab a towel and spray bottle to wipe down the tables.

I move to the garbage cans and pull them from their containers before sorting through the bulletin board that sits above the cans. People come in and pin different things on the board. Mostly advertisements for services. They tend to be things like editorial services, website design, and audio remastering. The occasional headshots for actors or models, but those are rare — it's Indianapolis, not Hollywood.

I take down the ones I know have been up at least a month and the ones advertising things with deadlines that have passed. Then I reorganize what's left. A summer special on a photography package, an advertisement for a personal chef for hire, and a missing persons poster.

We get a few of them every couple of months. This one shows the face of a young woman, college age. She's smiling and looking off to the side like she didn't know the picture was being taken. It strikes me as a genuinely candid shot, not the ones taken to look candid. I've seen her posters before.

She's been missing for quite a while, but a girl comes in every other month with a new poster for us to pin on the board. Always a new picture of the same girl. It's sad that she's missing, but how nice that someone cares enough to keep creating new posters to put around town. I take the bags of garbage out back and wonder if anyone would put up posters for me.

The sun is in the center of the sky when I finally leave work. I don't make it a block before I'm sweating through my shirt. My hair sticks to the back of my neck, and I pull my hair tie off my wrist and start wrapping it around my hair. As I pull the strands through the last time, I hear a snap and the tension disappears. My hair falls back onto my back.

I clutch the broken hair tie in my fist and whip it to the ground, fighting back tears of frustration. This day needs to be over. I practically stomp the remaining two blocks to the parking garage that Café Rêvasser pays for me to park in.

The rest of my shift was a nightmare. Brice left the café an hour before me, face pinched, and with a clipped tone he told 'us' to make sure someone stayed behind the counter at all times.

I wanted to tell him that Donna took breaks more than she worked, but she was standing right beside me, and I'm not trying to make enemies with the person I have to spend a large portion of my week with.

The back of my silver Honda pokes out from a line of cars, with a large dent and yellow paint on the bumper from the time I backed into a fire hydrant. It's impossible to miss.

I climb into the sauna-like vehicle and crank the windows down, then blast the air conditioning. A hot gust of air smacks into me. Cursing under my breath, I jab my finger at the dash to turn it off and begin backing out.

After a few minutes of driving with the windows open, I begin to cool down. My bad mood eases just enough for me to remember the part of the day that didn't suck. Theo Connor.

The anticipation of looking at the rest of his search results has me pressing my foot a little harder on the accelerator. The drive home feels even longer than usual.

I step through my apartment's front door and climb the three flights of stairs to the top. I'm winded by the time I reach my door and make a mental note to look into gyms in the area.

The more I think about my encounter with Theo Connor, the more self-conscious I feel. I go to the bathroom and cringe at my reflection. My mousy brown hair: flat and frizzy. My skin: oily and broken out. And I'm looking rounder and softer than I ever have. I know I've gained a bit of weight, but looking at myself as someone else might see me makes me realize it's a lot more than I thought. I slap at the light switch to cast the image of myself into darkness and go back to the living room.

My apartment is far from aesthetically pleasing. It isn't the type of place you'd show off on Instagram, with the ripped couch, cracked kitchen tiles, and wood floors that look as though someone tore up the carpet and stopped mid-project rather than a design choice. It isn't much. But it's all I can afford without a roommate. And I refuse to have a roommate. So instead, I live farther out of the downtown area, in a neighborhood that isn't as nice or as safe, in a building that should probably be condemned.

I plop onto my secondhand couch and grab my laptop from the side table. First, I open Facebook and type Ethan's name into the search bar. We were dating for six months before he broke up with me. He went from surprise visits to see me at work to ignoring my calls and texts in what felt like overnight.

Two days after texting me that he didn't want to see me anymore, he was tagged in a picture on Facebook. He was in a bar with a few friends that I'd met before, sitting on a barstool, a redhead standing between his knees.

But now, his profile doesn't show up when I search for him. He's blocked me.

I slam the lid of my laptop, annoyed and offended. Taking a minute to cool down, I go to the kitchen and pour myself a glass of red wine. After a long drink and a deep breath, I go back to the couch and to Facebook. I log out of my account and type in another email and password. It logs me into the account of Sarah Frazier. The fake profile I made a year ago. I search for Ethan's name again and his profile is the first listed.

A burst of adrenaline pulses through my fingertips as I click to message Ethan.

> *Hey! Totally don't mean to be creepy, but I'm pretty sure you're in Mr. Philbern's 1800s Lit class with me? I missed today and was wondering if you could send me the notes?? THANKS!*

Ethan went to college in Illinois and moved here for an IT job. But Sarah is a senior at Holloway University, and I've found it's the best way to strike up a conversation with someone. Pretend to mistake them for someone in my class. They'll correct me, apologize (for what, I don't know), but they almost always attempt to continue the conversation. Because Sarah is young and attractive and bubbly.

After I hit send, I browse the girl's profile whose pictures I borrow for the Sarah profile. She posts new pictures often, and I save them to my computer and upload them to Sarah's Facebook. It's important to update her profile often so it looks legitimate.

The man from the café pops into my head.

I consider myself decently skilled at the art of online stalking, but Theo Connor has somehow kept much of his life offline in this digital age. He has no social media profiles that I can find, and besides his staff photo, the web doesn't seem to have anything else to offer.

I'm about to close the window and admit defeat when I spot something on the third page of my search. It's an obituary for someone named Don Connor. It lists Theo Connor as a surviving grandson. I read through the posting and then search Don Connor's name. Surprisingly, I get a few more results than I did for Theo.

I click through some of the results, mostly local articles about donations made by the Connor family to various foundations, causes, and to Holloway University. It seems their family comes from a long line of supremely successful businesses. The most prominent, and lucrative, being Connor Consultants INC., which is still operational today. It looks like Theo's great-grandfather founded the firm right here in Indianapolis.

I keep digging through articles and conclude that Theo Connor and his family are basically Indianapolis royalty. Their donations have helped build half the city.

And yet . . . Theo is an English professor. Not part of his family business. I am thoroughly intrigued.

* * *

Morning comes far too soon. I can barely keep my eyes open as I drive to the parking garage. The sun isn't yet up, and I find it a bit ridiculous that I have to be. I miss my night shifts.

I spend the morning helping my co-worker with opening duties and thanking God Donna is off today. I can't, for the life of me, remember the girl's name, but she's quiet and much easier to be around.

After I've had my second shot of espresso, I perk up a bit.

"Can you watch the counter while I run to the bathroom real fast?" I ask the girl when I finish tapping in the order for the last waiting customer.

"Sure," she says.

I hurry to the bathroom and check myself over in the mirror. It's around the time Theo came in yesterday, and I don't want to miss him. I smooth down my hair, grab the lip gloss I stuffed in my pocket this morning, swipe it across my lips, and run back to the counter.

I scan the café, but he's not here. I really hope he comes back today. I haven't been able to think of much else since our encounter yesterday. I pace the small space behind the counter and wipe my clammy palms on my apron.

A crowd of women approaches the glass door and I sigh, deflating when I don't see Theo among the crowd. I put on my big smile and prepare to take their orders as they gather around the register. I type in the first order, and when I look up to confirm she's done ordering, I see him.

I try not to look at him, but he is magnetic. My eyes keep straying past the brunette telling me her order, and when Theo's eyes meet mine, I fight back a grin, but lose the battle. The side of his mouth lifts, and my own smile stretches wider. So much so that the woman glances behind her to see what's going on.

"Medium cold brew with sugar-free vanilla and a strawberry Danish. Anything else?" I say to get her attention back to me.

"That's all."

I tap it into the computer and take the remaining two orders. When Theo steps to the register, I have to remind myself to breathe.

"What a pleasant surprise," he says. "I was hoping you'd be working today."

"I'm here most days. It's harder to miss me than to catch me." I cringe internally, wondering if I made myself sound stupid.

"Good to know. I was at a bookstore downtown last night and saw this and thought of you." He pulls something from the inner pocket of his jacket and hands it to me.

I glide my fingers over the smooth surface of a metal button like the Edgar Allan Poe one on my apron as I read what it says.

*"Nevermind" — A passive aggressive raven.*

I laugh. "I love it. Thank you." I button it onto my apron, grinning like a schoolgirl.

"I'm glad you like it."

Still smiling, I remember to do my job. "What will you be having today?"

I type in his coffee order, the same large black coffee. The girl making drinks starts pouring coffee into the cup for him, and I say a silent thank you that Donna isn't here.

"Have a wonderful rest of your day, Laura," Theo says, taking his coffee and turning toward the door.

# CHAPTER THREE

*"From childhood's hour I have not been as others were. I have not seen as others saw . . . And all I loved, I loved alone." — Edgar Allan Poe*

I wipe down the already spotless counters for the third time. We haven't had a customer in almost an hour, and we have officially run out of things to do. I feel the need to keep busy, keep my hands moving to distract my brain. The incident with Brice the other day has me on edge, afraid to look like I'm slacking off.

Although, the edginess I feel could be the text I got last night from my mother. Her texts always make me tense, but the invitation to dinner that felt more like a subpoena filled my gut with a heavy dread.

"I'm gonna have a smoke," Donna calls over her shoulder as she leaves the front counter.

I sigh. Maybe I should take up smoking. Apparently, it's the only way you can take a break around here. The door opens and I perk up, eager to finally have a distraction. But my stomach drops when I see Theo Connor. Not in a bad way, but in the way you feel right as you begin a steep downhill on a rollercoaster. The panicked excitement of the freefall.

He smiles as he approaches the counter. "You again."

"Me again." I smile back at him. "How's your day so far?" I ask, forcing myself to be brave as I tap his order that I have memorized into the computer.

"I can't complain, but far better now. Caffeine and a pretty face have been known to improve a man's day by at least sixty percent."

I laugh and turn to make his coffee. "Well, mine wasn't going great. But a compliment from a handsome man has been known to improve a woman's day by at least thirty percent."

"Only thirty?"

I turn back to him, lower my brows, and slide his coffee across the counter. "Oh, yes. It takes a lot more than a compliment to keep a woman happy." I grin, and he holds my stare. My breath hitches in my chest at the hungry glint in his eyes.

"I've always liked a challenge." He takes a sip of his coffee, never breaking eye contact. "I hope your day improves another seventy percent. I'll see you later, Laura."

He turns and walks out, and I stand in silence, watching him. I press my fingers to my cheeks, feeling their heat, and then smile goofily like a teenage girl. With no one in the café to witness, I even do a little spin.

A noise in the back prompts me to get a handle on myself, and a moment later, Donna is back. "Anything exciting happen while I was gone?"

"Nope," I say, still smiling but not turning toward her so she can't see my face.

"This place is getting so slow lately."

"We had that big rush the other day." I turn to her now and lean against the register.

She makes a sound like a grunt. "That wasn't nothin'. It's been getting slower every year. I think it's the prices."

I shrug. "This is a high-end café. It's kind of the point."

"Gonna be a bankrupt café if they can't get more people in here."

I repress the urge to roll my eyes, and I wipe down the counters again.

I search for more distractions when I get home. Usually, I enjoy having the rest of the day after a morning shift, but there is too much time between now and dinner with my family. It looms ahead of me like a death sentence.

Theo Connor is a worthy distraction. I pull out my laptop and click on the open tab of his search results.

I still can't find much about him, but I keep reading articles about his great-grandparents. My fingers pick idly at the tear in my couch cushion as I learn about them. It makes me feel closer to him. I know his history. Where he comes from. I know all about the generations that came before him, and I want to know more. Everything.

My phone alarm belts out a loud chime that tells me it's time to get ready for tonight's dinner. I run through the shower and get changed into my nice jeans and a flowy black shirt. It's a little too hot for jeans, but my shorts are less forgiving and just a little too tight right now.

My parents live in Wolcott. The hour-and-a-half drive is only part of the reason I don't see them often. As I cross the street to my car parked on the curb, I search through my phone for a podcast to listen to. I need something to get invested in for the long drive. I tried audiobooks once, but it felt too millennial. I like my books the old school way. On printed pages.

Moisture hangs thick in the air. The clouds are a silky gray, too light to actually rain so the humidity will probably hang around through the night. I can't find a podcast that catches my attention, and I'm not in the mood for music. I toss my phone into the passenger seat, sighing, resigned to drive in silence.

I turn the key in the ignition, and my '95 Honda sputters to life. It sounds like an old, rusted lawn mower, and I hate the way the sound makes nearby people look over at me. I put the car into drive and ease off the brake, crawling onto the road and making my way to the highway. A car pulls out in front of me, and I slam on my brakes, swearing. The black sedan speeds up, only to be stopped at a red light just ahead of me.

I stop behind him and glance at the license plate. Of course. "Fucking Illinois drivers," I mumble.

I pull into my parents' driveway far too soon. I force myself out of the car the moment I shift into park so I don't work myself up again. The window to the left of the door glows a warm yellow in the darkening night. It frames the dining room table, and I stop, watching my family.

My mother, always full of anger or elation. She knows no middle ground. My father sits at the far end of the table, staring off like he usually does. Never mentally in the room he's in. His too-thin arms poke out of a blue T-shirt, knobby elbows resting on the table. My sisters are engaged in conversation. I can hear their muffled voices through the glass. Bethany throws her head back, laughing like a maniac. Shelby throws her arms in the air.

They all talk and laugh comfortably, and I bite back the feeling that always creeps up when I'm around them. They always seemed to fit with each other, and I always stood off to the side like a puzzle piece that got thrown into the wrong box.

Walking up and knocking on the door feels like an intrusion, but I rap my knuckles against the weather-worn front door. Bethany, my youngest sister, answers the door.

"Hey, you're late," she says.

I press the button on the side of my phone I'm clutching. It's 6:53.

"No, I'm not."

"Well, everyone else is here."

"You all live here." I walk through the door and step on the backs of my shoes to get them off, my annoyance already mounting.

"There she is!" my mother shouts.

"I'm seven minutes early," I say defensively, with irritation clear in my voice.

"What's the matter with you?" she says. All her features pinch together, and I try to backpedal. I'm not in the mood for an all-out battle, and her temper has always burned hotter than mine. It's how she wins arguments. So long as she's the angriest, she is in the right.

"Nothing, it was just an awful drive in. Sorry."

Her face immediately softens. "Oh, no. Was there traffic on 65?"

"Yeah. Construction has it backed up again." I exhale, relieved I've avoided a fight.

My dad chimes in. "They never finish that construction. I never see anyone out there either."

I shake my head and walk through to the kitchen where two boxes of greasy pizza sit on the stove. Dinner has always been fast food. Help yourself. I open the first box to find cheese pizza. Shelby's preference. The rest of them eat pepperoni, so I can guess what the other box is. I open it anyway to check. Yep. I curl my nose at the small, round greasy things and take a slice of Shelby's pizza. The slice falls limply when I move it to my plate, and I consider passing on the food. I prefer sausage, but I can't remember them once getting the option I preferred. I'm supposed to be getting into better shape anyway.

But it isn't worth the line of questioning and disapproving sneers I'll get if I tell them I don't want the pizza, so I take my plate back to the table.

Shelby and Bethany are talking about some television show I've never heard of, and my mother is leaning in, asking them questions about it. I tune them out, looking across the table at my dad. He's staring off, and I wonder if he sometimes feels as out of place as I do.

I watch his eyes focus in, and I know he's mentally back in the room. He turns and sees me looking at him. "Laura, you still working at the coffee place?"

"The café. Yeah, I am."

Disappointment spreads across his face, though I can tell he's trying not to show it. He exhales a little too loudly. "You applying anywhere else?"

"No. I like my job. It gives me time to write." It's not entirely the truth. I don't like my job. But I won't admit it to him. Especially in the middle of his 'you're a disappointment' talks.

"You've been there for years. Writing doesn't pay your bills. You gotta have a backup plan. You're damn near thirty years old. You need a job with benefits and good pay."

You need to, you haven't, you, you, you.

My pulse throbs in my head, and I resist the urge to cover my ears with my hands like a child. But that's exactly what they make me feel like every time I'm in this house. A bad child.

My mother and siblings, who have been lost in their own conversation, are now engrossed in ours, and I can feel the heat spreading up my chest and across my face. "Can we please just not talk about this?" I snap.

My youngest sister has never had a job for longer than a month, and Shelby works at a department store folding clothes, yet I'm the one getting torn into. They'll call it 'tough love.' But I've never felt loved by them. And without the love, it's just being an asshole.

Bethany resumes talking to Shelby, bored with me and my verbal lashing.

They're all bored with me, apparently, because they go on talking as if I'm not there. Discussing things they know I know nothing about. Talking about things that happened when I wasn't here. Why was I even invited?

"I need to find some boxes tomorrow so I can start packing," says Bethany.

"Jeremy doesn't have any extra?" Mom asks.

"I'll ask him, but I don't think so."

I do not know who Jeremy is. I'm assuming her newest boyfriend. But I'm confused on why they both need boxes. "Are you guys moving in together?" I ask.

Bethany nods emphatically. "Our offer was accepted on a house in town."

I choke on a small bite of pizza. "You guys bought a house together?"

Her brows pull in, forming a line down the center. "Yes."

I nod, unable to keep the disbelief from my face. I don't know why I'm shocked. I've always known her to be an idiot. And it's just like my parents to go along with it.

I know little about Bethany's personal life, because I'm not at all interested. But I do know she was single on Christmas, which was seven months ago. She wouldn't stop complaining about it over dinner. I consider myself a romantic. I understand the quick rush of love. But Bethany isn't smart. And she's young. Too young to be buying houses with some guy.

"What is that look for?" Bethany says.

"What look? I just didn't know you were seeing anyone. Let alone buying houses with them." I take another nibble from my pizza.

"Why would you? You know nothing about me, so keep your opinions to yourself." Her face is screwed up, and her eyes shine with tears ready to fall.

"I didn't say anything!"

"Laura, stop!" Mom snaps. "That's enough. I don't know why you come over here just to cause problems."

My mouth hangs open. "What problems am I causing? I didn't say anything. And you invited me here. I didn't just show up."

"Yeah, well, I'll think better of that next time."

I wince. The sting of her words making my face heat up again.

"This is a happy time for your sister, and you're making it about you because you can't control your jealousy for one dinner." She is practically baring her teeth at me, white spit gathering in the corners of her mouth.

"Jealousy?" I laugh. "You have got to be kidding me. How could I be jealous of people who fucking disgust me?" I stand from the table, chair grinding against the wood beneath it, and rush for the door.

I hate them. With everything I have, I hate them. My breaths are coming in too fast and too shallow. My chest burns with a fury I haven't felt in a while. It's still humid, and it feels like the air is closing in on me.

I walk to my car and slam the door. I need to be back home. In the city and away from the ignorant hicks that I somehow share DNA with. I remember being convinced I was adopted. Even the striking resemblance between my mother and me couldn't persuade me I'd actually come from her.

The thought of going back to my shitty apartment by myself is crushing. I spend the entire drive trying to think of someone I could text to hang out somewhere but come up empty. Ethan has blocked me on everything. There is a girl I've hung out with a few times, but she's been busy the last few times I've asked to get together, so I don't want to ask again.

I turn down my street but keep driving past my apartment. I drive twenty minutes to the east side of the city and find a place to park down a side street. The air conditioning in my car still isn't working right, so my clothes stick to my damp skin. I walk to my favorite bench and get comfortable.

His light is off. I check the time on my phone. 9:52 p.m. He's usually awake until at least midnight. We'd bonded over being night owls the night we met at a bar downtown. He spent the evening telling me about the app he was helping develop for smart homes. I didn't understand most of what he said, but I liked that he wanted to impress me.

He must be in the living room then. Maybe his roommate is out of town and he's taking advantage of having the place to himself.

I get up and walk around his building. I've only done this two other times, so I'm a little nervous. But I gather myself and climb the fire escape on the building across from his. He's on the fifth floor, and I'm out of breath and sweating clear through my shirt by the time I reach the top.

The living room light is on. I was right. I sit on the grated metal surface and let my legs dangle over the side. He's leaning against his kitchen island to the right of the living room. It's an open concept like my own, so it's really just one big room.

He's wearing a button up. Which is odd because he usually changes as soon as he gets home. But then I know why. A woman enters the room, exiting the bathroom, I believe. He stands up and hands her a drink. She takes it and smiles but sets it on the counter behind him as she rises on her toes and kisses him.

I watch them through the warm light of the window, like a glowing, moving picture. I watch as she unbuttons his shirt and Ethan bites his lip, gazing at her. I watch him help her out of her too-tight dress. And I watch as he bends her over the arm of the couch. I watch until I am bored and then descend the fire escape stairs.

I expected the sight of Ethan with another woman to bother me. To ignite the rage in my gut like a chemical explosion. But I feel nothing. In fact, the only thing I think about is whether I'll see Theo Connor again tomorrow.

## CHAPTER FOUR

*"I desire the things which will destroy me in the end." — Sylvia Plath*

I know I should sleep. Morning will come far too soon, and I struggle to get out of bed enough as it is. But I can't get into bed after sweating this much. I need a cool shower to rinse the salty film that coats me like a snake-skin.

I pull the shower curtain to the side and twist the knob to turn on the water. But no water comes. I turn the knob off, then on again, like it might make a difference, but the tap remains dry. I don't pay utilities here. It's the reason I can afford an apartment on my own. But I wouldn't be the least bit surprised if Hans, the landlord, forgot to pay the bill. His name always reminded me of a Disney character. But with his greasy, long, gray hair and yellowed teeth, he'd definitely be the villain.

What am I supposed to do now? My skin feels tight with dried sweat, and I feel gross. I go to the kitchen and try the sink, but that doesn't work either. I open the fridge and take out the one bottle of water I have. Grabbing a washcloth from the closet, I wet it with the bottled water and take a whore's bath in my kitchen.

My eyes sting with embarrassment, even though there is no one here to witness my shame. How have I allowed my life to look like this?

I climb into bed and pull out my phone, searching for Theo's name again. When nothing new comes up, I search for his name on every social media platform I can think of. I've done this all before. Of course. But it's like a compulsive tic. I can't help but perform it over and over again.

When I'm satisfied that I can find nothing new, I put my phone on the nightstand and roll onto my back. I close my eyes and listen to the muffled roar of the city through the poorly insulated walls. The constant noise and movement have always been a comfort to me. Filling the silence with life. I drift off to the sounds of distant sirens.

* * *

The next morning, I wake up early to get myself ready for work. The water is still off, and my hair is oily, so I pull it into a slick ponytail. I put on make-up and my best pair of jeans that I normally avoid wearing to work so I don't ruin them.

Today, I will ask Theo for his number. If he comes in.

Despite the very little sleep I got last night and the lack of a shower, I'm bouncing with energy. I could have a date with Theo by the end of the day.

Jess is my partner behind the counter today. I finally remembered her name. She smiles a perfunctory, closed-lip smile and nods as a greeting when I enter the front area. I return the smile and start helping her get everything set up. There isn't much to do. The café opens at the same time my shift starts today, so mostly everything has already been done.

The hours pass slowly as I watch the clock and the door. Each time Theo has come in, it's been late morning. I wonder if that's when he has a break between classes at the university. When eleven o'clock hits, my heart races. Any minute now.

I try to keep still, but I move around the small space, looking for any type of distraction. What if I fuck it up? What if I stutter or come off too eager? What if I have something in my teeth? I run my tongue across them, hoping to dislodge anything that might be there. But I haven't eaten yet today so I should be okay.

The door opens, and I suck in a breath. A small blonde woman enters. I deflate but then see Theo behind her, and I straighten, a smile already spreading across my lips. The woman gets to the counter first, so I do my job and ask what I can get for her.

"A small vanilla latte, please."

"Sure. What kind of milk would you like?"

"Whole milk is fine."

Wow, I almost wish Donna were here to see the first order with whole milk that we've had in ages. "Great. Would that be all?"

"Oh, and a medium dark roast. Black." She pivots and looks back at Theo, who smiles at her. My stomach sinks.

"That'll be $15.53," I say over the lump in my throat.

She hands me her card, and I run my thumb along the protruding letters of her name. Astrid Connor.

Could she be a relative?

I swipe her card.

A sister, maybe?

I extend the card back to her. She takes it with her left hand. A large gold ring with a white diamond stares back at me from her ring finger.

A sister who is married but kept her last name?

But when I look at Theo, his eyes evade mine, and instead he looks down at her, his hand on the small of her back, and I know she is his wife.

I'm too stunned to say anything. To mention to his beautiful, petite wife that her husband likes to flirt with the barista when she isn't here. To ask Theo by what percentage his day has improved today. But the words are all lodged in my throat, weighed down by my heavy heart.

Jess sets the coffee cups on the counter and tells them both to have a great day, but I don't want them to have a good day. I want them to get struck by a bus right outside the café so I can see it. They turn to go, and because I can't look away, I catch Theo's glance back at me. When he sees me looking, he winks.

My mouth falls open. The door shuts behind him, and I can feel Jess's eyes on me, but thankfully, she stays silent.

Theo is married.

I want to run. To the bathroom to hide. Or home to cry. But I'm trapped behind this counter, and I cross my arms over my stomach. How could I be so stupid? Of course Theo has someone. And she's beautiful. I am trash in comparison. I was a fool to think I had a chance with him.

But he *did* flirt with me. He just winked at me, for Christ's sake. What does that mean? That he's looking for an affair? That his marriage is unhappy? They didn't look unhappy. But he looked back. He looked back and winked.

The time drags on and on, and I am on autopilot. I listen only enough to tap orders into the machine and let Jess do the rest. I keep replaying the encounter with Theo and his wife. Over and over, I repeat it in my head and wonder what it means.

Maybe it means nothing. Maybe I'm looking entirely too hard into this. But I can't stop myself.

I couldn't help but notice how nice her ring was. How her black, flowy dress looked expensive.

Theo is the man of my dreams. He is exactly what I've always looked for. With him, I wouldn't be alone anymore. I wouldn't be crushingly poor anymore, either.

The door opening interrupts my thoughts, and I poise myself at the register. But it's just Jackson, the owner. I suppress the urge to scrunch up my nose. He creeps me out. He disappears through the door that leads to the back without so much as a word to Jess and me.

A moment later, his voice is behind me, making me jump. "Laura, can I see you in my office for just a moment?"

"Uh — yeah. Sure." I follow him to the back. I hate being back here. It's a stark contrast to the front of the café. Instead of old wood and natural light, it's linoleum and overhead lights a sickly shade of yellow.

The butterflies in my stomach flap wildly, triggering my gag reflex. I have to fight back the urge to puke. I sit at the black folding chair on the visitor's side of his desk as he does a shuffle to wedge himself behind it. Is this about the other day when Brice came in and I was in the bathroom?

He lets out a breath, and I stare at the beads of sweat forming atop his pink forehead. "Listen, Laura . . ." I hate when people say that. You know I'm listening. There is no need for instructions. "You know, hours have been tight recently. We're just not as busy right now as we are earlier in the year."

I nod, remembering Donna talking about how slow it's been lately.

"Well, upper management has decided it isn't fair to the veteran employees to lose their hours during this slowdown period. So that being said, we're going to have to let you go."

All the butterflies drop dead and plop into the pit of my stomach. Who the fuck is upper management? He owns the place. My ribs seem to contract around my heart as I open my mouth to speak. "What?"

Jackson looks away. "We just don't have the hours."

"I've worked here for three years. Can't you just cut hours?"

He shakes his head. "That wouldn't be fair—"

"But it's fair to fire me?"

He sighs loudly. "Your performance hasn't been great lately. You know, Brice told me about the incident the other day."

"The incident? You mean when I used the bathroom?"

"You were gone for a long time and left the counter unattended."

"Long enough to use the bathroom! Donna takes a smoke break every fifteen minutes. Fire her!"

"You can head out now. We have your address on file. We'll mail you your last check."

I nod, fighting back tears. There is nothing left to say. He's made up his mind. I walk to the front to grab my things. Jess is taking an order but looks over her shoulder when I slam the cabinet shut after retrieving my purse. "Hey, Jess, how long have you worked here?"

"A little over a year," she says, her voice meek and uncertain.

"Well, you're about to get fired. They don't have enough hours for us non-veteran employees." I go around the counter and shove the door open. I look back over my shoulder and shout. "In the event you don't get canned, make sure to never use the fucking bathroom!"

I rush through the door, my chest rising and falling heavily with my breath. Only once I'm in my car do I allow the tears to fall.

How dare he fire me? I'm one of his best employees. The 'veteran' employees are shit. Donna smells like smoke and doesn't know how to use a shower. But she gets to stay because she's been there for nearly a decade.

What am I going to do? Can I file for unemployment? I don't know how any of this works. All I know is, now I have no money coming in and I'm going to end up losing my shitty apartment.

My hands grip the steering wheel, shaking with rage and something like fear. What am I going to do? Café Rêvasser pays far better than the other coffee shops nearby. Maybe I can waitress? It's a similar job. Maybe I can see what I can do with my degree?

I have a bachelor's degree in English and Literature, but I never really intended to be anything other than an author. Café Rêvasser was only ever supposed to be temporary. A way to pay my bills until I got published.

I feel lightheaded as I make my way through my apartment door. I go to my sink and grab a glass, turning the tap on with shaking hands. Nothing happens. The water is still off.

I scream, clutching the glass. I turn and whip it against the far wall, breathing hard as it shatters.

## CHAPTER FIVE

*"Here I opened wide the door; — Darkness there, nothing more." — Edgar Allan Poe*

Sleep won't come. My mind won't rest, and why should it? I am nearly thirty years old and losing a stupid barista job has completely shattered my entire life.

I never imagined I'd be here. When I was eighteen, starting college and naively optimistic, I would have cackled at the idea that I'd one day be thirty years old working as a barista and living in a crumbling apartment with not one book published.

The time just passes too quickly. Eighteen feels like a year ago as opposed to over a decade. How have I let all this time pass and done nothing? Accomplished nothing?

The face of Theo's pretty blonde wife flashes in my mind. It must be nice. To be born pretty and wealthy. To marry someone like Theo and never have to worry about a thing. I bet she lounges around their mansion all day in designer pajamas, living off Theo's family money.

I lie in bed and let the day fade to night and the night fade to day. It feels like days have passed by the time the sun finally comes up on another day.

My rent is due in a week. And without this week on my last paycheck, it won't be enough to cover it.

I force myself out of bed and call Hans about my water. He swears he paid the bill and says he will come by today to look for what's causing the problem.

I have to ask him for an extension on my rent. The thought alone makes me nauseous, but I decide it would be better to do it in person, when he comes to check on my lack of water.

Hans is grouchy. Mean, even. I've heard him call me 'stupid' at least twice under his breath on the occasions I've been able to get him here to fix something with the apartment. He once left the entire building without heat when the furnace broke because the man on the first floor called him a 'fuck face.'

I just have to hope that he'd rather wait a few weeks for his money than go through the trouble of trying to find another tenant to replace me.

I sit on the edge of my couch, bouncing my leg as I wait for Hans. A knock sends me jumping to my feet and rushing to the door. I take a deep breath, pushing down the nerves and nausea as I open it and let him in.

I smell the liquor first. I can't help but glance at the time on the stove. Not even noon. His hair is scraggly and clumps into stringy strands. "The water works in the bathroom?" he asks, his voice like gravel.

"No. It doesn't work anywhere in the apartment. Do you know if it's working in the other apartments?"

His brows lower. "The water is fine. I told you, I paid it."

His voice is loud, and I shake my head. Backpedal, backpedal. I don't need him more annoyed with me.

"No, I know. I just wondered if whatever is wrong with it is just affecting my apartment or maybe others too."

He makes a scoffing sound in the back of his throat as he lowers himself to the cabinet under the sink. I want to ask him how that specific pipe to one sink could tell him anything about my entire apartment not getting water, but I hold my tongue.

I watch him fiddle around in silence for a few minutes before he struggles back to his feet. "I'll be right back. Leave this door open," he says, nodding toward my front door as he exits it.

In his absence, I pace the living room, going over and over how to bring up being late on rent. He clambers back into the kitchen, and I follow him nervously. He turns on the tap, and miraculously, water flows.

"Wow, thank you," I say. I stop myself from asking what the issue was, assuming it will annoy him.

He heads toward the door without a word. It's now or never.

"Hans, um—" I stammer. He turns halfway back to me, still positioned to walk out the door. "I was wondering if you might be able to give me a small extension on rent this month. I kind of lost my job, but I'll have a new one in just a few days, and I'll be able to pay it." The words rush out as I try to ask for the extension, explain why I need it, and assure him he'll get his money soon, all before he can form a reaction to me not being able to pay him.

He doesn't speak or move for a minute. I hold my breath.

"I don't usually do extensions," he says finally.

"I know, I know. And I don't normally ask for them. Or need them. I swear this is a onetime thing."

A rising feeling of annoyance and anger builds inside me at the need to plead to stay in a place like this. I'm begging for squalor, but what choice do I have?

Hans shrugs, eyes cast to the floor. "We could work something out."

I clasp my hands under my chin. "Really? Oh my God, thank you. I swear I will have it to you before next month's due."

He still doesn't look up. "I have terms."

I nod. "Of course. I can pay extra. Maybe an extra hundred as a late fee?"

He shakes his head and finally meets my eyes. "Nah. I only give extensions when they're worth it to me." His eyes float down my body. Then back up. My stomach rolls.

He can't mean what I think he means.

He takes a step toward me.

I take a step back.

"Take your shirt off," he says, dissipating any doubt I had of his meaning.

I recoil, unable to keep the disgust from my face. "You're kidding."

"No. Take it off and we can talk about the terms of your rent."

"No way." I cross my arms over my chest and take another step away from him, scanning the room quickly, looking for a weapon.

His face reddens, anger creasing the loose skin on his face. "You call me over here on a fucking Saturday to fix your fucking water and then have the nerve to ask me for an extension on rent. Fuck you. You're a fat, nasty whore. I wouldn't fuck you with a ten-foot pole, you bitch."

He's stepping toward me, slurring and spitting with his rant of ugly words.

"Get out!" I shout and move behind the couch, putting a physical barrier between us.

He jabs his thick, dirty finger at me. "You get out! Stupid bitch. You got twenty-four hours and I want you out. I'll call the fucking police. Take all your shit." He swings his arm around, indicating my belongings. "Anything you leave gets thrown into the trash."

He moves toward the door. "I'll be back tomorrow, and you better be gone."

He slams the door, and I fall to the floor. Adrenaline, fear, disgust, and hopelessness surge through me all at once. I can't stop the tears, but I jump to my feet and run for the door, locking the handle, the deadbolt, and sliding the chain lock into place. When I'm certain it's locked, I grab a butcher knife from the knife block on the counter.

What am I going to do?

# CHAPTER SIX

*"I am malicious because I am miserable." — Mary Shelley*

I'm out of options. I have nowhere to go and no time to figure it out. Though I doubt the legality of kicking me out with a twenty-four-hour notice, I don't feel safe challenging him on it and have no plans to be here when he comes back.

I hold my cell phone in my hand, staring at my mother's contact, finger hovering over the 'call' button. I'd rather call my dad, but I know my mom makes the decisions, so it would only delay getting an answer.

What will I do if she turns me away? I'd like to believe she wouldn't, but that possibility honestly feels more likely than not.

I take a deep breath and tap the button. My jaw clenched so tight it aches.

It rings and rings.

I'm about to hang up, expecting her voicemail to click on, but I get her breathless greeting instead.

"Hello?" She sounds annoyed. Preoccupied. Normally, I'd avoid asking her for anything when she already seems irritated, but I don't have the luxury of waiting until her mood has shifted.

"Hi, Mom. What are you up to?" I keep my tone light. Friendly.

"Trying to clean under the fridge. What's up? What do you want?"

So much for pleasantries.

"I need your help," I say, trying to trigger a motherly instinct she's never expressed toward me.

"With what?" She exhales.

"I have to move out of my apartment — today. I have nowhere to go."

My pulse pounds in my ears in her silence.

"Mom?"

"Are you asking to stay here?" she says.

I clench my jaw, teeth ready to crumble. Do I literally have to spell it out?

"Yes. I have nowhere else to go. I have to be out today."

I technically have until tomorrow, but I refuse to sleep here one more night.

She sighs again, and I can picture her in my mind. Standing in the kitchen, graying brown hair in her signature braid down the middle of her back, hand on her hip with her also signature scowl.

"I guess you can stay on the couch in the family room," she says. "How long do you need to stay?"

Everything in me feels hot with resistance. With the urge to tell her never mind, and to fuck off, and that she's a terrible excuse for a mother and always has been. It takes everything in me to swallow my pride.

"A month at the most," I say, heart hammering hard in my chest.

"All right. I'll let your dad and sister know. What time will you be here?"

"I'll be there by dinnertime."

"Right. I guess I'll have to make more food for tonight if you plan on eating with us."

"I'd appreciate it," I say.

She doesn't ask what happened. If I'm okay. If I need help packing or transporting my things. Tears pool in my eyes and I want to slap myself. Her indifference toward me shouldn't affect me anymore.

We hang up and I pack my things into my car.

I end up leaving all my furniture. All that fits in my car are my clothes, books, and a few odds and ends. I considered taking my dishes, but where would I put them? Let that repulsive slug of a landlord deal with it all.

I'm covered in sweat and panting by the time I climb behind the wheel of my car. The sun is hot, with a single cloud to block its intensity. As my car rolls forward, I force myself to look ahead and not at the place that's been my home for nearly six years.

It's a dilapidated piece of shit.

The thought of living with my parents again is soul crushing. I've never felt welcome in their home, even back when I had my own room. Now I'll be banished to the family room couch with no privacy and nowhere to put my things.

It's hard not to feel sorry for myself. I don't know how to get out of this. How to get where I'm supposed to be. I've wasted so much time.

When I finally arrive at my parents' house, I decide to go in without any of my things first. That way I can see the space they set up for me and figure out where to put my things.

I raise my fist to knock on the door and hesitate, then reach for the handle, but stop myself again. Pushing out a loud breath, I knock on the door and wait.

I can hear the television on full blast and my mom's voice shouting over it.

The urge to turn around is overwhelming. To find any other option besides this. I almost do turn around. But the door swings open, and I freeze. Shelby stands in the doorway, a smirk on her face.

"Oh how the mighty have fallen," she says as I push past her.

"Shut up."

She laughs. "What'd you do to get kicked out? Why can't you just get another apartment? You didn't get fired, did you?"

I turn to face her. "Shut. Up," I say again.

She makes a snorting sound that I think was meant to be laughter, but I walk away from her and head toward the family room.

I sense her following me and I want to turn around and smack her like I did when we were kids. She's always been an instigator, in constant fights at school. There is something about her that demands to be hit.

I step down the four stairs into the family room and pause on the last step. It is packed with boxes, some open and spilling out. The couch is covered by stacks of clothes on hangers.

"What the hell is this?" I ask no one in particular.

"Bethany and Jeremy broke up. She moved out and back in in one day. So she's moving back into her old room." Shelby practically giggles.

"And that is the cause for all this crap in the family room, how?"

My mom storms down the steps, right past me to the far wall, where she scans the boxes like she can see through them. "Bethany just got here. We'll move this stuff in a bit. She wants to move the bedroom furniture around before she brings her stuff in," she says in a rush, never looking at me.

I sigh and walk back up to the main floor, deciding to just sit at the dining room table and stay out of everyone's way. Shelby follows me and sits farther down at the table.

"It's nice to have the whole family back under one roof," she says.

"Mmm. Yeah, it's great. I look forward to a lot of family bonding."

"You do it to yourself, you know."

"Do what?"

"Make yourself an outsider. You never wanted to fit in with us." Shelby stands and disappears around the corner.

My vision blurs as I exhale frustration, and I roll my eyes as I wipe at the unshed tears. Why would I want to fit in with uneducated, uncultured trash?

I stand up and walk to the front door. "I'll be back in a bit. I have to grab some things from the store," I yell out to anyone in earshot.

Back in my car, I pound my open hands against the steering wheel. My car rumbles as I turn the key and back out of the driveway. There's a twenty-four-hour diner in town. It's no Café Rêvasser, but they'll have coffee for cheap, and I need a place to think.

The place smells like smoke, despite the no-smoking sign on the door. Maybe they don't enforce the rules here. Or maybe the scent of smoke still lives in the walls from all the years people lit up with abandon. Yet another sign tells me to seat myself, so I scan a row of booths and lean down to see if any of them have an outlet.

"Looking for a place to plug in?" a deep voice says from behind me. I stand up and turn around.

"Yes. Do you have a table near an outlet?"

He turns and nods, prompting me to follow. He's a tall guy, with wide shoulders and light sandy brown hair. When he turns back to me, arm extended to a booth, I notice his features are handsome in a traditional sort of way. He looks like he may have been the small town's football quarterback ten years ago but ended up a waiter at a diner instead of 'getting out of this town' like all the characters in the movies say.

"Thank you." I scoot into the seat.

"Yup," he says and walks away.

I pull out my laptop from my bag and plug it in under the booth. My Word document sits at the bottom of my screen, always open, but always minimized. I click on it for the first time in months.

This place isn't the least bit aesthetic. For a moment, I worry the faded green upholstery of the booths will be enough to seize my brain single-handedly.

My document. Always open, but never in use. Titled, but blank. The cursor blinks over and over tauntingly. Reminding me that in all these years, I've yet to finish a manuscript. I have all these dreams of publishing books and winning literary awards, but I haven't done even the very first step in making my dreams a reality.

I've started and stopped more than a dozen books. But by the time I get a few thousand words in, the story feels too flat, too mediocre, too . . . *bad* to continue.

Mr. Hometown Hero appears next to me, and I look up, seeing a name tag on his apron that I hadn't noticed before. 'Joe,' it says.

"Can I get you something to drink? Eat?"

"Coffee, please."

"You got it." He turns to leave.

"Oh, Joe. Do you have any specialty coffees? Lattes? Anything like that?"

"Nnno." He stretches out the 'n' sound. "Just the pot I brewed an hour ago. I got hazelnut creamer."

I deflate. "That works. Thanks."

"My name is Logan, by the way. Not Joe."

"Why are you wearing a name tag that says Joe then?" I ask. Unsure of why I'm even interested in knowing.

"Because it's fun to have this conversation five times a day," he says before walking away.

I catch the sarcasm in his voice, but I don't understand the intention.

Joe/Logan sets my coffee and a handful of hazelnut creamer cups on the edge of the table. "You working on something?" He nods to my laptop and, to my shock, sits down across from me.

I raise an eyebrow. "Yes. I am."

"What is it?"

My mouth falls open, but I recover quickly. What is up with this guy? "It's my manuscript."

"Like a book?" he asks, not missing a beat.

"Yes, like a book."

He frowns and leans across the table to look at the screen. "It's blank."

"I know that," I say through gritted teeth. "And that will continue to be the case for as long as you're distracting me."

He holds his hands up, placating. "Say no more!" He gets to his feet and disappears.

I exhale a long breath, trying to clear my head. My mind is foggy and I'm already telling myself trying to write just now is futile. I take a sip of my coffee. It burns my tongue and tastes cheap and stale. I miss the coffee shops in the city.

I manage to get a few pages written in an hour. And better yet, I actually don't hate them. I find myself wanting to show the typed words to Logan. Show him that there is something written in my Word document now. But a small redhead comes to my table with my check.

I passively scan the diner on my way out but don't see him. His shift must've ended.

The sky is darkening as the sun dips behind the trees. The heat is more enjoyable now. Especially now I'm not moving boxes of my belongings down three flights of stairs.

Back home, I fight the discomfort of walking into the house and push the door open. My mother breezes past me on her way to the stairs. She stops when I enter the house and throws her hands up before continuing to the second floor. I watch her, and she pauses again on the top landing. "You know, we could use your help around here. We've been moving your sister's stuff up and down the stairs all damn day and you take off for hours."

She doesn't wait for a reply. Just stomps down the hall, and there is no way I can stay here for a month. Not a single person has offered to help me with my stuff. And I was only gone for an hour. *For fuck's sake.*

# CHAPTER SEVEN

*"She could no longer borrow from the future, to help her through the present grief." — Nathaniel Hawthorne*

By ten o'clock, Bethany decides she's done moving and unpacking boxes for the night. Which leaves most of the family room still crowded with her stuff. I bite my tongue because I am outnumbered. I move the remaining boxes off the couch myself.

I bring pajamas, toiletries, my pillow, and a blanket in from my car and get ready for bed. The stillness is eerie. I've grown accustomed to the sound of cars and life outside my walls. While I'm trying to fall asleep, the house in a rare moment of silence, I play with a terrible fantasy in my mind. I imagine starting a large fire on the first floor of the house. Starting at the stairs so they can't escape. I'd slip out the front door and watch as the house flickered in the night.

The next morning, I jump from the couch, eager to get up and ready to leave before my family is awake. Luckily, they like their sleep, so I should be safe. I tiptoe to the bathroom with my small bag of toiletries and get cleaned up as quietly as I can.

When I step into the dining room, I nearly jump out of my skin. My dad sits at the table, a cup of coffee between his hands. He looks just as startled as I feel. I hold my hand to my chest and exhale. "You scared me."

"Ditto. I'm usually alone till at least eleven on the weekends."

"Sorry. I'll get out of your hair," I say, walking through to the kitchen for a bottle of water.

"No, I just wasn't expecting anyone to be up. Sit with me."

I hesitate. I can't remember the last time I spent even a moment with my dad alone. The others are always crowded around. Squawking and circling like pigeons around a picnic. I grab the water from the fridge and sit at the table, unsure of what to say.

"Sorry about your sister's stuff in there." He nods toward the family room. "I'll make sure she gets the rest of it out when she wakes up."

I nod.

We sit in silence, drinking our beverages and staring ahead. I wonder if he feels as uncomfortable as I do.

He breaks the silence. "You got work today?"

I haven't told anyone I've been fired. I don't intend to. If nothing else, it's a lie that gets me out of this house without a lot of questions. What would be a three-hour round-trip drive only adds to the time I won't have to be here.

"Yeah. I have the afternoon shift today."

He nods and takes a sip of his coffee. He looks like he wants to say something but takes another sip instead. When he finally sets his mug down, he says, "I know it isn't ideal. Having to stay all the way out here. But it won't be so bad, you know. Having . . . you know . . . having you around a bit more. It'll be nice."

Unexpected tears sting my eyes. "Yeah. It will be nice." I stand up, not wanting to sit in these weird emotions. Because it won't be nice. Not for me. Not with my mother and sisters. I fantasized about burning them all alive just last night. But I have to admit, the words feel good. It's the first time anyone in my family has expressed a desire to have me around.

"I have to get on the road, Dad. Long drive, and I have some errands to run before my shift."

"Sure. Drive safe."

I nod and hurry to my car.

Safely behind the wheel, I contemplate where to go. I'd love to go to Indy. But without an income, I don't have the gas money for trips back and forth. But I need to go somewhere my family won't run into me and a place I can hang out for a while and figure my life out.

I drive through town, but nothing stands out. When I'm over the search, I decide to go back to the diner from yesterday and hope that my sisters don't eat there. My parents won't likely leave the house on a Sunday.

I haul in my laptop bag and set up in the same booth that gives me access to the outlet. While I wait for the server, I take out my phone and check my bank balance. $107. And my phone bill will come out in a few days.

It's then I realize my last check is supposed to be mailed to my apartment that I no longer live in. I grab my things and sprint to my car, passing the waitress on my way out. I need that last check. Even if it is only half a check, it'll be worth more than the gas it will take to drive there and back.

I drive to the apartment first. My heart hammers against my rib cage as I search the street and sidewalk for any sign of Hans. When he doesn't materialize like a phantom super villain, I step out of my car and sprint to my old apartment building.

It's odd being here now. Just yesterday, it was my home. And even though I knew it was a disaster, I must have gotten used to just how bad it was. I must have become blinded by over-exposure. Because standing in the doorway now, I see the yellowing white walls peeling along the top. I see the stained brown carpet and smell the different meals cooking mixed with garbage.

Just inside the door, I check my mailbox. Junk mail. No check. I look up the stairs and, steeling myself, I take the climb up to the third floor. My hand hovers at my apartment door before I twist the handle. To my surprise, it turns, and I push it open. It's quiet inside. And dark. I step over the threshold and take it in.

Hans made good on his word. Only the couch remains. The dishes I left on the counter, my coffee pot, even my plants are all gone.

I don't really want to see the rest. I don't need to. As I walk out the front doors of my former apartment, it feels like I'm shedding a skin. I hold no sadness or nostalgia for the place that kept me acting like a prisoner, living in ruins and doing nothing to get out of it.

My neck aches with tension as I drive to Café Rêvasser. Without thinking, I drive into the parking garage. I don't like the idea of paying for parking now that I don't work at the café, but the street parking is time limited, and now I'm in the city, I'd like to hang out here for the day. After all, I have nowhere to be.

The café is in sight, and I force myself to stand tall. I approach the door and chant a silent prayer: please don't let Donna be working, please don't let Donna be working.

I walk through the door and try to experience the place like a customer. I don't work here anymore. I don't have to worry about whether the night shift cleaned up properly or if Brice remembered to order more almond milk.

Donna's eyes connect with mine the moment I walk through the door. Fuck. Taking a subtle, deep breath, I walk to the counter. Her face is all pity, and I want to slap it off her.

*Don't let these cockroaches pity you.*

"Donna. Hi," I say as her mouth opens to spew what is likely a bunch of crap. "Is Jackson or Brice in?"

I keep my voice even. Casual.

"Brice is in the back. I can get him for ya."

"Would you? Thanks."

She waddles to the back, and within thirty seconds, they both approach the front counter.

He scrunches his forehead in an unattractive way. "What can I do for you, Laura?"

"Jackson said they were mailing my last check, but I've moved apartments. I checked with my building, and they haven't yet received it, so I thought I'd pop by while I had a free moment."

"Oh. I have it in the back. We were going to send it out today."

"Perfect. I'll take it now."

He nods and retreats to the office.

"I actually need to get some writing done. Donna, can you make me a vanilla latte with whole milk?"

"Of course, doll." She taps it into the computer. "I gotta charge you."

My face burns. "Obviously," I say, handing her my debit card. Does she think I expect a free drink?

She swipes it and hands it back to me. "If he wasn't here, I wouldn't."

I don't respond and wait for my check and my far-too-expensive coffee. Brice reemerges with a white envelope in his hand. "Here you go."

I smile politely. "Thanks."

Donna hands me my coffee. I take it and move to the seating area before either can say anything more. I pick a table in the far corner. The farthest I can get from the front counter.

Telling myself not to worry about Donna or anyone else, I take out my laptop from my bag. While it's booting up, I take a sip of my coffee and suppress a sigh. It really is worth the nine dollars.

I try to let all the stress from the last few days go.

But it doesn't go. It stays. Like a rock in my chest.

"Okay, time to figure my life out," I whisper to myself.

I open a new document and start typing. It's the way I process everything. And my life needs a lot of processing.

*What is my problem? I've lost my job. Is that all? No. My whole life is a problem. Maybe this is a good thing. Maybe the universe saw me slacking on trying to achieve the life I swore I'd have and did something to wake me up.*

*Okay, say that's the case. I'm awake. What do I do next? I need to finish my book, but how can I focus on that when I'm going to run out of money, and I'm living with my parents?*

*Come back to this.*

I lean back in my seat and take another sip from my drink. How am I going to fix my mess of a life?

And then, like a sign from God, I see it. Or rather, I see her.

She moves purposefully to the counter. Her hair, so pin straight and platinum blond, contrasts against her black sleeveless blouse. Her confident posture, shoulders back, gaze straight ahead, makes her look taller than she is.

I pack up my things as quickly as I can without looking conspicuous. I take another drink of my coffee as she leaves.

Then I stand and follow Astrid Connor.

## CHAPTER EIGHT

*"Whatever satisfies the soul is truth." — Walt Whitman*

She walks quickly. I nearly have to jog in order not to lose her in the swaths of people on the street. I've fallen a bit behind, and then I can't see her at all. My nerves in my chest feel sharp and my fingers tingle.

Did I lose her? Did she somehow realize I'm following her, and hide?

No. I see her. Unlocking a large black wooden door of a storefront. The sign is a beautiful dark wood with black cursive letters: La Galleria.

Is that Spanish? Italian?

I keep walking past the gallery, make a loop to the other side of the block, and find a bench to sit on and wait.

The universe handed me the answer to all my problems just as I asked for it. Astrid Connor is living the life I've always wanted. She is married to the man of my dreams. The answer is suddenly so obvious. All I need to do . . . is replace her.

I have nothing to do and nowhere to be — so I wait. The city offers anonymity. Which is funny, if you think about it. Most people move to bigger cities in order to become someone. They want to be seen and known, but with so many people with the same goal, they often fade into the crowd. Indy is not New York City or LA. No one moves here to be famous. No, Indianapolis attracts a quieter subset of creatives. The ones who hide behind laptops and canvases. We're not the type to thrive on stage or in front of a camera.

But that's only one part of this city. The rest of it is filled with the other types of people that dwell in every city. And they all bustle up and down the streets, to and from their destinations, making me blend into the background.

I take out a book, just to look less suspicious in case someone does notice I've been here for too long, but I only pretend to read it. I'm afraid to miss Astrid leaving the gallery.

The more time that passes, the more I am afraid she's left through a back entrance or something. I want to do an internet search on her and this gallery she seems so fond of, but again, I don't want my eyes distracted.

Does she work here? Own it?

I assume if she planned to be somewhere for this long, she'd park in the parking garage where I'm parked. Street parking on this block is limited to two hours, and we're going on three and a half. My ass is numb.

But what if she didn't drive? Plenty of people take Uber or Lyft into the downtown area. I tell myself it's okay if I lose her now. I have enough information to learn about her, and I know where she likes to get her coffee. But something keeps me rooted to the bench and searching for her anyway.

Has she always been a customer at Café Rêvasser? I hadn't been on the morning shifts long, but I don't think she would've stood out to me anyway. Not without Theo. She looks like all the other wealthy women that come in there.

A flash of blonde hair snaps me to attention, and I catch her strolling out of the gallery, her coffee from hours ago miraculously still in her hand. I jump from the bench and walk in the same direction on the opposite side of the street.

She's heading toward the parking garage. I break into a jog. I'm on the first level, so if she's parked there, I can follow her out. My heart races, both from the excitement and the physical activity. God, I have got to get to a gym!

Astrid disappears around a corner, and I quicken my pace. I pick up sight of her, still en route to the parking garage. I can't believe my luck when she walks right into the giant cement structure.

I jog to my car, right near the exit. I don't see her, and I do not know which level she's parked on or what her car looks like. As quickly as I can without hitting another car, I reverse out of my spot and back into it so I can see more easily and pull out after her quickly if it's her leaving.

A blue pickup truck passes me. I duck down, out of sight, but I'd be surprised if this was Astrid. A peek over the dashboard proves my instinct, and I watch a bearded man exit the parking garage.

The next vehicle, seconds later, is a small white car. It looks expensive. I get a glimpse of blonde hair through the windshield, but the rest of the windows are darkly tinted. It has to be her.

I throw on my sunglasses and pull out behind her. Adrenaline makes my fingers tingle. I've never tailed someone before, but I've read enough books about it. Though fictional, they have to be at least somewhat realistic, so I rely on them now.

It's a little difficult to stay far back from the car in front of you in the city without looking even more suspicious. It isn't easy to change lanes at the last minute, and there are stop lights and crosswalks that cut through traffic randomly and frequently.

But as luck would have it, she turns off the main strip almost immediately. The white car, a Porsche, I see now, makes its way farther and farther from downtown. Now I can hang back a little more. I even take a few risks and wait at a stop sign before turning down the road she's on.

I have to hang back even farther when she turns onto a street with giant mansion-looking houses. They're spread so far apart you can barely see the neighboring houses. My car clearly doesn't belong here. Maybe I can pass for someone's maid, but somehow, I expect even the help drive luxury cars.

The white Porsche turns, and I slow down. Following the driveway with my eyes, I see one of the most impressive houses I've ever seen. It looks like a Victorian castle. Like an old, prestigious university rather than a home. Two hexagon-shaped towers rise up on each end of the home. The middle sits just slightly back from the towers, and the whole thing is brick with a vast number of arched windows. Ivy climbs the walls like it was perfectly painted on.

The house sits far back on the property, and I'm kept out by a large black iron gate, which is as much a piece of art as the house, with ornate shapes, flowers, and creatures twisted into the iron.

I keep driving because they probably have cameras. I clumsily tap at my phone to GPS my way back to my parents' house. Do Astrid and Theo Connor really live in that mansion? She could have been visiting someone. But my gut tells me that is their home.

I need to know more about Astrid. I need to know everything.

## CHAPTER NINE

*"I was born for something greater than I was and greater I would become." — Mary Shelley*

There's an argument going on inside the house when I get back. Muffled shouts and clanging objects ring out like the soundtrack to my childhood. The only guarantee is that my mother is involved. Even if it's an argument between Bethany and Shelby, Mom would have picked a side, likely Bethany's, and joined in like the fight is her own.

I just want to sit in peace and do the research I need to do. I reach for the gear shifter to reverse and try the diner, but just as I'm about to lift my foot off the brake pedal, the front door swings open and my mother, flared nostrils and lips curled, spots me. If I leave, her anger will only shift to me. Not that it won't anyway.

I put the car in park and slowly climb out.

"Where have you been?" she snarls as I climb the front steps.

"Work."

She makes a noise like she doesn't believe me, but I walk through the front door and into the family room. I'm not taking the bait.

The family room has been emptied of boxes, just like my dad said it would be. I set my laptop bag down on the couch and look around, considering if I should bring some of my things in from the car now.

As though she could read my mind, my mother's voice comes from the landing. "I don't want you treating this like it's your bedroom or something. Don't leave shit lying around everywhere."

I sigh through my nose, but don't respond. She wants to draw me into an argument. But it's not happening. I dig through my purse and grab two twenty-dollar bills. Climbing the stairs, I hand them to her.

"What's this for?"

"Just a little something to go toward food or whatever since I'll be eating here," I say as I walk to the kitchen and open the fridge.

"Your father went out to get pizza," she says, and I see her stuff the money into her pocket. "I don't know what's taking him so long, though. He left like an hour ago."

The argumentativeness in her tone is fading, though now shifting to my dad, like a virus that desperately needs a new host. I close the fridge just as the front door opens.

"Helen. Grab these pizzas, will you?" Dad says from the doorway.

My mom jogs over and takes the pizza boxes from him. "What are you doing? What is that?"

I walk closer to the front door. My dad comes in hauling a large wooden box. A dresser?

"I saw this on the side of the road on my way home. A guy was selling it for twenty bucks, so I grabbed it."

"For what?" Mom says.

Dad looks up at me. "For Laura. So she has a place to put her clothes and things."

My heart constricts. And even though it's a disgusting, side-of-the-road, hand-me-down dresser, I'm touched by the gesture.

"She isn't going to be here forever, Tom. What the hell are we going to do with it when she's gone?"

Dad moves past her, carrying the dresser down the steps and into the family room. He calls over his shoulder, "She can take it with her. If she don't want it, we can put it out on the curb. I'm sure someone will take it."

I fake a stomach-ache to get out of eating pizza and sitting with my mother and sisters. I don't quite know how I'm going to take Astrid's life just yet, but I know I won't be able to do it with the love handles and soft arms I have now. Instead of dinner, I sit propped on the family-room couch with my blanket and my laptop.

I check Facebook first. Sarah's profile, not mine. My own will not have anything new. There is a little number three next to the messages icon. My fingers tingle in that familiar way as I click on it. Ethan has messaged back in exactly the way I knew he would.

> *Sorry, you must have me confused with someone else. I don't go to school anymore. 1800s Lit sounds like my nightmare haha I'm a tech guy.*

He's so predictable. I message him back with a flirtatious message, saying how smart he must be, because I know he loves a good ego stroke. The woman in his apartment the other night must not have meant much.

I open a new tab and search for Astrid Connor's name. There are a few results. Online articles, a LinkedIn and Facebook profile, and a website. I click on the website first. LaGalleria.com.

Her name in a beautiful cursive font spans the top of the page. I think it's the same font that was on the gallery sign downtown. When I scroll down, there are paintings for sale. Are they her paintings? Is she an artist? The prices aren't listed, which, in my experience, means I can't afford it, so I click on one.

I copy and paste the artist's name in my search browser. A few social media pages and junk results come up, but none of them looks right. I type the word 'artist' after the name and try again. Still nothing. He must be one of those artist types that avoids the internet.

I click through the other paintings listed and learn that none of them is made by Astrid. So, she's an art dealer, not an artist. And a high profile one. The pieces she's selling are listed for hundreds of thousands of dollars. Even a few in the millions. Though I can only find a few of the artists online.

I click on the 'About' page on the website and read about how Astrid Connor opened the gallery five years ago. I click through the other pages of upcoming events. There is an exhibition open to the public four weeks from now.

I continue my search and click on her Facebook profile. In her profile picture, she stands in a sleek black dress, long blonde hair in a wave down her back as she peeks over her shoulder at the camera. But the rest of her profile is locked down.

I lean over and grab my phone, pulling up Instagram to search her name. Theo didn't have an account, but I bet she does. My assumption proves right. But it's private.

Who uses their privacy settings these days?

I open my document from this morning and begin making a plan.

*Astrid Connor. How to replace her? She has the money, the husband, the opportunities, the life I want.*

*I have to get Theo to choose me over her.*

*Money*

*Look*

*Proximity*

I have my solution, but how do I make it happen? I'm broke, unemployed, and living at my parents' house an hour and a half away from where I need to be.

I need money. I need another apartment in the city, or at least closer to it. I search online again. I watch several videos on 'side hustles.' I hate that term. But the search for making money triggers all kinds of ads to be sent to me. Ads for credit cards. Ads for personal loans.

* * *

After taking out several loans, applying to every credit card I could think of, I proudly have a grand total of fifteen thousand dollars. It's far more than I expected to get.

It's a lot of debt, but I have to think of it as an investment in my new life. There is no option but to succeed in my plan to make Theo leave Astrid for me. I have to make this work.

Every sign has pointed to this. Astrid is beautiful, wealthy, and successful. She doesn't need Theo like I need him. She can find someone else. I picture those few times in the café, the way he looked at me. He wouldn't have looked at me like that if Astrid was the love of his life.

The money is slated to be in my account within the next twenty-four hours. It's one of the rare times I'm grateful for the age of instant access and gratification. By this time tomorrow, I'll be fifteen thousand dollars richer. By this time tomorrow, I'll have the means to put my plan into action.

The next day, when the money has hit my account, I feel lightheaded with possibilities. I've never had this much money at one time. I drive into town and sign up for a gym membership. Then, I hit the grocery store and load up on frozen vegetables and chicken breast.

I book a hair appointment with a salon whose prices make me woozy. But the difference between a $60 dye job and a $400 one is clear. And I am now the woman that has $400 hair. The picture I show the stylist is the one I screenshot of Astrid's profile picture. After a few hours and the sting of bleach on my scalp, I'm looking at myself in the mirror and I'm blown away. I was definitely meant to be a blonde.

I start spending a lot of time at the gym or in the city. Now that gas money isn't an issue, it's the best place to do research. I go to high-end bars, making notes to perfect my new persona. Being a writer works to my advantage because I know how to people watch. I notice the small things that make a person who they are.

I'm intrigued by a tall brunette during a busy night at the Zombie Club, an expensive bar frequented by wealthy young people. She moves through the room with her shoulders back, easing in and out of conversations. I watch men's eyes linger on her as she moves on to a new group.

Her confidence commands the room. She smiles a lot. Nods her head when people speak to her. She looks genuinely interested in the people around her, and I think that is what people are drawn to. We all want to be listened to.

Her outfit is killer, too.

Another night at the same bar, I watch a woman hang on the arm of several different men. They chuckle at her when she goes to the bathroom. She's trying too hard. There is something desperate in the way she clutches at their forearms. The way she tries to pull a man away from his group of friends to dance. She's drunker than everyone else, though she isn't wasted. Just at a level no one else is on quite yet.

I note everything about the women I admire and the ones I don't. Some nights, I practice my desired skills, perfecting my personality while waiting for the work I've been doing on my body to pay off.

The extra weight melts off easier than I thought it would. Turns out, working out in place of a full-time job and consuming nothing but chicken and vegetables gets you a pretty decent body.

Picking out clothes is by far the most fun part. It's such a different experience when you have money and a flattering frame.

The last part of my preparation is to move back to the city. This is something I waited on for as long as possible to save money. I needed to become the new me first. And I need to get myself into the Connors' orbit next.

Just four weeks since the day I was fired and the day I found out that Theo and Astrid were married, I step out of a cab and onto the sidewalk a completely different woman. My black trousers are loose and soft and trendy. They pair beautifully with the nude lace top, so delicate, that shows off my newly slender shoulders and just the slightest strip of my midsection. It's the exact outfit the confident brunette from the Zombie Club wore. I styled my hair the same as hers too. Straight and slicked back, just a little on the sides. I feel like a supermodel.

I wear my newfound confidence through the front doors of the gallery. They're having an art event tonight, and it's one that has been largely talked about in the art community for some time. The ticket cost a fortune. But a look around tells me it was well worth it.

"A drink, miss?" I turn to see a server in a black-and-white tuxedo holding a gold tray of wine glasses, a polite smile on his face.

"Yes, please."

"White or red?"

"Red."

He hands me a glass of red liquid and I take a sip. It's so much better than the cheap stuff I used to keep in the apartment. I prefer an old fashioned, but they're expensive and take a lot of ingredients. So red wine is my go-to.

I scan the room, taking it all in. The art on the walls, well-lit by the lights on the ceiling, the people, both young and old, but all elegant in a way that only this community can be. My preferred form of art is that of words, but I can appreciate all the other mediums too.

And then, what I've been looking for. My entire purpose in this trip and the culmination of all my hard work has come to this moment. I take a deep breath and stride to a painting that is red and blue flowers in the shape of a heart.

“This one is beautiful,” I say.

“Isn’t it? It’s one of my favorites by the artist.” She looks at me and smiles warmly.

“You’re the owner of the gallery, aren’t you?”

Her smile brightens. “Yes,” she says, sticking out her hand. “Astrid Connor.”

## CHAPTER TEN

*"Look like the innocent flower, but be the serpent under it." — William Shakespeare*

"Olive Tate," I say and shake her hand.

"Wonderful to meet you, Olive. What a lovely name." We both hear her name being called from somewhere a few feet away. She looks over her shoulder and smiles at someone, and I know I'm about to lose her. My brain doesn't work fast enough. "I hope you enjoy the exhibition. There are a few assistants around. They're wearing gold, and they can help you if you'd like to know anything more about the painting or if you're interested in purchasing one. Will you excuse me? Have to make the rounds." She laughs, and her smile is just so damn dazzling.

"Of course. It was nice meeting you." I turn back toward the painting, trying to play it cool. I try not to feel defeated. I just got here. I could have another chance to talk to her later. In the meantime, there must be people here that know her. Plus, these are all people in her art scene. The more of them I become acquainted with, the more chance I have to 'run into her.'

I move from painting to painting, trying to look like I know what I'm looking at, but focusing more on the people huddled around them. There is a small group just behind the viewing section of one painting that I move to and stare at while listening in on the conversation behind me.

"It really is quite the event," a woman says.

"A little overdone, don't you think?" says another.

"Not at all. These paintings are exclusive. It had to be done up. It'd be offensive otherwise."

I take a sip of my wine and move to the next painting. A couple is looking at the one next to it as they chat. I catch something the man is saying, but I've tuned in mid-sentence.

"—can leave by eight, then I can catch the end of the fight."

"Will you stop talking about your stupid fight? We can't leave early."

"I hate these types of things!" he whisper-shouts. "Art functions are boring, and I hate abstract paintings. They creep me out. You can tell Astrid in yoga that it was my fault we left early. I don't care."

"She is our friend, and we are supporting her," she says. "You're a music composer, for Christ's sake. You should enjoy these types of things."

They move to the next painting, walking away from me.

I back away from the paintings and find a server, exchanging my empty wineglass for a full one. Then I approach the couple from behind. "Do either of you know what we're looking at?" I ask as I come to stand beside the woman.

They both turn to me, and I can tell they're fumbling for a response.

"I mean, I never really understood abstract paintings. A toddler could do that." I stare at the mess of color on a canvas.

"I literally just said that," the man says. "Didn't I just say that?" He turns to the woman, eyebrows raised.

She shushes him, looking around like the artist might overhear us insulting the painting. "You did say that, honey."

She laughs and looks uncomfortable, shifting the hem of her dress with her free hand. "This is admittedly not our scene, but we're here to support Astrid. She's a good friend of ours."

"Oh, wonderful. I just met her a bit ago. She's lovely."

I catch the quizzical look she gives me, though she does well to hide it. She's wondering why I'm here. I don't get the art. I'm not a friend of Astrid's.

"I'm a writer. I'm here for research on a book I'm working on."

"Oh, are you a student of Theo's, then?" she says.

"No, no. I have a book contract with BH Publishing. I graduated from school long ago." I laugh and suppress a cringe. Did that sound braggy?

"I just thought you might be one of his writing students. He teaches writing courses at the college that aren't part of the school's degree programs. I'm pretty sure anyone can sign up to take them."

"Oh, I'll have to look into that. It sounds like it could be interesting." She nods and I stick out my hand. "I'm Olive Tate, by the way."

The man shakes my hand first. "Neil Sigurdsson. This is my wife, Tessa."

"Pleasure to meet you both."

"Oh, look." Tessa points behind me. "Astrid is free. Let's go say hello so she knows we were here. Then we can leave to see your stupid fight." She loops her arm through her husband's and begins tugging him forward. "Enjoy the rest of the exhibition. It was nice to meet you, Olive."

The name sends happy chills down my spine. I picked it because it is unique and weird. It says that I am interesting. Much more than 'Laura' ever said. I changed it legally last week. I am legally and officially Olive Tate.

I infiltrate several more groups of people, ebbing and flowing in a subtle and natural way. My customer service experience has given me many skills, one of which is being able to fake a conversation and feign interest. I'm with a group of women, all so beautiful that my old self-consciousness starts to creep in before I remind myself that I am beautiful now.

"Look at them," one woman says. Janine, I think her name is. She makes a puking sound, and it's an out-of-place noise coming from such a beautiful woman in such a beautiful dress. But I turn and look.

Astrid is laughing at something said to her by a man whose arm is wrapped securely around her waist. Theo. She looks up at him, eyes filled with stars, and he stares down at her, looking just as smitten. I almost make a puking sound of my own.

"Not to be mean, but people like that freak me out," says Janine.

A brunette with boobs the size of my head laughs. "What do you mean?"

"They're too perfect. No one is that perfect."

"I don't know. Some people just have it all figured out."

Janine is mid-drink but pulls the glass from her lips while shaking her head. She swallows the wine. "Uh-uh. They've got bodies in the basement. I just know it."

Miss Boobs snorts. "That would be something."

"Have they been together a while? Maybe they're just in that honeymoon phase," I say.

Basketball Tits takes a slug from her glass. "They've been together a decade. Since college."

"Damn," Janine says. "Far removed from the honeymoon stage."

I shrug and take a sip from my own glass. The liquid struggles down my strained throat. Ten years together.

"That's a long time to spend with one cock. Must be a good one." I risk the crude remark because Janine and 34 Double Gs are the type to appreciate it. And they do. They cackle, and I even get a friendly shoulder push from Janine.

I don't move in on Astrid or Theo for the rest of the night. It's not the time. I introduced myself to Astrid, and that is all I need from her tonight. For Theo, I pass his line of sight several times, never making eye contact with him despite the intense pull I had to look at him. I wanted him to see me, but to remain a mystery. I leave after a few more people begin to filter out. I don't want to stick out by being one of the last here.

I am too wired, thrumming with the excitement of a successful night and the first step in my plan. I don't want to go home just yet. The energy is churning in my mind, and for the first time in a while, I feel creative and capable. When my taxi drops me off at my car a few blocks over, I drive back to Wolcott, tapping my fingers to the beat of the music.

I pass my parents' street and continue into town, parking at the twenty-four-hour diner. I have the urge to write. I lug my laptop bag through the door and set up in the booth with the electrical outlet.

"Well, check you out. You didn't get all dressed up for me, did you?" Logan plops into the booth across from me.

I roll my eyes. "You have an inflated ego."

He laughs. "Says the girl that walks around with her nose so high she'd drown if it rained." He drums his hands against the table and gets to his feet. "Coffee?"

"Yes, please." I pay him no attention, focusing instead on opening my Word document.

"You finally have something written. Congrats," Logan says, making me jump. He sets a cup of coffee and a tray of hazelnut creamer on the table.

"Can you stop sneaking up on me like that? Just approach the table like a normal person."

"Aye, aye." He salutes me and walks away.

I shake my head and try to concentrate. I've been here quite a few times in the past four weeks, but Logan was never working. I need to figure out his schedule so I can avoid him and his distracting antics.

When he's gone, I find myself thinking about his comment on my outfit. It seemed like a compliment, but barely. I was a tubby brunette when he first met me. Now I'm lean, blonde, and in designer freaking clothes, for crying out loud.

Shouldn't that warrant more than an observation of the fact that I'm dressed up?

What the hell is wrong with me?

Why am I even worried about the waiter at a small-town diner? I need to get it together. I need to focus.

Time ticks away and I tap at the keys, only to highlight and delete what I've just written. I can't get my mind into the story. Thoughts about Astrid, Theo, the gallery, and all the interesting people I just met keep blocking out any thoughts I have about my story. I exhale and slam my laptop shut.

"That bad, huh?"

I jump and bang my elbow against the edge of the table, then spin around to see Logan leaning against my booth. "Why? Why do you do that?" I say, rubbing my elbow.

"Do what? Make conversation with customers? I don't know. It's in my nature, I guess. I've always been social." He pours more coffee into my mug.

"What is your work schedule? I need to—"

"You asking me out on a date?" He raises an eyebrow with a stupid smirk.

"No," I say flatly.

"Good. Because I'm not just some piece of meat you can pick up and show off around town." He crosses his arms over his chest, and I sigh.

"I want to know so I can avoid coming in here on your shifts."

He narrows his eyes with a sarcastic, tight smile. "Likely." He mouths the word 'stalker' dramatically and slaps my bill on the table.

I take a $5 bill from my bag, lay it over the bill.

"But if you must know," he says, changing his voice to a whisper. "I don't really work here."

Now it's my turn to raise an eyebrow. "Then why *are* you working here?"

He shrugs. "It's my grandpa's place. He's been having a hard time finding servers lately, so I'm just helping out here and there."

"Total Hometown Hero," I mumble, more to myself.

His lips stretch into a lopsided grin. "What?"

I shove my laptop back into my bag and fling it over my shoulder with a huff. "Nothing. I have to go."

He nods a goodbye and grabs my dirty dishes from the table as I walk to my car.

# CHAPTER ELEVEN

*"I have laughed, in bitterness and agony of heart, at the contrast between what I seem and what I am!" — Nathaniel Hawthorne*

It's late and my feet are aching from being in heels all day. But I feel on top of the world, unable to wipe the grin from my face. I collapse onto the family-room couch that has doubled as my bed for the past few weeks with a glass of cheap wine. I wiggle my feet free from my expensive shoes and sigh with relief.

My family has gone camping for the weekend, so I have the place to myself. I was able to get out of going with the excuse of having to work. I take a small sip from my glass and set it down, picking up my phone.

I met a lot of new people tonight. I have a lot of research to do.

Neil and Tessa Sigurdsson were the first people I met. I remember the guy saying his wife did yoga with Astrid. It would be the perfect place to run into her again, so I search for Tessa on various social media platforms.

Instagram seems to be her poison of choice, and she doesn't believe in privacy settings. I scroll her pictures using my new Olive Tate profile. A few hundred people have already followed the account. I've posted a handful of pictures so far, starting with a shot of the city at night from a top-floor apartment that I stole from another account. I captioned it, saying, "I finally caved and started an IG!"

Scrolling through Tessa's photos, I come across a picture of her in sunglasses and a sports bra outside a tan brick building taken a week ago. She's tagged Solstice Yoga in the photo, doing all the hard work for me.

Before diving deeper into her Instagram pictures, I look up the yoga studio. They have an online registration for classes, and I book a morning class for three days from now. Ideally, I'd wait at least a week to 'run into' Astrid so it doesn't seem too weird. But I've waited long enough for the things I want, and so three days will have to be enough.

Once the class is booked, I continue learning about Tessa. She's one of Astrid's friends. Or at least, one of her acquaintances, and she might be useful in getting closer to Astrid.

I learn Tessa is a mother of two small children. She hashtags her pictures 'two under two' and spends her time online making motherhood look easy. Showcasing her perfectly clean, all-white house, her cute outfits with perfectly done hair and make-up, her colorful salads, and the well-balanced meals she makes for her kids. I close out of the app when I see a photo of her hunched in front of a mirror in an effort to produce rolls that she doesn't have for the sake of #bodypositivity. Her yoga instructor deserves a bonus because Tessa doesn't look like she could have possibly been pregnant at any point, let alone eleven months ago.

The house is quiet, and the silence that I usually enjoy feels empty after the bustle of the gallery. Being around so many interesting people made me feel alive in a way I never have before. But then my mind summons the image of Astrid and Theo looking at each other and the knowledge that they've been together for ten years. Can I really compete with that?

I sigh and grab my laptop from the side table. I think it's time to find a new apartment. I'll need to be close by to have any shot of getting acquainted with Astrid and her friends.

I search the internet for hours. I want a nice place. But they cost more than I'm willing to spend right now. I have a little over eleven thousand dollars left. I'll need that to keep up with them. I can't spend it all on a few months of rent. I find one I think I can afford for a while. Close to downtown, but no better looking than my last apartment. It comes partially furnished, but I'd rather peel off my own skin than sleep in a used bed or sit on a couch I know nothing about. I shiver just thinking about it.

But I send an email asking to view it tomorrow.

Sliding my laptop to the floor and closing my eyes, I remember how it felt when Theo's gaze was on me instead of Astrid. When he complimented me and laughed at the stupid Edgar Allan Poe joke. I have to compete with Astrid. I deserve to be happy too, and if Theo would prefer me over her, who am I not to take him up on that?

I roll to my side and pull the button that Theo bought me out from underneath the couch. I run my thumb across the smooth surface. His gift to me. His signal that he was thinking about me. That he wants me.

* * *

I'm early for the 6 a.m. yoga class. I'm normally not much of a morning person, but I felt like a kid on Christmas and just couldn't stay in bed any longer. I wait in my car, not wanting to be the first one in. My heart races every time I see someone approach the door. I look for her telltale blond hair, but when there are only ten minutes until the start of class and I still haven't seen her, I rush from my car with the yoga mat I got from Amazon and hurry into the studio.

The class starts, and there is still no sign of Astrid or Tessa. I deflate and consider leaving. But then the instructor is talking and walking through the room, and maybe it will be a good thing to have been here once before running into them. And I won't have to go to the gym later.

We're in our fifth downward dog when I decide that I loathe yoga. Which part of this is supposed to be relaxing? I'm in the best shape of my life, but still, my wrists feel like they're going to snap if I try to hold my bodyweight up a second longer.

When we get to Savasana, I've never been so happy to lie still in my entire life. That is, until I'm ready to leave, but the instructor hasn't told us we can get up yet, and everyone is still lying on the floor. I peek through one eye to check if anyone else has gotten up. How long are we supposed to lie here? My whole body tingles with impatient rage.

I'm nearly shaking when she finally signals us to start wiggling our toes and fingers back to life. Lady, I've been wiggling for five minutes.

I roll up my mat and run for the door. I feel like I need to go for a run to shake off the irritation of staying still for so long, and the fact that I'll have to do this again until I run into Astrid makes me want to fistfight someone.

From yoga, I head over to my possible new apartment. I'm more interested in seeing if the landlord is a creep than anything else. I know what the place looks like. I know it sucks. But I refuse to deal with another Hans.

I park outside the building, and it has a similar feel to my old one. Like you're probably safe, but you walk a little faster than normal to get inside.

There's a woman leaning outside one of the apartment doors. She looks up when she hears me approach.

"Hi, are you Olive?" she says, stepping toward me with a warm smile.

"Yes, I am. Hi."

She sticks her hand out and I shake it. "I'm Mackenzie. I'm the building owner. If you follow me, the unit is right here."

She seems nice. And it helps that she's a woman. Less chance of her telling me to take off my shirt if I'm ever late on rent.

"I've done a few updates since we listed. I was just about to update the pictures when you emailed. But this is it." She steps aside and I walk in.

It's better than the pictures. The updates are nice. It's still a piece of shit, but the countertops are decent. "It's great," I say. "Do the updates affect the amount you listed for rent? Because it's already at the top of my budget—"

"Oh, no, no. The rent is still the same. Don't worry about that."

"Perfect. I'll take it."

"Really?" she says, sounding surprised.

"Yes. When can I move in?"

She hands me the key, eyebrows raised and a small smile on her lips. "Whenever you want."

She pulls paperwork from the kitchen drawer, and I sign my new name across several pages, committing myself to a year lease. I get butterflies drawing a swooping *O* and a curvy *V*. Every day I become Olive a little more. Every day I leave Laura behind.

I drive to my parents' house, practically vibrating with excitement. Living with them has been near torture, and I can't wait to be back in the city and to be able to execute on my plan full force.

I'm on my second trip to my car loading up my things when my parents' car pulls in beside me. I'm sure my mother will be thrilled to learn I'm moving out. She steps out of the passenger seat, eyeing my backseat.

"Are you leaving?" she asks.

"Yep," I say with a grunt as I hoist one of the full dresser drawers into my trunk.

Bethany slides out of the back of the car. I catch an eye roll as she walks past me and into the house. I follow her in to grab more of my things. My dad appears behind me. He grabs the next drawer I pulled out of the dresser from me. "Will the dresser fit in your backseat?" he asks as he carries the full drawer to my car.

"I think so. If I scoot the front seats up, it should slide in on its side."

I carry my laptop bag, toiletries, and purse out and put them in the passenger seat before reaching for the bar to slide the seat forward. Then I go to the other side, getting into the car and scooting as far forward as I can while still being able to drive.

"I'll grab it," he says.

"Thank you, Dad," I say softly. He's the only one stepping in to help me. My mother and sisters have disappeared into the house.

I wait by the front door to hold it open and guide him down the steps and to my car. We lift the dresser up, flip it onto the side, and start trying to push it into the backseat.

"Where is it, Laura?" Bethany screams from the doorway.

I jump, almost dropping the dresser. My dad wiggles it side to side, and it slides in more.

"Where is what?" I call over my shoulder.

"Go to the other side and try to pull it to you. I'll push it," Dad says.

I do as he says and round the front of my car. As I do, I catch a blur of movement, and then I'm checked into the side of my car by Bethany storming past me. She throws clothes out of the drawers sitting in my trunk. I run and shove her away.

"What is your problem?" I shout.

"I know you took it. I left it here, and I get back and it's gone. Give it back, you fucking thief."

"What are you talking about?"

"My engagement ring from Jeremy! It was in my room on my dresser and now it's gone." She pushes past me again and flings fistfuls of clothes onto the ground.

"Stop!" I grab her arms and try to wrestle her away. "I don't have your stupid ring. I didn't even know you were engaged. I thought you broke up."

My dad grabs her just as she latches onto my hair and shirt. She yanks as she's being pulled away, and I feel both tear. I scream and claw at her arms, hoping to God I've drawn blood.

"Go back in the house," Dad says to Bethany as he sheepdogs her to the front door. I notice Shelby standing off to the side of the front steps, arms crossed, a smirk on her face.

My mother steps onto the porch, red-faced with wild hair like she's been doing jumping jacks in the living room. "Laura, give her the ring back. I know you took it. Just give it back and get the hell out of here."

"I don't have the ring, Mom!" I yell. My scalp stings, and I wish I had a brick to throw at her thick, dim-witted skull.

"Laura, just go," Dad says, pushing Bethany and my mother back into the house.

Heat spreads across my face and I stand there for a second, wanting to say something but not knowing what.

"It's okay, Laur. Just go."

I shut the trunk and the doors and get into the driver's seat. I watch as my dad holds his arms out, trying to reason with crazy women who will never so much as sit in the same room as reason. I watch Shelby sneer from the driveway.

I reverse and drive away.

Back at my new apartment, after two hours of hauling in all my things, I finally sit on the living room couch that I draped a sheet over, so I don't have to touch the mysterious fabric.

I did it. I'm out.

I twist to the side and pull the silver and diamond ring from my pants pocket and twirl it around my index finger. It's tacky and exactly Bethany's taste. I'm hoping I can get at least a couple of grand for it. I grab my laptop and prepare the listing.

* * *

It's my fourth class this week and I'm nearly ready to call it. I no longer wait for people to file in. I'm one of the first to class and pick a spot in the back so I can see everyone that comes in.

I'm trying to grip my toe, just out of reach, when I see Tessa walk in. My heart hammers as I watch behind her. And sure enough, her blonde ponytail swings through the door, and there she is.

I look away and focus on my warm-up stretches and calming the fuck down. I glance up at the flick of a mat being unrolled and slapped down in front of me. It's Tessa.

Here we go.

"Tessa?" I say and she turns, searching my face for recognition. "Tessa Sigurdsson, right? Olive, from the art exhibition."

Tessa's face lights up. She remembers. And she's more pleasant in her own comfort zone. "Olive! Hi! Oh my gosh, I didn't know you came to this yoga studio. Have you been coming long? Have we been coming here together, not even knowing it?"

She laughs and I'm thrilled. Women like her usually annoy me. The ones that act like they know you far better than they do. You'd think we spent the whole evening getting to know each other instead of exchanging barely more than our names. But her over-inflated false sense of familiarity works in my favor now.

"I've only been coming for a few days actually, but wouldn't that be so funny?"

"Oh my God, Olive, this is Astrid Connor. She owns the gallery the exhibition was at."

My smile stretches even further. "Oh, yes! I think we met that night. Just briefly, though. You were the woman of the night."

"I remember." Astrid smiles. "How could I forget a name like Olive?"

The instructor starts speaking and asking everyone to take their places on the mat.

"We'll chat after class," whispers Tessa.

I have to fight back a smile the whole first half of class. Until a particularly uncomfortable pose that she has us hold for entirely too long wipes any signs of joy from my face.

When the never-ending Savasana is over, I begin rolling up my mat, letting them strike the conversation back up so I don't seem too eager.

"Olive," Astrid says, and I hold my breath, looking up to meet her eyes. "We're going for coffee down the road if you'd like to join?"

"Sure." I try not to sound like an overly excited puppy dog. I'm hoping they decide to walk because I haven't yet upgraded my car and there is no chance I'm letting them see my rusty beater. When they turn away from the parking lot and toward the road, I breathe a sigh of relief.

"Astrid came across this cute little place a few weeks ago. You're going to love it," Tessa calls over her shoulder.

For a quick moment, fear spreads like needles into my fingertips, thinking she's talking about Café Rêvasser. All I need is to run into loud-mouth Donna, and for Astrid to put together who I am. But we're on the other side of town. I'm safe. For now.

"Here it is." Tessa swings open a door to a very plain building. It's one of the newer constructions built to house anything. It's bland and unassuming. But when I step inside, my mouth drops open at the unexpectedness of it all. The coffee shop looks like an 1800s tavern, but it's filled with art and books in every free wall space.

"It's incredible," I say, closing my mouth so I don't look like an idiot. I follow them to the counter, and they let me order first. I order the drink that Astrid ordered in the café the day she broke my heart and my plans for my future with Theo.

"How fascinating, that's exactly what I get," Astrid says.

I smile and make a face like 'no way.' Fascinating? Really? Such a strong word for having the same boring coffee order.

When we get our drinks, I follow them to one of the corner wooden booths. Tessa and Astrid sit on one side with me across from them, and I feel like I'm being interviewed. But I'm a good interviewee, and I'm excited for a challenge after all this preparation and work.

"So you were at the exhibition last week? What did you think of it?" Astrid asks.

"It was incredible. It was the first exhibition I've ever gone to and now I'm eager to go to more."

Astrid smiles, her perfectly sculpted eyebrows stretching toward her hairline. "Wow, I'm honored to have been your first." She places her hand on her chest like a Southern belle. "What brought you there? If you don't mind me asking."

"Book research," I say, looking over at Tessa, who nods mid-drink.

"Mmm — yes, you were doing research for your novel," Tessa confirms.

"A novel writer? Wow. My husband will be thrilled to know I've befriended a writer." Astrid laughs.

I beam. "Oh yeah? Is he a writer as well?"

Tessa mentioned he taught at the university, but I don't want to make her feel weird to be called out for talking to a stranger about her friends.

"He is. He's an instructor at the university, but a writer through and through."

"What an artistic household you have!" I wonder what he's written. I wasn't able to find any of his writing online, but maybe he uses a pen name. Especially since his family has such a big name in this city. Maybe it was his way of separating from that.

I imagine their conversations over dinner are far from the ones I have with family over dinner. They'd talk of art and literature. Conversations on literary theories in the morning over coffee.

"I can't lie. It's everything I've ever dreamed of having as a little girl." Her lips turn up in a soft smile and her eyes glisten. And even though I should be jealous, and part of me is, I'm more in awe. How incredible that someone's life has turned out to be everything they've ever hoped it would be. And how sad that it will soon all be taken away.

"But enough of my sappiness," Astrid laughs. "Tess, you never finished telling me about Devin's birthday party."

Tessa's eyes go wide with the excitement of having the floor. I've learned from Instagram that Devin is Tessa's oldest son. He's turning four.

"Yes. So, we've booked the caterer. I was telling you that the other day." She turns to me. "We had a different caterer booked, but they bailed last minute, so we've been struggling to get another one this short notice."

"Oh, thank God," Astrid says.

"Anyway, so everything is in order and ready for Saturday. The theme is Summer's Last Hurrah, so the pool will be open."

"Fantastic. You know I'll be in the pool."

Somehow, I can't picture Astrid in a pool. She seems too elegant to swim at a kid's birthday party.

"Olive, you're more than welcome to come," Tessa says.

My heart skips. "Oh, no. I don't want to intrude."

"Please," she says. "It's a kid's birthday party. The more the merrier."

"Well, okay." I smile, grateful. Truly.

"Here," she says, taking out her phone. "What's your number?"

I read it out for her, and she types it into her phone. A moment later, my phone dings with a text. So does Astrid's.

"I texted you in a group chat with Astrid, so you have both our numbers. Mine is the one that ends it 7108. Astrid's is the other. Obviously. But I'll text you the time and address so you have it."

"Thank you," I say and look at the women sitting across from me. Both smiling politely.

I take a second to soak in this moment as Tessa starts telling Astrid what they got Devin for his birthday. This is a moment I've wanted for so long. To be the woman on the other end of the counter.

I look over at the barista standing behind the register. She's younger. Probably in college. Her hair is pulled back into a tight ponytail and her eyes are rimmed with dark circles. I wonder what she daydreams about between customers. What or who she aspires to be. If she sees me as someone to envy. A target to aim for.

# CHAPTER TWELVE

*"I do not suffer from insanity. I enjoy every minute of it." — Edgar Allan Poe*

Tessa texts me with the address, time, and theme of the party. She tells me how to dress and what to bring and leaves literally nothing to be figured out. I've picked out a white bikini and put a white dress over the top of it. I look like the character in *White Oleander* with my white-blonde hair.

I bought the kid a gift from a toy store that wrapped it up for me and saved me the work. Tessa told me to get him race cars, so race cars I got. I decide to call an Uber. I don't need anyone seeing me get out of my old beater of a car.

I hear the music as I step out of the car. Above a white privacy fence, I see the top of a yellow bounce house swaying and jutting up and then back down. A cacophony of voices and laughter floats toward me, both adults and kids. I can't help but smile as I approach the door.

A sign on the door, orange with white writing, says to 'come on in and party!' and so I do, pushing on the large blue-painted door. I've seen the door before on a few of Tessa's posts online, and it looks just as beautiful as the pictures.

I follow the voices to the back of the house and emerge into the kitchen. It's weird to experience this place in the flesh after seeing it online. I've never been here until now, but I know from a reel where she keeps her silverware and which cabinet contains the coffee mugs. I know what I'll find in her fridge and where she got her sugar and flour containers from. I know she keeps baked goods in the oven because it's something her parents used to do, and it drives Neil crazy because he sometimes turns on the oven, forgetting that Tessa may have a boxed Danish or a loaf of bread stored on the top rack.

It's a fire waiting to happen.

"Olive! I'm so glad you could make it. Come out back." Tessa has her hands full and is trying to move the French doors with her elbow. I hurry over to her and take a few things from her arms. "Thank you," she breathes out.

"Of course. How can I help?"

"Oh, no. I've got it. Go out back and grab a drink. The gift table is next to the hors d'oeuvre table. You can't miss it," she says as she runs to the oven. Baked goods safely stored away.

"What are you making? The caterer didn't flake on you again, did he?"

"No, no! It's Devin's cake. I want it to be a tradition, baking their cakes every year."

"That's so sweet," I say. "Are you sure you don't need help with anything?"

"I'm sure, thank you, hon."

I head out back and try to remember if anyone has ever baked me a cake. We always got the pre-made ones from the store for our birthdays. The bakery would open the box and write our names in icing across the top.

The backyard is a well-orchestrated, high-end circus. There are jump houses, slip and slides, and a pool with a slide. And off in the corner of the yard is a tent with a bar and a bartender, tables of food, and a DJ. It's insane and wonderful. My life in this world will look different. I have no intention of having kids for one, but I love the endless possibilities that come with this kind of money.

I spot pale blonde hair under the tent and walk toward her. My life in this world will look like Astrid's. It will be Astrid's. I set my present on the gift table, and as I approach Astrid, Theo appears next to her and hands her a drink. Pulses of excited energy shoot through me like lightning in my veins.

This is it. He likely saw me at the exhibition, but not up close like he's about to. I look different from a few weeks ago, but someone who spent a lot of time with me would recognize me. Theo and I spent nearly no time together before I was fired. Before I learned he has a wife. But he has looked into my eyes. Scanned my features.

"Astrid, how are you?" I say when I'm next to her.

"Olive! I was hoping you'd be here!" She smiles, happy to see me, and hugs me like a close friend. Her hair smells like roses, and I make a mental note to find out what shampoo she uses.

When we separate, she immediately turns to Theo. "This is my husband, Theo. Love, this is Olive, my writer friend I was telling you about."

I hold my breath as he reaches out a hand and I take it. His hand is cold, despite the heat of the afternoon. His touch sends shivers down my back. I look into his eyes and try my best to keep my expression neutral as I search his eyes for recognition.

"Nice to meet you, Olive. I've heard a lot about you."

He shows no sign that he knows who I am. That he's seen me before. Though it's what I wanted, what I needed, to keep moving on my plan, there is a sinking feeling in my stomach.

"It's great to finally meet you. I've heard a lot about you too."

"All good things, I hope."

"Mostly," I say, winking at Astrid, who laughs.

"Can I grab you a drink from the bar, Olive? What would you like?"

"An old fashioned, if they have it."

He nods with an approving grin. "I think they do. I'll be right back." He kisses Astrid's cheek, and I fight back the urge to turn away. And then I fight the urge to stare at him as he walks away to fetch my drink. He's just as breathtaking as I remember, and I've waited so long and so patiently to see him again.

When he returns, I take the drink from his hand and hold my breath, waiting for his fingers to touch mine, but they don't, and I deflate as his hand falls back to his side.

"Astrid says you're working on a novel," he says. I try to picture Astrid and Theo sitting in their grand living room with wine in front of a gigantic fireplace, talking about me.

"Yes," I say. "I sold the book this past spring."

"That's fantastic. What genre?"

"Literary fiction."

"Wow. Those are hard to sell these days," he says. "Very impressive."

"Thank you. I have to turn it into my editor by the end of next month, so I've been locked away with my laptop."

Everything I've told him is a lie. I've never sold a book. I've never even finished writing one.

But he doesn't need to know all that. Because Laura is the one who failed to achieve her dreams. Olive is successful. Olive gets what she wants.

Astrid's eyes float over my shoulder and she smiles and waves. I look behind me and immediately recognize the two women headed our way. The two women I talked to at the exhibition. The vulgar one and the big-breasted one.

"I didn't know you guys were coming!" Astrid says, hugging them. "It's so nice to see you." She steps aside to include them in our little circle, and I bite back my annoyance. Three is a crowd, but five is a traffic jam. Astrid introduces everyone. I remember Janine's name and learn DD's name is Corrie. When she tells them my name, Janine's eyes light up.

"That's it!" she says. "I thought you looked familiar. I met you at Astrid's gallery."

I nod and smile. "Yes, that's right." I'm almost surprised she brought it up. She talked a bit of trash about Astrid and Theo that night. If the roles were reversed, I might be a little nervous to see that they'd obviously begun a friendship. But I haven't tattled on her to Astrid. And if she's going to be around more than I thought, I might need more gossip from her later.

"I didn't realize you two were friends," Corrie says.

Astrid shakes her head. "We weren't. We actually ran into each other later at the yoga studio."

I'm glad Astrid explained it. It looks less suspect than me trying to explain it. Despite that, she looks at me with obvious curiosity. But then she shrugs with a blinding white smile and changes the subject.

Drinks flow from the open bar, and while I try to slow down, aware I'm at a kid's birthday party, everyone else is going full steam ahead. The sun is beating down, and even under the tent, I feel like I'm baking through. When there is a lull in the conversation, I excuse myself to the bathroom.

The air conditioning feels better than an orgasm when I walk into the kitchen. I sigh out loud as I make my way to the bathroom. When my bladder is empty, I let the cold water from the sink run over my hands and wrists and then dab my chilled hands at the back of my neck and my cheeks.

I don't want to be away from Theo and Astrid for too long, so I leave the bathroom to make my way back to our table. Something clatters in the kitchen as I round the corner. Theo stands at the counter with an armful of red solo cups and a box of juices tucked between his elbow and body. He looks up when he hears me come into the room and smiles in a self-deprecating way when our eyes meet.

"Did they put you to work?" I ask as I approach the island and lean against it.

He lets the drink supplies fall to the counter. "Eh, I offered to help the guy for the kids' bar restock."

"These kids are such lushes."

He laughs. "Almost as bad as the adults."

Now I laugh. "I thought I was the only one who realized how drunk everyone is getting."

"Oh, no. Just wait till tonight. You're staying, aren't you?"

"I might. I have a long day of writing planned for tomorrow. Deadline's looming."

"You have to stay. It's a blast after the kids head out." His smile is flirtatious. Welcoming. Daring.

I make a face like I'm considering and then narrow my eyes at him. "It better be worth the inevitable hangover."

His grin turns triumphant. "It will be. Now make yourself useful and grab that box of juices for me." He winks, and my heart hammers against my chest. That fucking wink.

I walk over to him and stand a little closer than necessary, reach across him to put my hand on the box of fruit punch on the counter. "Anything else?" I ask, my voice low.

The door hits against the wall as it's flung open, and I jump about a foot back from Theo.

"Hey, the juice guy is looking for his cups," Corrie says from the doorway.

"Got 'em here. I had to find another arm for the juice," Theo says, casually picking up the plastic cups he'd dropped.

I place a hand on the box of juice, slide it to me, and pick it up, plastering a smile to my face. "You should have seen him trying to carry it all himself."

Corrie doesn't hide her suspicious glare. "Bet it was something to see."

I walk past her back into the heat and I wish, not for the first time, that my face didn't flush so damn easily. I can feel the heat in my cheeks, and it makes me look all the more guilty. Nothing happened. But Corrie barged in before there was a chance for anything to happen.

Stepping back out into the oppressive heat, I search the yard for Astrid. I spot her kneeling down next to the pool, consoling a crying child. Is it her child? Theirs? I realize I have no idea if they have kids. Astrid wipes tears from the little girl's cheeks and says something that makes the girl giggle. Another woman runs over to them just as Astrid stands.

They have a small, smiling exchange, and the woman walks away with the little girl, hand in hand. Astrid watches the mother and little girl walk away with a smile still on her face, but a hint of sadness underneath.

Throughout the rest of the party, I feel Corrie's eyes on me. When I'm standing and talking to Astrid about her upcoming trip to Europe to look at a few paintings and sculptures to buy, I glance to my left and startle a little to see Corrie standing by herself, sipping from her drink and staring right at me.

I swallow hard and turn back toward Tessa, who is complaining about something.

"He set the whole thing up while I was out of town visiting my mother. I have no idea how to use it."

Neil throws his hands up. "You can figure out every social media app with no problem. I thought you'd like managing the house through your phone since you're on it all the time."

Everyone makes an *ooooh* sound, and Tessa elbows him in the stomach.

"Be nice!" she shouts. He laughs and hugs her to his side.

Corrie and her crew join our group. Everyone in the small circle steps back to allow them in. I avoid looking at her but feel her eyes on me. She stands next to Astrid, and I hear her mm-hmming to everything she says, weaving her way into the conversation.

"I have to be in London next week for a few days," says Astrid.

"That sounds lovely," I say before Corrie can chime in. "Will Theo be going with you? It would be a great little vacation for you two."

"Theo has to work," she says with a frown. "He's got a lot to keep up with, so he doesn't usually come with me on my buying trips."

"That's too bad," I say.

Corrie steps forward, misshaping our circle of friends. "You really should think about hiring out for an art dealer. It would save you so much time."

"I know, I know," Astrid says. "I just have such a hard time relinquishing control. I'm still not used to the way the gallery has grown. I'm used to doing it all myself."

"Totally understand," Corrie says. "But it has grown so quickly. You won't be able to keep up with it all alone. It would give you more time to focus on the shows and give you more time at home."

Astrid nods. "I'll give it some thought."

I idly wonder why Corrie seems to care about how Astrid runs her business and make a mental note of it.

The number of kids running around has dwindled, and then Tessa is standing behind her own two kids, each with backpacks on. The little girl looks ready to topple over. "Devin and Leah wanted to thank you all for coming to Devin's birthday party and for all the generous gifts."

The boy mumbles a thank-you and then she ushers them back into the house. Astrid leans into me. "Now the real party starts."

A team of people tears down the bounce houses and all the other kid party things. I watch them transform Tessa's backyard from a kid's wonderland to a luxury adult spot. Tessa reemerges, now dressed in a black one-piece bathing suit and a black wrap around her waist. She walks to the bar and makes herself a drink now that the bartender has been dismissed.

"All right, let's celebrate that being over," Tessa shouts as she raises her drink in the air. Everyone whoops, and I raise my drink with the rest of them, beginning to get a little anxious about what I may have gotten myself into.

"Where did her kids go?" I whisper to Astrid.

"To their grandparents' house. It's a birthday tradition."

Interesting.

Before I can say anything else, Astrid is running full speed toward the pool. My mind can't comprehend what's happening before she cannonballs into the water, and everyone is cheering and whooping again. I stare at her as she emerges from the water, a huge grin stretching across her face. Astrid Connor does not seem like the type of woman to cannonball into a pool. She continues to surprise me.

A few more people get into the pool, none as abrupt as Astrid. I sit on the edge with my feet in the water, sipping my old fashioned. I feel a little tipsy, but I can tell I'm one of the most sober people here. Corrie and Janine are huddled off to the side of the pool with a guy I don't know.

I jump when a voice on the other side of me speaks right next to my face. "Olive, I want to introduce you to a friend of mine." Tessa squats down beside me, but the friend she's referring to is standing and I have to lean back and strain my neck to look at the man standing next to her.

He extends his hand down to me. "Hi, I'm Ken."

I take his hand, intending to shake it, but he grips my fingers and tugs upward.

Okay, I guess we're standing now.

As I awkwardly get to my feet, I spill some of my drink down my leg. "Oh — I'm sorry. Shit," he stammers. He bends and uses his hand to wipe the spilled liquid from my leg. I step back.

"It's fine. I'll just grab a napkin." I move toward the bar. Tessa has already disappeared, so I can't scold her for so obviously trying to set me up or to tell her I'm not interested.

After cleaning myself up, I make another drink and return to the poolside. Ken is still standing there awkwardly. "Sorry about that," he says again.

I smile instead of verbally reassuring him again that it's fine.

"I know a fantastic drink," he says, nodding toward the glass in my hand. "I guess I should have said that before you made yourself a new one." He laughs nervously and I feel bad for him.

"What kind of drink?" I don't know why I'm entertaining him.

"Come on. I'll show you."

I'm about to object when he turns and walks away from me and to the bar. I stand awkwardly, not really wanting to follow him, but not wanting to hurt his feelings. I scan the area for Theo and spot him on a plastic chair on the opposite side of the pool.

I walk toward Ken, and he spins to me, holding a drink out.

"Here, try this." I eye the concoction suspiciously. It's pink, which isn't a good sign. "Go on, take a sip."

I do, despite ever-present warning bells about a guy I don't know making me a drink I didn't watch him make. I make a face at the mouthful of sugar that comes through the straw. His face falls when I try to scrape the taste off my tongue with my teeth.

"Sorry," I say. "It's a lot sweeter than I was expecting."

"Yeah." He shakes his head self-deprecatingly. "It's definitely on the sweeter side."

"I can show you how to make an old fashioned, if you'd like?"

He smiles. "Sure. I need another specialty drink up my sleeve."

I have to force myself not to look back at Theo. I can't appear too eager. Especially after my half-assed attempt to make a move was interrupted. As I'm pouring in the whiskey, we hear a sharp intake of breath — a sniff, not a gasp. I look over and see Corrie and the guy she was talking to bend over the table. When Corrie sits back, I spot the white line before it disappears into the guy's nose.

My hand trembles and the glass of alcohol clanks into my rocks glass. I blink hard, trying to re-focus on the drink tutorial. So this is what everyone meant by the real party? I'll find a way out of it. I'm not snorting cocaine.

"That's not nearly as difficult as I thought it'd be," Ken says when I finish the drink.

"Now you have a not-sweet drink in your arsenal."

He grabs himself another beer from the ice cooler and we walk back to the pool. I strip off my white dress and sit on the pool's edge again but slide into the water instead of just dipping my feet. The water is the perfect temperature. Warm enough to be comfortable, but not so warm that it feels gross.

Ken takes off his shoes and takes my place poolside with his feet in the water. I take a big sip of my drink before submerging myself beneath the surface. Using the concrete edge, I kick off and swim underwater to the other side of the pool. When I come up for air, I'm right beside Astrid and in front of Theo, who still sits in a chair just outside the pool.

"There you are," Astrid says, swinging an arm around my shoulders. Her eyes are enormous. Dilated so much that I can barely make out her blue irises. I'm taken aback by how beautiful she is. Her make-up has been washed away, and even though I know she's in her thirties and she's high as shit on something, her face looks so young and innocent that I feel a pull to protect her.

It's a primal feeling. One that has no place in this civilized age. She doesn't need my protection, and she won't get it. I'm here for one reason. I look over at him and he's looking at me. He doesn't look away and neither do I. My chest warms under his stare, and I know I would do anything for him. It's more than wanting the life I deserve to have. The money and the opportunities. He is meant for me. I can feel it.

Arms snake around my neck, and Astrid pulls me to her. She presses her forehead to mine, and she smells like chlorine and sweat with hints of her rose-scented shampoo, and it's intoxicating. The alcohol has made its way to my head, and everything sways like we're swimming in treetops.

I wrap my arms around Astrid, trying to anchor myself. The swaying of the branches — no — the water — is making me dizzy. I focus on her eyes because it's the only thing I can really see with her face this close. And then her lips press against mine. I freeze, not kissing her back, but not pulling away. Her mouth parts, and this is not the Connor I intended to be kissing tonight. I don't know what to do, so I kiss her back. A rejection would surely be awkward, and I can't have her not talking to me.

I can taste the vodka on her tongue and something else. Something hard slips into my mouth and it's sweet and chalky. Before I can think better of it, I swallow it. Astrid pulls away, a silky smile on her face, her eyes nearly closed.

I duck under the water again and swim the length of the pool. The rest of the night comes in blurred flashes. Faces laughing manically, too close to mine. Too close. Too loud. Spinning. Dancing? Falling. Hard. My face hurts. Black. Swirls of color. Black again. Nothing.

# CHAPTER THIRTEEN

*"Oh, what a tangled web we weave . . . when first we practice to deceive."*
*— Sir Walter Scott*

I wake up in a bed that is not my own, and I'm overwhelmed with relief when I discover I'm still clothed in my damp bathing suit. While disgusting and uncomfortable, it's better than waking up naked in a stranger's bed. Or even in pajamas you don't remember putting on. No one is in the room with me. Another relief.

Light is flooding the room from a row of windows on my left. I push myself up and groan as piercing pain shoots through my head. Pressing my hand to my forehead with my eyes clenched shut, I try to keep moving to get off the bed. The white sheets seem to stretch on forever.

My feet finally find the edge, and I force myself to stand. My mouth waters and I know I'm about to vomit. I look around me and see that there is an attached bathroom. I sprint to it as fast as the pain in my head will allow. Maybe a little too fast because my vision starts to go black as I hit my knees in front of the toilet.

My mouth fills with sour acid, and I continue to heave even after my stomach has finished emptying. When my stomach finally settles, I roll onto the floor, covered in sweat and shivering against the cold white tile floor in my damp white bathing suit.

It takes a while to get back to my feet. Everything hurts, but I can't stay here forever. And I don't want Tessa or anyone else to come to check on me and find me in this state. Back in the room, I see that the bedside table is filled with things. A few bottles of water, a small bottle of ibuprofen, a package of hydration powder, folded pajamas, and a protein bar.

I almost cry.

I pour the contents of the hydration stick into the water bottle and take small sips. I don't want to throw up again, and my body needs the water and the electrolytes. I sit on the edge of the bed, staring at the bottle of painkillers. I decide to chance it and take two of them. I have to take deep breaths to fight back the wave of nausea that comes from swallowing them.

When I haven't vomited after a few minutes, I get back to my feet and inspect the shower. There are towels rolled up on a shelf that I hope are for use and not just decoration. There are also full bottles of shampoo, conditioner, and body wash. The shampoo is an expensive brand, and I say a silent thank-you for my hair.

By the time I shower, change into the pajamas, and get myself looking halfway decent, I can hear people outside the room. The sound of plates and cups and soft laughter. It's a sound I've heard on rare mornings I've woken up at a friend's house as a kid, but the sound never played for me at home. My dad was gone before the sun came up, and my mom remained asleep until after we left for school. My sisters and I would tiptoe through the house to get ready.

As I'm leaving the room, I realize I haven't seen my bag or my phone. I turn around and search the room, having to stop and take a few breaths as my head swims and my stomach turns. I feel much better, but not a hundred percent.

My things aren't in the room.

My heart races as I think about what is in my bag. I still have my old driver's license with my old name on it. And my phone. It's password protected, but also opens with my thumbprint. I don't remember the last time I cleared my history, so all my searches of Astrid, Theo, Tessa, and Neil would be easy to find if they're looking.

I walk toward the noise of people and breakfast hesitantly. Theo and Neil sit on stools at the kitchen island and Tessa stands on the other side of it, pouring a cup of coffee. She spins when I enter the room. I don't know how she heard me.

"Olive, good morning!" she says, excited, but her tone is mercifully low. "There is breakfast here, coffee, orange juice, mimosas and Bloody Marys if you're a hair-of-the-dog type."

"Thank you," I say, and it comes out hoarse and broken, being the first time I've spoken today. I clear my throat and try again with a self-deprecating grin. "Thanks."

I take a piece of toast from a pile and munch on it, taking in the scene. Tessa has walked to the back of the kitchen where Corrie and Janine both sit at a small round table. The hangover anxiety is thick in my chest. My face burns as I remember the kiss with Astrid when she slipped drugs into my mouth. As though he can hear my thoughts, Theo says, "Astrid is still asleep. She's not a morning person at the best of times."

"Why does she do morning yoga, then?" I ask with a small laugh.

"You should see her before she leaves the house on those yoga mornings. She's a mess."

"You couldn't be talking about me." Astrid's voice comes from behind me, and Theo smiles over my shoulder.

"Never, my love. My wife a mess? Never heard of such absurdity," Theo says in a bad English accent that makes Astrid giggle, and I bite back my grin.

Astrid leans in front of me, grabbing a piece of toast. She glances up and meets my eyes. "How are you feeling?"

"Good," I say, trying to look it. "Definitely tired, though."

"I'm going to sleep the rest of the day away when I get home."

"Me too."

"Oh," I say, turning to Tessa. "I must have misplaced my purse at some point. I didn't see it in the room . . ."

"Go up the stairs and it's the first bedroom on the right. It's our room. I locked everyone's things in there last night to make sure no one tried to drive home."

"Right." I smile. "Good call."

I climb the stairs and push the door to the bedroom open. It's a giant room. As big as my entire apartment. There is a daybed against the far wall that has my bag and two others on it. I grab mine, opening it to ensure my phone is there. It is. I press my thumb to the unlock button but get a message saying that I have to input my code.

Usually, it only requires the code if the thumbprint didn't match up or if my phone has just turned on. The thought of someone attempting to unlock my phone makes me queasy. But then, maybe it's just the hangover.

I look around the room, taking it in. I have to see her closet. I tiptoe quickly to the closet door and peek in and exhale all my breath. It's amazing. It's as big as my living room and kitchen area. There is even a chair with a table in the corner. Why would you need to sit in here? I don't know, but I love it.

I walk in and run my hands along one of the white fur coats. As my hand trails down the soft fur, I hear a crinkling. I do the motion again and then move the coat around, trying to find the cause. My hand finds the pockets and I pull out the culprit. Dozens of crinkled up bills. Money. I look at the door, my heart pounding.

I smooth a few of them out. Fifties. Hundreds. Twenties. A few singles. I shove them all into my bag. Quickly, I check more pockets and find more cash. I want to look for more, but I've already been up here too long. I move out of the closet and push it closed.

I walk to the bedroom door and pull it open, jumping out of my skin when I nearly collide with Corrie.

"Shit! Sorry," I say, hand on my chest.

"Careful, there. Where's the fire?"

"At home, actually." I hold up my phone. "Missed a couple of calls and emails from my agent, and I have to get back to put out a few fires."

"Right. Well, I'm sure I'll see you around." She walks into the bedroom, presumably to get one of the remaining bags on Tessa's daybed.

* * *

I only sleep for a few hours before my mind starts racing, and the stress won't allow me to sit still for another moment. It's the fact that Theo is at home with Astrid right now. The fact that I still don't know how to get him alone. The fact that I have six minimum payments to make on loans and credit cards, and another hair appointment tomorrow morning. Blonde is beautiful, but it is a son of a bitch to keep up with.

I pile my hair on top of my head and throw on my sweats. They're loose now, falling off my hips. After making a cup of coffee, I climb into the corner of my couch and pull all the cash I found in Tessa's coats out. I pile it in front of me.

Smoothing and sorting each bill, I add it all up. $1,107.

This woman has over a thousand dollars in crumpled bills sitting around, forgotten in her coat pockets. It had to have been in there a while. It's the end of August, and there is no way she's worn fur coats recently. Her forgotten chump change just paid next month's rent and my next hair appointment.

I pull my laptop onto my lap, unsure of what I'm looking for at first. I can't count on finding cash lying around, and my money is going to run out sooner rather than later. I need an income of some sort. But I need the freedom of not having a job. Isn't that everyone's problem?

I search for remote jobs first. There are a few that look like they might work. Data entry. Customer service hotline. But both require set hours, and that's not possible if I want to keep up with Astrid and Theo's life.

Then another idea strikes. Freelance writing. Or editing. I have a master's degree in English. I've been too proud to use my writing that way in the past, but I'm desperate now. I don't need a lot. Just enough to make my minimum payments. The credit and loans I have will sustain me for a while longer.

I find an overwhelming number of people searching for writers. Article writers. Copywriters. Ghostwriters. Editors for blogs, online articles, and manuscripts. Fiction is my strong suit. I apply for a few ghostwriting jobs for fiction works and then I create a profile on a freelance site for writing specifically and offer my services for editing and ghostwriting.

With that done, I allow that stress to be set down for the moment. I've taken action and now I have to wait. Now it's time to figure out my next steps with Theo. I still think that my best bet is just staying present in their lives. He can get to know me that way. He can have time to realize I am the one he wants to spend his life with. And the best way to do that is through Astrid.

* * *

I continue going to yoga three times a week with Astrid and Tessa. We get coffee afterward each time. No one has so much as acknowledged the party at Tessa's, and I'm realizing that's part of the deal. They get drunk, black out on drugs, and whatever happens, happens. You just don't bring it up again in the light of day. I keep waiting for Tessa to bring up missing a large amount of cash, but it never comes up.

I got one of the ghostwriting jobs I applied for. It's a three-book series of romance books. Part of me hoped I wouldn't get this job, but it had the largest listed pay of any other posts. I don't enjoy commercial fiction, and it's proving difficult already. But she paid me a thousand dollars up front and signed a contract to pay four thousand per finished book. I can't pass it up.

As I'm working through a particularly tough scene, my phone chimes with an incoming text. My heart skips when I see Astrid's name on the screen.

*Dinner party at my place this Saturday at 6 p.m. Will you come?*

*—Of course. Special occasion?*

*Just a friendly get-together! (: Dress is formal. No need to bring anything. See you then!*

My heart is pounding at the prospect of a formal dinner party at Astrid and Theo's home. I finally get to see the place I've been imagining. The place that, if I play my cards right, will be the home I share with Theo.

I jump up from the couch, tossing my laptop to the side, and go to my closet. The only formal wear I have is the outfit I wore to the exhibition. Which I cannot recycle. I need a new dress. I text Tessa and see if she's free this week for a shopping trip. She can help me pick something out, and I can try to get dirt on Astrid.

My phone chimes. A response from Tessa:

*Omg I'm so glad you asked. Only if you let me pick everything.*

*—Deal!*

I meet Tessa at the store of her choice. A fancy boutique full of beautiful dresses. I came into today knowing this would be an expense that would make me nauseous. I try not to think about it and tell myself, as soon as I finish this book, I won't have to worry about it.

Tessa scans racks of clothes, handing different pieces to a boutique worker to put in a dressing room for me. "Okay.

This is a good place to start, so I can get an idea of what colors and cuts fit you best."

The saleswoman leads me to a spacious room lined with mirrors. I start to undress and wipe my palms on the designer jeans I wore here. Being around all these expensive clothes is making me nervous. What if I rip something? Or sweat into it. My heart hammers in my throat as I change into the first dress.

I turn and let the white fabric sway around me. It's beautiful and I don't dare look at the price tag. I walk out of the room to show Tessa.

"Oh, that's stunning on you. White really is your color. It's Astrid's color too. I could never pull it off. My complexion does better with warm tones."

"I love it." The compliment of being compared to Astrid makes me feel lightheaded and tingly.

"Go try the others on," Tessa says, shooing me with her hands.

The next one is a champagne color. I like the cut, but the color washes me out. I bend my arms behind me, trying to get the zipper up in the back.

"I never did ask . . . how did you end up going to Solstice?" Tessa asks through the door.

I freeze. "Uh — I just searched for yoga studios in the city and picked one that looked nice." I open the door and step out. "Can you get this zipper for me?"

She looks me up and down. "Don't bother, that color washes you out. Next one."

I turn and go back into the room.

"That must've given you at least twenty different studios. What a coincidence you picked mine and Astrid's studio."

My throat tightens. "Seriously. Small world."

I hang the champagne dress back on its hanger and go to the red one. I can't remember the last time I wore anything red. It's a bold color, and I wouldn't describe myself as a bold person. But maybe I can be now.

"Astrid has taken a liking to you. It's not often she invites strangers to her home."

I walk out of the room once more, my face feeling as red as the dress I have on. "Well, I'm flattered she seems to enjoy my company. I enjoy hers too. And yours. As far as being a stranger, I'd say we're a little beyond that, no?"

Tessa smiles, staring directly into my eyes. Her expression is cold. Cautious. "This is the one. I'll wait for you by the shoes."

She turns and strides away, leaving me standing there with my breath caught in my chest. I force myself to move back into the changing room. Why is she so suspicious of me all of a sudden? She just invited me to her kid's birthday party.

I remember needing to input my passcode in my phone. Was she trying to unlock it? Has she realized her cash is missing? I have to figure out why she's on my case. And more importantly, I have to get her off it. Maybe she's jealous. She's Astrid's best friend, from what I can tell so far. At least Astrid is hers.

I find Tessa by the shoes, and she hands me a pair of Louboutin's. "These are perfect. Size eight, right?"

"Yep." I smile and we walk to the cash register together.

"That will be $1,824.92," the woman behind the cash register says.

I feel lightheaded. I try to keep my face neutral as I hand her my card. I'll be needing another cruise through Tessa's closet to pay myself back for this little shopping trip.

We walk out together. The sun is an assault on my eyes, and I sift through my purse to find my sunglasses. They're Prada and I found them on eBay for a steal.

"Are you headed home?" Tessa asks, putting on her own sunglasses.

"Yes. I have to get back to work."

"Astrid and I have girls' wine nights, and we alternate houses. We should do one at your place next," she says.

"Absolutely, I'd love that."

That is absolutely not happening.

"Well, I'll text the group and set something up." Tessa leans forward and wraps me in a hug. Over her shoulder, I spot a familiar face, and my whole body goes rigid.

"Laura! Hey, Laura, is that you?" Donna calls a few buildings down. The street is busy with afternoon shoppers and I'm hoping her voice is drowned out.

"Okay, see you later," I say. I turn and walk as quickly as I can.

"Laura!"

I look over my shoulder and Donna is now closer to me than Tessa. Tessa is walking in the opposite direction, but she stops when Donna shouts my name again.

Shit. Shit. Shit.

Donna breaks into a jog, and there is no way to avoid her unless I start sprinting. "Laura, I thought that was you. Wow, you look great. So different. How are you?"

"I'm sorry, you have the wrong person," I say, looking over her shoulder. Tessa has stopped walking and is watching our interaction.

"No." Donna laughs. "Laura Tate. From Café Rêvasser."

"That's not me." I try to smile and laugh it off like an awkward situation and not the detrimental one that it's quickly becoming. I turn away from her and start walking again. Donna doesn't follow or yell after me. But the damage has already been done.

# CHAPTER FOURTEEN

*"I loved her against reason, against promise, against peace, against hope, against happiness, against all discouragement that could be." — Charles Dickens*

Sitting in the back of the Uber, I bounce my legs and chew my lip, trying to figure out how to handle this. Should I text Tessa? Make a joke about the crazy woman who chased me down the sidewalk? Or would addressing it make it seem more like a lie?

I feel sweat tickling my hairline and gathering at my lower back. I take out my phone and tap out a text to Tessa.

*Did you see that nut job run after me outside the shops? Remind me to buy a Taser haha.*

I let my face fall into my hands. Fucking Donna.

My mind won't stop racing as I climb the stairs to my apartment. Tessa hasn't responded to my text yet. But she's probably still driving. I work the key into my door handle.

"Hey. I know you," a male voice says from behind me.

What now?

I spin and meet eyes with Logan. Hometown Hero from the diner.

"You have got to be kidding me," I say, irritation mounting.

"You know, not the typical reaction I get from women."

"And yet, it still isn't enough to wipe the cocky grin from your face. Why are you here right now?"

"Oh, it would take a lot more than that to kill my confidence. And I live here. What are you doing here?"

I shake my head. No. Nope. Not dealing with this right now. I walk into my apartment and shut the door without responding to him. What in the actual hell is happening?

* * *

I don't leave my apartment until it's time for the dinner party at Theo and Astrid's house. I spent the week forcing myself to write the book for my ghostwriting gig because, after my shopping trip with Tessa, I could really use a paycheck.

Tessa never responded to my text. Tonight will be the first time I've seen or talked to her since the incident with Donna, and I'm so nervous that I keep dropping things and bumping into furniture as I'm trying to get ready.

My phone chimes with the alert that my Uber is here. I peek through my front door, searching the hall for Logan. When I'm confident he's not there, I hurry down the stairs to the shiny black car waiting for me. I chose the Lux option for tonight, making sure I don't stick out in any way.

Seeing the Connors' house again brings such an incredible mix of feelings. I'm almost euphoric as the car drives up the long driveway. I'm delighted to see more of the house. To see it up close. To touch the stone. To know what it smells like. I want the full experience.

"You having dinner with the president or something?" says my driver as he pulls in front of the house.

I step out without answering and tap on my phone to give him a rating and a tip. Both modest for his last-minute comment. And because I'm only playing at being rich.

The front door is twice the size of the tallest person I've ever seen, and it opens as I lift my hand to ring the bell. "Please come in, Miss Tate," says a middle-aged woman in an all-black uniform.

I smile and let her take my shawl and my purse. I follow the woman through the house. I want to stop and take it in. Look at the art on the walls and the ornate woodwork. But I have to keep up. She leads me to a sitting room where Astrid, Theo, Tessa, and Neil all sit with crystal glasses in their hands. A fire crackles at the back of the room in a fireplace large enough to stand in.

"Olive, I'm so glad you could make it," Astrid says as she stands and glides across the room to hug me and kiss my cheek. Her dress is white, and the bottom is cut at a slant. Theo sits in a leather armchair behind her in a black suit with a white tie. His hair is shorter than the last time I saw him, but his face is covered in facial hair that is just barely more than a five o'clock shadow. I have the overwhelming urge to run my hands across his cheeks.

"What would you like to drink?"

"An old fashioned if you have it. If not, wine would be just as welcome."

Astrid nods to the corner of the room, and I see a man behind a wooden bar that I hadn't noticed before. I make my rounds to hug and kiss everyone as the man makes my drink. Tessa is stiff and a little too cool for my comfort.

When I get to Theo, my heart is hammering so loud that I'm sure he must hear it. He smells like spices, oranges, and leather. He leans down to kiss the air beside my face and his facial hair brushes my cheek.

"Nice to see you again, Olive."

"Dinner will be ready in about ten minutes," Astrid says. "I hope you're all hungry."

We sit around a long, dark, wood table. A couple dozen candles of all different sizes are gathered along the center of the table, flowers and greenery woven between them. Large built-in bookcases surround us, and it looks as though it was built straight from my dreams.

Dinner is served, and my mouth waters. My calories have been lacking lately, trying to keep up with these ultra-fit women. I haven't eaten at all today, saving all my calories for this meal so I can look like I eat what I want. It's not attractive to show restrictive eating. Men want you to eat like they do but look like a starving twelve-year-old. It's asinine.

"This food is incredible, Astrid," Tessa says, dabbing her mouth with a white linen napkin.

"Thank you." Astrid beams as though she cooked it herself instead of the kitchen full of staff.

"So how did you two lovebirds meet?" I ask, glancing between Astrid and Theo. They look at each other, and Astrid nods her head toward him.

"You want to tell it? You're a better storyteller."

Theo grins, his eyes on hers as he leans forward like he's about to tell everyone a secret. "It was quite the scandal," he says.

His eyes leave Astrid as he begins his story and scans the guests at the table. When he gets to me, my stomach does flips, and his eyes linger. "I was a sophomore at Holloway. Astrid was a freshman. She was dating my best friend, and I was dating hers."

Tessa makes an "ooooow" sound like a child when someone does something bad. She must have heard this story before. I'm thoroughly interested. My eyes haven't left Theo's and his haven't left mine.

"That's how we met. We'd been on a few double dates together, and from the beginning, we just really hit it off."

"You dog," Neil says with a boyish grin. It's the first time I've heard him talk all night.

Theo laughs and continues. "We were at a party one night. My girlfriend and I had gotten into a fight, and she left, but I stayed behind and drank my sorrows. Astrid and her boyfriend were still there, all cozied up in a corner. I had begun to admit my feelings for Astrid. Only to myself, of course. But looking back, I think that's why my girlfriend and I had been fighting so often. So seeing them together was upsetting, and I was drunk. I asked my buddy to play beer pong with me to get him away from her."

I finally allow myself to look away from Theo. His eye contact was broken when he laughed at Neil's remark. Astrid is smiling and staring over at him, and I feel like college Theo.

"Well, I'd managed to get my buddy properly wasted. By the time we stepped away from the table, he was swaying on his feet. I had him sit down for a while and he passed out almost immediately. Astrid was nowhere to be found, so I searched around for her. I found her sitting on a window ledge in one of the bedrooms of the frat house we were at. She looked more beautiful than I'd ever seen her."

Theo leans over and kisses Astrid's head. I smile, but inside I want to whip one of these candles at her.

"I walked right up to her and kissed her. She was shocked at first, but she kissed me back. We were getting pretty heated when both our partners walked into the room to find us."

"Oh, no!" Tessa says.

"Apparently, my girlfriend had come back looking for me and saw my friend passed out on the couch. She woke him up, asking where I was, and they both came looking for us. Needless to say, we were both dumped. But we started dating each other a few weeks later. And then, like the crazy kids we were, we got married six months after that. The rest is history."

Astrid takes a long drink of her wine, her face a little flushed.

"Well, that's a relief to hear. I was starting to think you guys might be too perfect to hang out with. At least now I know you're both terrible people." I laugh to let them know I'm joking. Though I'm not. Not really.

"To terrible people," Theo says and raises his glass.

We all lift our glasses. "To terrible people," we say.

"I want to know more about you, Olive," Theo says.

I force my face to stay neutral. "What do you want to know?"

"Anything, really." He nods toward Tessa and Neil. "We've been friends for so long. It's been a while since we've had fresh blood in the group."

I glance over at Tessa for the first time since we sat down to eat. She's staring at me like vomit on the sidewalk.

I look back at Theo and lean forward, taking a sip of my drink. "I'm an open book."

"Do you have a family?"

"I mean, I come from a family. But I don't have one of my own."

"So no kids? No husband?"

"Nope."

"Ever?"

"Nope. No ex-husbands. Just a few unlucky ex-boyfriends. No kids."

"Do you want kids? A husband?"

"I'd love to get married one day. But I've never wanted kids."

Theo nods. "And the family you come from? Local?"

"No. I grew up in northern Indiana. I moved down here to go to college and never went home. I have parents and siblings, but we don't talk."

No one from my family has contacted me since the day I left the house. I thought my dad would call me, at least. But it seems I've officially been cut out. Fine by me.

"At all?" he says.

"Not at all."

He nods again, and I wait for him to ask why. But he seems to decide that the question is maybe beyond a line and changes direction. Thankfully. "Have you always wanted to be a writer?"

"For as long as I've wanted to be anything at all."

"Do you have many other writer friends?"

"No. Writing is a solitary profession," I say, because I've heard that it is. I've only ever wanted to be a writer.

"It definitely can be," Theo says. "You said you moved here for college, didn't you? Did you go to Holloway?"

"I did."

"I'm sure Astrid told you, but I'm a professor there. I run a writing course on campus too. You should come by. Maybe you'll be able to connect with some like-minded people."

"Sure, I'd love that." My cheeks grow warm at the invitation.

I glance over at Astrid. She's been quiet since the story of how she and Theo got together. She stares into her glass, eyes unfocused.

When dinner is over, we reconvene in the lounge room we were in earlier. I request another drink from the barman, and I watch the room while I wait for him to make it. The men are talking off to one side of the room and Tessa has excused herself to the bathroom. I turn, looking for Astrid, and see her slipping through a door that looks like it leads outside.

I take my drink from the barman and follow Astrid.

It's cool outside. Fall is on its way in. The backyard is more incredible than the front. I have no idea how many acres there are, but it must be a lot. There is a pool off to the left, illuminated and curving in a way that makes it look like a natural occurrence. To the right is an outdoor fireplace with couches. Open yard stretches back for a long distance and then mature trees block off whatever else might be out there.

I spot Astrid on a chair by the pool, a puff of smoke floating up over her head. I walk over and sit next to her. "Got another?"

She hands me a cigarette and a lighter.

"Are you okay?" I ask. "You seemed a little off after dinner."

"Oh, yeah. I'm fine."

I raise an eyebrow, and she blows out a hard breath laced with smoke.

"That story. How we met. It always brings back some tough emotions," she finally says with a small smile.

"I'm so sorry. I shouldn't have asked. That was none of my business."

She shakes her head. "No, no. It's a normal question to ask someone."

I'm quiet for a moment. Trying to decide whether I should pry a little or let it go. I decide to pry.

"It was so long ago, and you guys have been together ever since. Surely you don't still feel guilty."

"No, it's not that. My ex wasn't as good a guy as he led people to believe. But I guess Theo and I aren't either. 'Terrible people.'" She laughs through her nose.

"You know neither of you are terrible."

She raises her eyebrows and does a head tilt like I don't know what I'm talking about. Then she looks at me, seeming to consider something before she takes another drag of her cigarette. "There's more to that story. The part Theo always skips when he tells it. I got pregnant a few months after we started dating. It's why we got married."

My mouth drops open, so surprised that I can't hide it.

"We lost the baby. I had a miscarriage at sixteen weeks." I notice a tremor in her hand as she puffs on her cigarette once more before dropping it to the ground and grinding it beneath the toe of her high heel. She stands before I can say anything.

I stand with her and put my hand on her shoulder, stopping her as she starts to walk away. "I'm sorry that happened," I say. "What a terrible loss to suffer at such a hard time in your life."

She's looking down, and I watch as a tear falls and hits the ground. I wrap her in a hug before I can think of all the reasons not to. She looks so sad that it pulls at my heart. She hugs me back, and while I stare over her shoulder, I remind myself that I cannot afford to feel sorry for Astrid. She may have lost a baby, but look at all she's gained since then.

She has no idea how much she will soon lose.

I follow her back inside where the rest of the group sits in large chairs sipping drinks like they did before dinner. I like the idea of drinking with friends being the bookends of dinner.

"There you two are," Theo says as I close the door behind me.

Astrid smiles. "I just needed a little air. Olive wanted to see the back of the property."

I glance at her out of the corner of my eye. She's standing tall, smiling casually. "It's beautiful. You have an incredible home."

"Theo, why don't you show her your study? You writer people geek out over writing spaces. I know Theo does, anyway," Astrid says.

Theo stands. "Have you seen Stephen King's office?"

"I've seen pictures." Surely, he can't have seen it in person . . . I follow him across the house and through a large oak door. The room is expansive with a monstrosity of a desk sitting in the center, made of the same oak as the door.

Interesting.

I remember reading something about King's writing room. How he once had a large oak slab desk in the center of his writing room. But after years of misery and drunkenness, he got rid of that desk and got a smaller one to put in the corner of the room. I wonder if Theo knows that.

The wall to the right of the desk boasts a huge fireplace framed by shelves decorated with expensive-looking vases and old books. I take a step closer and read the leather spines. They're all classics. I run my finger along the gold letters of Dracula.

"Beautiful, aren't they? Every time we go on a trip, I try to bring back a rare book and a handcrafted vase."

"They're incredible," I say, my voice a whisper. I trace my finger along the painted clay.

"Theo," a voice shouts from down the hall. Astrid's. "Where is your cigar cutter?"

Theo sighs. "I'll be right back."

He strides out of the room, leaving a breeze of citrus and smoke in his wake. I cross the room and trail my fingers across the surface of his massive oak desk. It's cool to the touch, and I like the textured feel of the wood. I move to the large, leather computer chair and sit down. I take a deep breath and inhale the leather and oak. I want to remember this.

My curiosity gets the best of me, and I pull open a drawer. A line of expensive-looking pens sits on top of personalized stationery, and I wonder what he uses it for. I reach farther back into the drawer where I can't see and feel around. My fingers land on something that feels like paper and something hard. I pick them up, and with a quick glance at the door, I look through Theo's things. There are two polaroid pictures and a ring. The ring is a men's class ring. Class of 2010. I slip it into my bra.

I pull the first picture closer. It's a little blurry. A man and a woman stand next to each other, arms slung around each other's shoulders. They're standing in front of the university. I squint. They're too far from the camera, but I'm almost sure it's Theo and Astrid. I flip to the next picture. Another of a man and woman, but this one is newer.

I hear footsteps and I return the pictures, shut the drawers, and stand up, opening one of the books on his desk.

"That's one of my favorites. I reread it when I start a new writing project. It always helps me get my tone right."

"I hate to admit that I haven't read this one. But it's on my list now." I close it and place it back on the desk. "Should we get back to the party?"

I love any time I can get alone with Theo, but I'm anxious about leaving Tessa alone with Astrid. She's been cold toward me all night, but she seems to have said what she needed to say that day at the boutique. Hopefully, she decides to mind her own business from now on.

He sweeps his arm across his body, holding his hand out toward the door. "After you, madam."

I cross the room, walking a little slower than necessary.

And just a little closer to him than necessary.

## CHAPTER FIFTEEN

*"We would be together and have our books and at night be warm in bed together with the windows open and the stars bright."* — *Ernest Hemingway*

Theo's writing course starts at eight in the morning. I'm not much of a morning person, but neither is Astrid, and I have to be better than her. So I wake up at five, go for a run, and now I'm sitting on my couch with a cup of coffee while I work on this awful romance book I need to turn in soon.

I'm hoping to get some helpful tips somehow in Theo's class. I'd never admit to ghostwriting a romance novel, but I can ask for help with what I'm struggling with in roundabout ways. Maybe he can even help me with my own book. That's what I'll be telling him I'm struggling with. Which isn't a lie.

I get to the university campus thirty minutes early. It's strange to be back here. I take in the tall stone buildings as I walk toward Theo's class. The atmosphere instantly makes me feel like I'm eighteen again. Awestruck with the beauty and the possibilities. Too bad all those possibilities went rotten. All but one. This one will be different.

A bulletin board on the front of the building catches my attention. Ads for tutors, DJ services, and upcoming campus mixers are scattered across the surface. Off to the side of the board is a white paper with a color photograph of a young girl, a freshman maybe. The same girl from the posters at Café Rêvasser. MISSING GIRL typed in bold font across the top of the poster. She probably went to school here.

I keep walking and find the classroom. I peer through the glass window of the door. Theo is sitting at the desk at the front of the classroom. Rows of chairs with desks attached line the room in front of him. His head is bent down over his phone. His expression is serious. Is he texting Astrid?

I twist the handle and push the door open. He sits up straight at the sound of me entering and quickly locks his phone. "Olive, you made it."

"I did. I couldn't turn down such valuable writing insight." I walk down a row of desks, tracing the tops with my fingers. "This book is going to be the death of me, I swear."

I turn back to the front of the room, and Theo is watching me, standing now, leaning on his desk, his hands flat on the top. "Oh, I doubt that. I won't allow it to be the case." His crooked half smile, my favorite of all his smiles, plays on his lips.

"My savior," I say, my voice low.

The door to the classroom opens and Theo straightens up, his expression shifting into that of the friendly writing teacher as two other women step into the room. They're young and pretty. In that way teenagers are. Taught skin, perky tits, and bright eyes despite the dark circles that ring them from sleepless nights.

I wish I had seen myself at that age how I see them now. I was self-conscious, painfully shy, and so uncertain of myself. My skin may be losing its elasticity, but the shyness has eased, and thanks to my new diet and exercise routine, I have more confidence than ever. I'm far from the same girl who sat at these desks ten years ago. She didn't have what it took to get to where she wanted to be. It took me ten years, but I have it now.

A few more students wander in with unkempt hair, cups of coffee, and sleep still in the corners of their eyes. This isn't a college credit course, so it's interesting to see the students who force themselves out of bed to make it here. Only one other person looks older than me.

Theo talks as he writes his name on the chalkboard. 'Professor Connor.' "This is a workshop class. So I won't be lecturing on specific writing topics. I'm here to help you with your own writing projects. So take out whatever you're working on. Make note of what you feel you're struggling with." Theo walks in front of his desk and leans against it, folding his arms. "If you'd like me to read through what you have and provide feedback, I can do that too. So for today, if you'd like, you can email me your file with specific questions or things you're struggling with. Otherwise, I'll just give you my general feedback. Or if you have a hard copy, you can leave a note with the same information and leave it on my desk. If you'd like to talk through anything, I'm going to make my way around to each of you. You're free to work on your project in the meantime until I get to you. Sound good?"

Everyone mumbles an affirmation. One student, a girl in sweats with her hair piled high, takes a giant stack of papers from her bag and begins scribbling on a piece of paper. "Can I leave this on your desk?"

"Yes. Please leave a way to contact you on the note as well. Thanks for coming." He turns to a man in the front row and sits on the desk next to him.

I brought just a notebook, and in it I write out questions while I wait for Theo to get around to me.

The time passes impossibly slowly as I wait for my time with Theo. And before he gets to me, the hour-and-a-half class is over and all I've done is sit in a chair scribbling in a notebook. Theo stands and looks at the clock, alarmed. Like he hadn't realized the time had passed already. My annoyance fizzles as I take in his face. The boyish passion in his eyes, how he's lost track of time in a world of stories.

Me and one other girl are the only ones he hasn't gotten to. He looks around the room, coming to that same realization.

"Olive and Sandra, I'm so sorry I didn't get to you." He looks at his watch and considers something. "I have another thirty minutes if you have time. If not, you'll be first next time."

Sandra gets to her feet. "I have to get to work, but I was actually able to add another two thousand words to my manuscript, so it wasn't a loss at all. I'll talk to you about it next week."

"Sounds great. Thanks so much, Sandra. See you next week." He looks over at me, and I'd be damned if I'm going anywhere. This has actually worked better than I'd planned. Sandra disappears through the door, and we are finally alone.

"I'm free the rest of the day, so I can stay. This book is all I have to work on today."

"Great," he says, spinning the desk in front of me around to face me. "Tell me what you're working on. What you're struggling with."

I've had a lot of time to think about how I can ask for help without revealing what I'm actually writing. "I need help writing intimacy without it sounding cheesy or crude."

He nods, eyes pointing to the ceiling as he thinks. "Okay. That's not too difficult. Especially if you have those experiences to draw on."

"And a lot harder when you don't," I say with a self-conscious laugh. I think about the few boyfriends I've had. About Ethan. And it all falls short.

He doesn't miss a beat. "Definitely harder, but not impossible. You just have to find good examples. You can do that in entertainment and in real life. Pay attention and observe intimate moments around you. Intimacy doesn't have to be cheesy or crude. It's an exchanged look between two people who know each other so well that words are unnecessary. A subtle, comforting gesture. It can be found in complete silence or in a moment of chaos."

I hang on to every word he says and wish to know the intimacy he is describing. My envy of Astrid only intensifies. Does she even know how lucky she is to have him?

"I guess without ever having experienced true intimacy, it's hard for me to read."

"Intimacy requires vulnerability. Without it, it won't appear genuine."

I nod. "That makes sense."

Theo shifts in his seat, extending his leg. The inside of his leg scrapes the outside of mine. I shiver. He doesn't move it away. "I find it hard to believe you've never experienced intimacy."

"The men I've known before were all lacking," I say, my voice nearly a whisper. Before. Before him.

"Well, that's a shame."

All the incoming air seems to get caught in my chest as my brain searches for what to say to make this moment bigger. But words escape me, and the moment evaporates when I hear his phone vibrating against his seat. He leans to the side to retrieve it from his pocket, and that same serious expression that painted his face when I saw him before class is there again. A line forming between his eyes as he looks at the screen.

"I'm sorry," he says, sounding far away. He snaps out of it and looks up to meet my eyes. "I have to go."

"Of course," I say, a little thrown with the sudden change in his demeanor. "Yeah — uh," I stammer as I look around me, trying to gather my stuff. He's already on his feet. And moving to his desk to gather his own things. We get to the door at the same time, and he locks it behind us.

He seems to gain a little composure as he turns to me. "Sorry for the abrupt ending there. I have another class tomorrow. Maybe you can make it if you're not busy." He smiles and leans in for a hug. I wrap my arms around him and hope he can't feel how hard my heart is slamming into my ribcage.

"Yeah, I'll check my schedule and see if I can," I say, knowing there isn't a chance I'll miss it.

We part ways and I head home, wondering the whole way what happened that had Theo hurrying out of class. I consider texting Astrid, but having just left Theo, it feels weird. If he's heading to her, and he likely is, I don't want him to see that

I immediately started texting Astrid, trying to pry and dig to see what's happening.

Instead, I stop at a drive-through for coffee and head back to my apartment to work on the book. I like what Theo had to say about intimacy. I've been brainstorming a way to write this romance book that doesn't feel contrived. And thanks to Theo, I've come up with a few scene ideas and new thoughts about the story.

I step through the front door of my apartment building and stop to check my mailbox.

"Are you following me? I knew you were some sort of stalker pervert." Logan opens his mailbox next to mine.

"The odds of you living in my apartment building just don't make sense," I say, slamming my mailbox shut.

"Hey, I lived here first. You're the one that looks suuuper sketchy in this situation."

"You are a very annoying person."

"Aw. Thank you."

I look up at him, and he's smiling sweetly. I want to kick him.

"Do you want to come by and watch the game with me?" he asks.

I laugh. "In what world . . . ?"

"Baseball is America's pastime, miss." He bends down to look at my mailbox. "Why's it say Olive and your card says Laura? Are you a spy?"

"I didn't like the name Laura, so I changed it." I don't know why I tell him the truth. Probably because I don't have a lie on hand.

"Hmm." He shrugs. "So, you sure you don't want to watch the game with me? It's going to be a good one."

"I'm sure." I climb the stairs and let myself into my apartment. I wonder how hard it'll be to get out of my year lease.

I spend a few hours typing out my ideas and even getting through a few new scenes. I'm on a roll when my phone starts ringing. I almost ignore it, not wanting to break this momentum now that I've finally found it. But curiosity gets the best of me, and I lean over the length of the couch to grab my phone. Astrid's name fills the screen, and I quickly swipe to accept the call before it goes to voicemail.

"Hey. Astrid, how are you?"

"Olive? Are you busy?" Her voice is strained, like she's holding back tears.

"Uh — no. Not really. What's wrong? Are you okay?"

"Yeah." She laughs, but it sounds strangled. "I'm okay. I just need to get out. I — uh . . . I need a friend." She makes a sound that I can't decide whether it's a laugh or a cry. "Can I come over to your place? I need to get away for a while."

Panic claws at my chest. She can't come here. "I'm actually having my floors replaced so unfortunately, there's nowhere to exist in my house right now," I say with a small laugh. "But how about we meet at Fredrick's?"

"Yeah, that works. Thank you, Olive."

"Of course. I'll be there in thirty minutes."

I have the Uber driver drop me off a block away and do a weird run-walk the rest of the way, hoping Astrid isn't there yet. I tried to get here early so she wouldn't see me arriving. I don't want to explain my commuting habits. I really need to look into getting a better car.

Astrid walks up just as I'm nearing the entrance to Fredrick's. She must have parked on Broadway and walked over. Her face is red and tear-streaked. There is a small pull on my heart that I ignore, though I wrap my arms around her all the same. "Oh my gosh, what's wrong? What happened?"

A thought suddenly occurs to me that something could have happened to Theo. My heart falls to my stomach at the possibility. "Is Theo okay?"

Astrid pulls away, rolling her eyes as she pulls open the door to the bar. I admire the way she isn't ashamed to walk into a public place in clear distress. She doesn't wipe her face or try to look like she hasn't been crying. She's so different than I expected her to be those weeks ago in the café.

She leads us to a booth in the back corner and slides in, and I scoot in across from her. She chews her lip as she stares toward the bar, likely trying to spot the bartender. I watch her, waiting for her to answer my question from outside, my chest tight with apprehension, though the roll of her eyes has made me think it is at least nothing too serious.

A bartender finally comes to our table, and we order drinks. When the bartender leaves to get our beverages, I look back to Astrid with a raised eyebrow.

"Have you ever felt utterly alone in the company of someone you love?" Astrid asks, still looking toward the bar.

The question takes me off guard. My first thought is what it means that she's asking it. If she's referring to Theo. But then I realize I need to answer her, and I consider the question. It brings up an ache in the back of my throat.

"I guess I have. It's been a long time, but I suppose I loved my family once. When I was young. When I wanted a connection with my parents, and later, my sisters. But I always felt different. They never got me. And I never got them. So, yeah. It was lonely."

I'm surprised by my honesty, but Astrid finally turns her attention to me with a thoughtful expression. She and her husband have the same way of never showing judgment in response to what someone says.

I've never talked out loud about my family. Never admitted how alone I felt those long years ago. And never allowed myself to verbalize that, at one point, I did want their approval and understanding.

"Theo and I got into a big fight," she says, finally answering my question. "We just feel so distant lately. Like maybe we're starting to want different things." Her face falls onto her hands as a sob escapes her. "And that scares the hell out of me."

The openness is almost too much. Because I keep feeling waves of sympathy and guilt. For Astrid and my intentions. I have to remind myself that this isn't personal. This isn't a vendetta against Astrid. I don't want to hurt her. She's just in my way. Theo and I have a real connection. This is everything I've ever wanted, and I can't let that slip away.

Astrid is strong and clearly has her own thing going with her gallery. And now I've finally discovered a crack in the armor that is their marriage. This is a very good thing. Astrid will land on her feet. She's already unhappy. They're growing apart. This might be easier than I thought. Maybe, after all is said and done, we could even be friends.

# CHAPTER SIXTEEN

*"The wicked envy and hate; it is their way of admiring."* — *Victor Hugo*

I'm the first one in class again. And again, I stand outside the door and watch Theo as he sits at his desk. He's not on his phone this time. He stares straight ahead, looking like he's somewhere else entirely. He's leaning forward, resting his elbows on the desk, and from the movement of his body, I can tell he's bouncing his leg.

I wonder if he's stressed about his argument with Astrid. I wonder if he knows we met up to talk last night. There's only one way to find out, so I take a deep breath and open the door.

His smile is immediate when he sees it's me. It warms something right in my center. "You made it," he says, standing from his desk.

"I did." I set my bag on a desk in the front row and turn back to him. "How are you?"

"I'm good. Considering," he says with a shrug and a look that says I know what he's talking about. So, he must know.

"You guys will work it out. You're perfect together," I say, though the words sting and stick like electric-charged syrup in my mouth.

Theo laughs humorlessly. "Anyway, thanks for talking with her last night. She needs a friend like you, and I appreciate you being there for her like that."

"Of course. That's what friends are for. She has Tessa too, though."

He makes a face. "Tessa is a good friend, but she's a shallow friend. Astrid can't talk to her about real stuff the way she can with you."

I only nod in response. Did Astrid tell him all of what she told me? More importantly, did she tell him all of what I told her?

The other students filter in, and I settle into my seat for the next hour. I love watching him work with the other students. His easy laugh and the way he throws his head back. His more serious expressions when he's focused on what they're saying and thinking of how best to help them. The lowering of his eyebrows. My mind conjures images of all the expressions I haven't seen. What his face might look like when he's making love to me.

I glance up and he's looking at me like he knows what I'm thinking about and my face warms. He grins and turns his attention back to the person he's working with. Is he flirting with me? That felt like flirting.

At the end of the class, I gather my things, moving slowly so the rest of the people leave the room first. I don't intend to hang around like last week, but I'm greedy for any moments I can get alone with him.

"Bye, everyone, see you next week. Email me if you need anything," he says. "Olive, are you busy?"

I'm halfway to the door and I stop, looking over my shoulder. "Not particularly."

"I was wondering if you might be free for lunch. My treat."

It feels like a flock of birds takes flight in my stomach all at once. "Perfect, I'm starving."

He smiles and starts packing up his things in a leather messenger bag.

The sun is warmer than it was just a few hours ago. Too warm for mid-September and the jeans and long-sleeve shirt I wore today.

"I'm parked just over here. I can drive, if you'd like?"

"Sure," I say and follow him. I'm glad he's walking ahead of me because I can't help the giddy smile at the thought of him driving me to a restaurant for lunch. It feels so much like a date that it's hard to remind myself he's still married to Astrid. For now.

His car is black and sleek. A Porsche, like Astrid's. He opens the passenger door for me. "Let me take your bags. I'll put them in the back."

I hand him everything but my purse and climb in, taking his extended hand to help me. I watch him go around the back of the car in the mirrors. The car smells like cedar and leather. It's a manly smell, and I wonder what it'd be like to fuck him in the back seat. Is there enough room? I'd manage.

He slides into the driver's seat and starts the car, the engine vibrating softly. "Have you been to Jericho?"

"In Palestine?"

He laughs. "No. The restaurant."

"No, I haven't," I say, laughing too. The way he laughs makes me feel like I've told a joke that he thought was funny, instead of making me feel like he's laughing at me.

"It's a small place on the east end of the city. Best food I've ever had."

"Wow. That's big praise."

"Well deserving. You'll see."

His hand rests on the gearshift, and I stare at his tanned fingers, wishing they'd work their way over to me. For a moment, I consider making a move myself, but I ultimately decide not to. Everything is working in my favor right now. He and Astrid are in a bad place, and I don't want to move in too soon and wreck that. I need to let them crumble further. Help to chip away at their relationship where I can and make myself available when the time is right. It's almost that time. We're so close. I can feel it.

He parks in a small lot off the main road, and I wait as he circles to my door and opens it for me, hand extended once more to help me out. His hands are cool and slightly calloused, which is surprising. How does a writer and a teacher acquire callouses?

Theo leads me to a brick building with a wooden sign — *Jericho* painted across it in cursive writing. I envisioned a quaint place, but this is anything but. Crystal chandeliers hang overhead, and the seating is all plush brown furniture that looks more expensive than everything in my apartment combined. A hostess in a black dress smiles at us as she approaches from within the restaurant.

"Mr. Connor, so nice to see you. Dining for two?" she says.

"Lovely to see you as well, Natalie. Yes, thank you."

If Natalie is confused as to why Theo is dining with a woman who's not his wife, she doesn't show it. For a tiny second, I wonder if he often takes other women out for a meal and drinks, but that's nonsense. The girl is just doing her job and minding her own business.

He stands beside my side of the booth and offers his hand to help me slide in. When he sits across from me, I can't help but grin like a schoolgirl with a crush. "This place is beautiful," I say.

"It's one of my favorites. Which is why they know me by name." He laughs.

A server appears beside our table. "Good afternoon, Mr. Connor. Will you be having the house red?"

"Yes. Thank you, Jonathan."

He nods and retreats to wherever he came from. "They make their own wine and age it in cellars below the restaurant. It's the best wine you'll ever taste."

"Best food, best wine? I don't know how I haven't heard of this place." Of course, I know exactly why I haven't heard of it. It's clearly out of my price range. Even with my borrowed money.

"Not many people have. But the ones who know come so often that they do quite okay."

"I guess so." I look around, taking in all the extravagance. The waiter returns with two glasses and a bottle of wine. He fills the glasses and leaves the bottle on the table.

"Olive, do you prefer seafood, beef, chicken, pasta, or vegetarian?" Theo asks.

"Seafood," I decide.

"Excellent choice. Jonathan, we'll both take the chef's seafood special."

Jonathan nods. "Yes, sir."

When we're alone again, Theo raises his glass. I raise mine to meet his. They clink together, and Theo takes a sip. I follow his lead, unsure why we just toasted to nothing. The wine is good. Better than good. You can tell immediately that it's expensive, though I don't really know how.

"Thanks for coming to lunch with me," Theo says.

"Thanks for inviting me."

"I'm so sorry about Astrid involving you in silly personal matters. It must've been a little awkward. But I am really thankful you were there for her. She doesn't have many friends she'll talk to about stuff like that."

"She didn't tell me much," I say honestly. I inferred a lot from what little she did say, but none of it was her words.

He nods. "Forgive me if this is too personal. But the truth is, we've been trying to have a baby for quite a long time."

My heart hits the floor. "Really? I had no idea."

He nods with a grim expression. "Astrid can't get pregnant. We've looked into different options, and nothing is quite right for either of us. That's what our disagreement was about last night. We don't agree on the path forward."

Saliva pools in my mouth. They want a baby. I've been thinking that they're falling apart, when really, they're trying to expand.

I force my breathing to slow down. I need to understand the full picture. "What paths are those?" We seem to be past a certain line of privacy, so fuck it.

Theo considers my question like he's trying to find the right words. I don't understand what is so difficult about explaining this. "Astrid wants to . . . stop pursuing a child. I want to keep going."

I nod slowly, taking this in. What does this mean for me? He wants a child with Astrid. Or maybe he just wants a child. I've never wanted to be a mother. But would I? For Theo?

"Anyway," he says, sitting up taller and smiling. "Enough of our drama. How is your book coming along?"

I'm thankful for the change of subject. I need a minute to process this new information and figure out how to move forward. "Great, actually. I'm nearly ready to send it off. Your advice has helped tons." And that's true. I should be ready to send the manuscript to my client in just a day or two after I look through it all once more.

"I'm glad to hear it. You'll have to tell me as soon as you have a release date."

"Of course. I think I'll throw a little party to celebrate when I turn it in for the final time. You know, when all the edits are done and everything."

"That's a great idea." He holds up his drink, a small raise-your-glass moment, and I mirror the gesture.

"What are we raising our glasses to?" A voice belonging to a woman makes me jump. I look over and Corrie is approaching our table, a glass of white wine in her hand. "Oh, Olive. I thought you were Astrid."

I scold myself internally for jumping when she spoke, making myself look guilty. But I laugh and flip my long blonde locks over my shoulder. "It's the hair."

Corrie nods toward Theo. "And the husband."

I stumble, trying to think of how to respond, the smile slipping from my lips, when Theo jumps in. "Hi, Corrie. What brings you here? I thought Astrid said something about you being out on a buying trip this week?"

She shifts her weight to her left foot, jutting her hip out. "I had to come home early. Pascal, my bird, got sick, and the house-sitter had to take him to the vet."

"That's terrible. I hope he's okay," Theo says with a genuinely concerned expression. I commend him. It takes everything I have not to roll my eyes.

"He's fine," she says briskly. "Mind if I join you?" She scoots in next to Theo without waiting for an answer. Theo moves farther in to make room for her.

I watch Theo, waiting for him to tell her to get lost in whatever Polite-Theo way he can. He looks only the tiniest bit surprised, but he doesn't seem like he's about to tell her no.

"So, what are we raising our glasses to? Don't leave me out now," she says, her glass poised in the air.

"To Olive finishing her final edits on her book," Theo says. I notice he doesn't tell her about the party I plan to throw. Giving me the option not to invite her. As much as I don't want her to be there, it would look bad not to invite her.

"I'll be throwing a small party to celebrate. The details are still being finalized, but I'll be sending out invites by the end of the month."

"Is that a thing?" she says. "Throwing yourself a party for doing your job? Writing books is your job, yeah?" She takes a sip of her wine, eyes locked with mine over the rim of her glass. I want to knock the glass into her mouth and see how sturdy her shitty veneers are.

"It is." I smile. "It's an artistic thing. I guess it would be different for those who create the art versus those who sell it. Less rewarding. You do get to wear those nice suits to work, though. So there's that." I rake my eyes down her blazer and back up, putting on a full smile when I reach her eyes again. "Pros and cons to every job, I suppose."

I feel a little guilty, as Corrie and Astrid have a very similar job. But it isn't really the same. Astrid owns her gallery. She puts together the events and coordinates the pieces herself. She is an artist in her own right. Corrie is an employee. A middleman between artists and buyers.

A nervous smile twists into shape on Theo's mouth. "Corrie, how long have you known about Jericho? I thought this was my secret little gem."

"A colleague brought me here for lunch a few weeks ago and I've been dying to come back. How sweet of you to share your secret gem with Astrid's friends. You've always been so generous." She squeezes Theo's arm.

He opens his mouth to respond, but our server appears beside our table with a tray of food. Apparently, they didn't miss Corrie moving to our table because her meal is set in front of her as well. Our wines are topped up, and we're left alone again in an awkward silence that I can tell Corrie is very much enjoying.

After the meal, the waiter brings the check and Theo grabs it. He must be paying for Corrie as well because she isn't brought a separate one. He's such a gentleman. Paying for someone so rude to invite herself to our lunch.

"Jonathan, can you have an order of crab cakes packaged for me to go?" Theo asks as he hands him his credit card.

"Of course." Jonathan nods and leaves.

"Afternoon snack?" Corrie asks.

"They're for Astrid. Her favorite."

"I thought she was allergic to shellfish?" Corrie's eyebrow shoots up.

"Hmm?" Theo looks over at her. "No. Astrid? She loves shellfish."

Corrie shakes her head. "Maybe I'm remembering someone else."

And she calls herself a friend of Astrid's.

# CHAPTER SEVENTEEN

*"You call it hope — that fire of fire! It is but agony of desire." — Edgar Allan Poe*

Corrie's house was easy enough to find. She posted a picture on Instagram two years ago when she bought the place. I only had to zoom in to see the address numbers. From there, I remembered her mentioning the drive to the gallery was bad because there was an accident on I-65 South. I scrolled a little farther back on her Instagram and found a picture of the Meridian Hills town sign captioned with 'House hunting today! Wish me luck.'

I searched the address numbers on Google maps and found a few streets with those numbers. Then I used the street view to virtually walk around the neighborhood until I found the house that matched her other picture.

And voilà!

Her Instagram stories tell me she has left for yet another buying trip. The hardest part will be getting inside. I have to hope that living alone hasn't made Corrie hyper-focused on security. She lives in one of the best neighborhoods in the state, for crying out loud. She should feel plenty safe.

I climb into my car with a bag of supplies: a brown wig, a baseball cap, sunglasses, and a small assortment of tools. It is easier to sneak around when I don't have very bright, distinctive blonde hair to give me away, so I had to splurge on an Amazon wig to better disguise myself.

Tormenting Corrie is a little off my course of winning over Theo. But I have things I need to figure out, and Corrie is pissing me off. So, I figured two birds, one stone. Step away from the problem at hand, clear my head while focusing on something else, get revenge on Corrie for being a rude bitch. So I guess it's three birds.

I park on the street and stride up the driveway. The sun is just setting. I debated whether to do this during the day or at night. Most break-ins happen during daylight hours because everyone expects them to happen at night and, therefore, are less suspicious of people during the day. In the end, I took too long to decide, and now here I am right in the middle.

The house is nice enough. Compared to any place I've lived, it's the Taj Mahal. But if I had her money, it's definitely not what I would pick. It's a two-story that looks like one of those mass-manufactured homes. White siding with small bushes lining the front.

I walk along the side of the house, assuming she locked the front door. Scanning the faces of the house for any obvious cameras, I walk casually up to the back door when I don't see any. It's locked.

I move to the windows, knowing a lot of people forget to lock them. There is one right beside her back door, but that one is locked too. *Shit.* Crossing my arms, I look around, trying to figure out a way in. I glance down and read the brown floor mat. "Gather." I make a gagging noise, step off it, and lift it up.

Laughing under my breath, I pick up the single silver key. People can be so dumb. The key glides into the deadbolt lock. I turn it and the door opens.

Corrie's house smells like lemon cleaner and artificial flowers. I wipe my feet on another mat just inside the door and then step farther into the house. The door leads into the kitchen and straight ahead is a living room. It looks nice. Expensive.

The furniture looks straight out of a catalog, and the room is expertly decorated. A set of stairs to the left beckon me, and I step quickly, not wanting to waste any time. I have a bird to find.

The first room is a bathroom. It's nearly empty, so I'm assuming she doesn't use it much. Though it's odd to leave a room untouched after living in a house for years.

The next room holds what I'm looking for. The red bird squawks from a cage in the far corner of the room. It's a bedroom. A large one with an ensuite. It would make sense to be the master bedroom, but it looks odd. Like the bathroom down the hall, there is barely anything in the room. The bed looks full size and sits on a metal frame. It has a tangled green patterned blanket crumpled on the end, a single black-and-white pillow, all on top of a beige sheet. Nothing matches. And it's a stark contrast to the downstairs of the house.

I cross the room and open her bedside table. The bird screeches again, making me jump.

"Shut up, bird!" I hiss.

The drawer has random things you might expect in a bedside table. Chapstick. An abandoned bookmark. An old flosser (ew). I close it. There is a dresser along the side wall. It clearly is not part of a set with her nightstand. How odd. She's some big shot corporate something or other. She's always wearing designer clothes, and she was just casually having lunch by herself at a restaurant that costs the same as groceries for a month. Why does half her house look as impoverished as mine?

I go to her closet and my jaw drops when I open the door. There are two items on a hanger. The pants suit she wore at Jericho's and a black dress. The rest of the large walk-in closet is completely empty.

No. Scratch that. A box of shoes sits in the back corner. I run my hand along the black dress, loving the feel of the expensive material between my fingers. Then I notice the tag still attached to the dress. $230. I move to examine the pants suit and find that it also has the tag attached. I guess it's possible it isn't the one she wore to the restaurant, but I'm pretty sure it is.

I know this trick. Leaving the tags on to return the clothes after you've worn them. It's a poor-girl trick. Or a cheap-girl one. But the difference between the lower level of Corrie's house and the upper level tells me it's likely the former. Why splurge on the common areas of your house, but live like a college student upstairs?

*Squaaaawk!*

I jump again, and I'm ready to throw the bird out the damned window. I exit the closet and walk to the birdcage. What did Corrie call him? Patches? Pablo?

"What's your name, bird?" I say, mostly to myself as I try to open the cage door.

"Hi, my name's Pascal. *Squawk*."

My eyes widen in surprise. "So you're one of those birds, huh? Well, how would Pascal like to be free?"

I get the door to the cage open, then move to the window. I unlock it and shove it open. "There ya go, buddy. Be free."

The bird stays put.

"Come on, stupid bird. Fly. Right out there. Be free." I swing my arm from the cage to the open window to show him the way. But he still doesn't move.

I sigh.

I grab the cage from its table and carry it closer to the window. Pascal flaps and squawks with the movement. I hold the open cage toward the window.

"Go on, Pascal. Fly away!"

He flaps his wings, and I think he's going to do it, but then he settles back onto his little perch.

*Seriously? Come on, stupid bird!*

I set the cage back on the table and shut the window. I hate birds. They freak me out. I was hoping he'd just fly through the window and Corrie would come home to find her precious bird gone. But maybe he can't fly? Don't people clip their wings to make sure they don't fly away?

I gather up my nerves and slowly stick my hand inside the cage. Pascal moves, and I yank my hand out, afraid he's going to bite me. *Damn it.* Okay. I can do this. I stick my hand back in and try to coax him out, but he doesn't move.

With a heavy exhale, I slam the cage door shut and carry it downstairs. "You're going to fly away, bird," I say, feeling stupid for the warning tone directed at a bird.

I walk outside, set the cage down, and lock the door. After returning the key to its terrible hiding place, I carry the cage out into Corrie's backyard and open the door once more.

"Time to go, bird."

I spend nearly thirty minutes trying to get the bird to leave its cage and end up sitting on the damp grass, my head in my hands and the bird still safely inside the gold cage. I'm too afraid to get him out with my hands. I have no desire to get bitten or pecked.

I've already been here much longer than I wanted to be. Every minute I'm here, I'm risking getting caught. My whole body freezes when I hear the crunch of tires on the driveway.

*No, no, no.*

She's supposed to be out of town. Is she back? Is it the police? Did she have a camera I missed and they're here to arrest me? I snatch the cage and run to the sparse tree line. I hear a car door slam shut and I inch forward. The bird flaps and squawks in his cage and I shush him.

I move forward and peek around to the front door, my heart hammering hard in my chest. I don't see anyone. There is a black sports car in the driveway. I don't know if it's Corrie's or not, but it's not a police car. I take a deep breath and sprint down the driveway, Pascal bouncing around in his cage beside me.

I make it to my car and open the back door, shoving the birdcage inside. I run around to the driver's side and race off.

My hands tremble, and I grip the steering wheel tighter. That was too close. I look in the rearview mirror at the red bird sitting in my backseat. What the hell am I going to do with this thing?

* * *

"Is that a macaw?" Logan asks as I struggle to unlock my door.

I whip my head around. "I don't know. Yes. Can you help me?" I ask and ram my shoulder against the door. "My door is stuck."

My pulse hasn't slowed since almost getting caught at Corrie's house. Now my door is stuck, and I've been spotted with a stolen bird. I move aside and let Logan try the door. He wiggles the handle, pulls on it, then pushes. He's standing close to me, and I can smell his laundry detergent.

The door finally opens, and I sigh with relief.

"I can fix that for you, so it doesn't stick anymore," Logan says as I move past him, bird in tow.

I hesitate, biting my lip as I consider just telling him to leave.

"It'll take ten minutes, tops."

"Fine," I say.

"Did you mean 'thank you'?"

"Yes. Thank you," I mumble.

He nods with that stupid grin on his face. "I'm going to grab my tools. I'll be right back."

I wave him off and pull out my phone to search for pet stores or bird rescues or wherever the hell might take this bird. I look up as Logan returns. He squats down in the doorway.

"Hi, my name's Pascal!" the bird says from my kitchen counter.

Logan laughs, standing up and walking toward the bird. "Hi, Pascal. My name is Logan. You're a pretty bird."

"Pretty bird!" Pascal squawks.

"Where'd you get him?" Logan asks, sticking a finger inside the cage to pet him.

"Don't do that. He'll bite you," I say.

But Logan's finger strokes the bird's feathers, and it doesn't bite him.

"Noooo," Logan says in a voice usually reserved for talking to infants. "Pascal is a nice bird. Aren't you?"

"Nice bird!" Pascal parrots.

"Where did you get him?" Logan asks again.

Why does he keep asking? "The place you get birds from," I snap. "Where else would I get him from?"

Logan laughs. "You're so aggressive." His hand falls back to his side, and he returns to the doorway.

"Well, you ask stupid questions."

Logan works on the door, and I try to find somewhere to take the bird, but I keep thinking they will want some kind of proof of ownership or something. Or that they'll have store cameras and Corrie will eventually find him and trace it back to me. Do people microchip pet birds?

"All set," Logan says.

"Great. Thank you." I try to sound appreciative, but the panic I'm feeling adds an edge to my tone.

"Are you okay? You seem upset. More than usual."

I narrow my eyes at him. "I'm not usually upset. And I'm fine. I just don't know what to do with this stupid bird."

I should have kept my mouth shut. I should have told Logan to leave after thanking him and revealed nothing more about the bird, but I'm panicking. My stupid, petty stunt is going to get me caught and ruin all the extensive and *expensive* planning I've done.

"What do you mean? Why do you even have him?" Logan says.

I make up a story about my sister having to leave town suddenly and asking me to care for her bird. I tell him I can't get a hold of my sister to ask her questions, and I don't know what to do with him. It was the quickest story I could think of, but now I'm stuck because I want to ask if he knows of a place that takes birds, but why would I be trying to get rid of my sister's pet bird I've been tasked to care for?

"Okay. Well, do you have his food?"

"I couldn't find it in her house," I say.

"All right. We can get some from a pet store. But just keep his food and water bowl full. You'll want to change out the bedding at the bottom of the cage every few days. But that's about it. Birds are low maintenance."

"I'm so overwhelmed." I let my head fall into my hands, unable to keep the facade up. I need time alone. To calm down and to figure this all out.

"Hey, it's going to be okay." Logan wraps an arm around me, and I feel myself soften into him. Tears sting my eyes.

My phone dings, and I pull away to grab it from beside me. It's a text from Astrid asking me to meet up at a coffee shop on the other side of the city. I almost tell her I can't. I need to re-collect myself, and I have a fucking bird in my house that I don't know what to do with or if Corrie can track it somehow.

"I have to go," I say. "Emergency."

Logan nods, stepping away awkwardly. "Sure. I'll go." He walks toward the door, then turns back. "I'll — uh — I'll see you around."

"Yeah. Thank you, again," I say.

When he shuts the door behind him, I scramble to change clothes and tame my hair. I'm halfway through the front door when I stop and turn back. I run back inside and fill the bird's water bowl, then run out the door to meet Astrid.

My fingers drum nervously on the steering wheel. I had no time to think about the situation with Astrid and Theo because of my stupid stunt.

They're trying to have a baby. But they're not on the same page about it. I slow down to stop at a red light, chewing on my lip. I have to convince Astrid that she shouldn't give in to Theo's insistence to keep trying. All of this would be so much easier if Astrid just walked away.

But there is a big question I've been avoiding asking myself. Am I willing to have children with Theo? I've never wanted to be a mother. I've never wanted to share my body with a small creature that relied on me for survival. Or to share my time with kids, who always seem to need something. I know my feelings are self-centered, but I'm willing to acknowledge that.

But it might be different with Theo. Everything is easier with money. We could hire a nanny so I could keep my free time. Then it might not be so bad.

And so it's decided.

I have to convince Astrid to leave Theo. Not to continue trying to have children. And I have to convince Theo that giving up having children is too big a sacrifice to make. And I will have Theo's children.

I park a block over and walk to the coffee shop, finally feeling a little calmer now I have something figured out. I push thoughts of the bird and Corrie from my mind. I'll worry about that when I get back home.

Astrid sits at a table with a lazy smile and a faraway stare. She seems to be in the opposite state from the last time I saw her. Her eyes focus on me when I enter the coffee shop. We smile at each other, and I walk to the counter to order a drink.

While I wait for my vanilla latte, I watch her stare out the window. She's happy. Which is not good for me. I have the overwhelming desire to take my coffee and walk straight through the door and go home. I'm in a cloud of mental exhaustion, and I really don't know if I have it in me to play this game right now.

The girl behind the counter hands me my drink and I take a big gulp, burning my mouth and throat. I wince but swallow it down. I take a seat across from Astrid and ready myself.

"You look happy today," I say, smiling. "Did you love-birds kiss and make up?"

She laughs. "We did. My stubborn, hard-headed husband finally conceded and agreed that we can stop."

"Wow. That's great." I try to look like I feel that way, but I'm afraid the smile isn't reaching my eyes. I wouldn't say I'm surprised that Theo gave in, but definitely disappointed. I thought I'd finally found the chink in their armor.

"Seriously," I say. "I'm so happy for you. That kind of stress hanging over you isn't good for anyone. It makes it hard to enjoy the other parts of life that are good, you know?"

"Yes." She nods. "That's what I told him. I can't enjoy this beautiful life that we have when . . ." She pauses. "When we're so focused on . . . that."

"Sure. That makes total sense." I stare off, trying to gather my thoughts. My crumbling plans. But Astrid must see my expression as concern.

"I think he really is content to stop," she says. She's trying to convince herself.

"That's a big decision. I mean, I'm sure you guys will be happy together no matter what. Not many marriages could make it through such a fundamental difference in wants. But you guys will be fine." I smile reassuringly.

"We've made it through a lot as a couple," she says.

I nod. "You're my friend. I want you to be happy. If you think you won't grow to resent each other for that kind of compromise, then I support you one hundred percent."

I hope I'm coming off genuine. She doesn't seem offended or put off by what I'm saying. She seems to actually consider it.

"Just know, you are whole all on your own. You don't need another person to have a happy life. And if you guys disagree on something this fundamental, maybe you haven't actually found your person yet. You did get married young and pretty quickly."

I hold my breath, hoping I haven't crossed a line. But Astrid just nods along, brows pulled together in thought.

"Thanks for being blunt with me. You're a good friend. I have to give it all more thought." She's no longer happy and relieved. I only feel a little guilty.

After coffee, we part ways with plans to get together in a day or two.

I climb the stairs to my apartment, ready to relax with a hot bath and a glass of wine. I pause when I see a few bags leaning against my door. Moving closer, I see the image of a bird on one of the things inside the bag and remember the annoying winged creature in my kitchen.

I crouch down and sift through the bags. Bird food, bedding, and a few toys to put in his cage. Logan must've gotten them. I glance behind me at his apartment door, feeling a pull to knock and thank him. But I can't handle another interaction right now. So I take the bags inside and close the door.

# CHAPTER EIGHTEEN

*"We are only as blind as we want to be." — Maya Angelou*

I wake up to the sound of a siren. I spring from the bed, eyes darting wildly. They're here for me. The bird is chipped, and they've found me.

But then the siren transforms to bird song. And changes again to a baby crying.

"Ughh!" I flop back into my bed and pull the pillow over my face. Why the hell did I take this stupid bird home with me? I panicked, that's why. I panicked, and instead of leaving the thing outside, I ran with it.

I force myself out of bed and walk cautiously into the kitchen.

"Hi, my name's Pascal," the bird squawks.

"Yeah, I know."

I step around the cage to start my coffee maker. Theo's writing class starts in a few hours, and I feel the tickle of anticipation in my stomach. I can't wait to see him.

No sooner than I think the thought does my phone ping with a notification. It's an email from Theo. Canceling class. He apologizes and blames a family emergency, closing with plans to hold class next week.

My mood instantly sours. My fingers itch to text Astrid for details, but I don't want to come off nosy.

I feel a little better after I've gotten a cup of coffee down. I clean and refill Pascal's food and water bowls, then eye the bottom of the cage, wondering if I can get Logan to clean the cage.

A knock on my door makes me jump. "Well, if it isn't the devil himself," I say when I open the door and Logan stands on the other side.

"Were you talking about me?" he asks, winking.

"Yes, actually. Will you clean Pascal's cage?"

His cocky grin slides off his lips. "I suppose I can."

I step aside for him to come in. "What were you here for?"

"To check on my buddy, Pascal, of course. You don't seem like a bird person to me." He eyes me over his shoulder mock-accusingly.

Lifting myself to sit on the kitchen counter, I watch him slide the bottom of the birdcage out and begin emptying it into my trash can. He glances up, looking at me through a row of dark eyelashes.

"You said you were working at that diner for your family?" I say because the silence makes me squirm.

"Yup. It's been in my family for two generations. My grandpa's health has been declining, and there's been a lack of willing workers as of late, so I help out when I can."

"What do you do when you're not being a waiter?"

"We prefer to be called *servers,* if ya don't mind." He makes a self-righteous expression, and I grin, which makes him smile. "I'm a nurse."

"Did not expect that." I laugh.

"Because I'm a guy?"

"Partly. But you just don't seem like a nurse."

"Well, I'm offended."

I roll my eyes. "Don't nurses make good money? Why do you live here?"

He grabs the bag of bedding from the counter and refills the bottom of the cage. "I'm still in med school. I want to be a surgeon, and I want to pay for it myself. So . . . I need cheap rent."

I nod, pulling the corners of my mouth down as if to say *impressive*. He finishes up and puts the cage back together.

"You know, you're supposed to offer me something to drink," he says, leaning against the counter.

I roll my eyes again. He is very eye-roll inducing. Hopping off the counter, I open the fridge. "What do you want? Or I have coffee, too."

"Coffee is great."

I make him a cup.

"Then you're supposed to say, 'I'll be right back. I just need to slip into something more comfortable.'"

I side-eye him. "This is not one of your cheap pornos. You're lucky you get coffee."

He laughs. "Okay, okay. Fine."

I hand him his cup and lean against the counter opposite him. Strangely, I feel at ease around him, though I certainly shouldn't. He has seen me as Laura and now as Olive. He lives in my apartment building and clearly has a thing for me. He could be a problem. But despite all of that, he's easy to talk to. I don't feel guarded like I ought to.

"Why have you never asked about changing my name and how I look?" My heart races with the words out of my mouth. It is safer to leave it alone. To pretend like it didn't happen, and he doesn't know. But I'm too curious.

He shrugs. "Well, it's not like we've had a lot of conversations. And it's none of my business. Girls change the way they look all the time. My sister looks like a different person every time I see her."

I chuckle. I'll leave the topic there. It *is* none of his business and I'm glad he realizes that. "Are you done with your coffee? I have things to do."

His eyebrows shoot up and his eyes go round, looking down and to the side. "Wow. Rude." He sets his cup on the counter, grinning as he walks to the door and lets himself out. "Let's do this again sometime soon," he says through the cracked door before he closes it.

Another eye roll.

I sit back on the couch and think about what to do with my day now Theo's class has been canceled. I don't actually have things to do, but it's best not to let Logan hang around too often. A straying thought of Ethan crosses my mind, but the idea of him bores me. All I can think about is Theo.

Before I can talk myself out of it, I throw my hair up in a ponytail, scrub yesterday's make-up from my face, and throw on a pair of leggings and an old university hoodie. I drive to campus and park in the student lot. I don't know what I'm hoping to find. I guess anything that makes me feel closer to Theo. Maybe I can find out why he canceled class.

It's the weekend, but there are still plenty of students milling about that live on campus, take weekend classes, or use the facilities on campus for homework.

I do my best to blend in, carrying my laptop bag on my shoulder. I make my way to Theo's classroom. Slowing down as I reach the door, I glance over to see if the light is on. It isn't. I figured he wouldn't be here, but you never know. I twist the handle, but it's locked. Shit.

I stand outside the door, looking around to make sure I don't get caught. I need to get in there. Security would have the key. But they'd never let me in there without reason. I can say I forgot something, but they wouldn't leave me alone.

Janitorial? They'd have a key and would likely be a little less strict. I might be able to get them to leave me alone inside. I walk to the cafeteria and purchase a tray of food. A bowl of chili, crackers, and a fountain drink. I walk the tray across campus and to the hall where Theo's office is and toss the tray onto the floor just outside of his office.

Oops.

There are campus phones all over. They link to security, janitorial, and the police. I connect with janitorial, put on an over-the-top whiny girl voice and tell the man who answers that "Someone just totally dropped their whole tray of food on the ground in the first-floor hall of the Parrish building and it's a freaking mess."

The man sighs and thanks me before hanging up. I wait around the side until I see someone in a gray jumpsuit walk into the building. I give it a few seconds and then hustle into the building too. I walk right past the man and try to open Theo's office door. "Dang it!" I exclaim loudly.

I walk outside the doorway and do my best to look stressed. The janitor looks up at me but goes back to cleaning the mess. Seriously? I start pacing, breathing quickly and shallow. I get myself worked up and make myself cry.

"You okay, miss?" he says. Finally.

"No. No, no. I'm not. Oh my God, I'm going to fail, and my parents are going to kill me. Oh my God." I'm gasping for air. On the edge of full-on panic and I'm impressing myself. "I dropped my flash drive in Mr. Connor's class yesterday and it has my paper on it that's due tonight. Oh God, oh God."

He stops cleaning but looks extremely uncomfortable. Like most men when a woman cries. He hesitates just a second longer, but then he's walking to the door, sorting through the keys on his key ring. "Go on. Hurry up and find it."

"Oh my God. Thank you so much!" I rush through the door and start crawling around on the floor along the rows of desks, trying not to think about the array of germs I'm sliding my hands through. I glance up, using my ponytail to block my gaze. He's standing in the doorway but facing the hallway. I need him to leave.

I keep searching the floor for my non-existent flash drive.

"I'm gonna be just out here, finishing cleaning up this mess, okay?"

"Uh-huh," I say, trying to sound distracted and focused on my task. I hear the door click shut, and I crawl as fast as I can to Theo's desk. I turn the computer screen away from the door and shake the mouse. Theo's profile avatar sits in the middle of the screen, asking for a password I'll never be able to guess.

I click the bottom option to change users and click the guest user that automatically logs me into a generic account that most of the students use. My foot bounces uncontrollably as I repeatedly check the door.

The guest profile loads, and I click the PC icon on the desktop, remembering how I was able to find so many assignments that I accidentally saved on the computer instead of on my flash drive back when I was in school. I go to the C drive. Then users. And click on the most recent user under the Guest account. I sort through the different places he might save things. The desktop and documents are full of documents. I slip the flash drive I brought into the computer and copy all the files to it.

Hurry, hurry, hurry.

The files finish just as I hear the door click open. I turn off the screen with the power button and drop to the floor.

"Miss?"

I crawl around the desk and jump up. "Found it!" I run over and squeeze him in a hug. "You are my hero. I owe you my life!" I run from the room to the parking lot, jittery and full of energy from the adrenaline.

I take my time sorting through all his documents when I get home. Even the ones that mean nothing to me. I love reading it, knowing he read them. Knowing they are his. I find his calendar for the semester. It has all his classes, his after-hours writing classes, and even things from his and Astrid's social lives. Astrid's trip to London in a few weeks. Her gallery expo. Dinner with Tessa and Neil. And my publishing party this Thursday. I lean over and grab the Edgar Allan Poe button he bought me. I've come so far already. My plan is working.

# CHAPTER NINETEEN

*"Hell is empty and all the devils are here." — William Shakespeare*

Tonight feels like a test. Like a chance to see if I can play in the big leagues, and I refuse to fail. I've been a failure all my life, so I'm owed a win, and I spared no expense to ensure I get it. I had to use all the money on my credit cards that I've managed to pay off. I'll have to figure out how to make this month's minimum payments, but that is a problem for tomorrow.

The sound of Astrid's heels against the hardwood floor announces her arrival. I turn to see her wide-toothed smile as she hurries toward me to pull me in for a hug. She smells like oranges and cigarette smoke.

"The decor team just pulled up as I was parking. What can I do to help?" She holds me by the shoulders like I'm a frightened child.

"Actually, I think I've got it all under control," I say, looking around the room as though to check, but I've already checked twenty times over before she got here. The only things left to do are things I've hired other people to do.

"Wow, really?" She looks around too. As if to check my work.

“Really.” I smile. “Come have a drink with me.” I walk to the bar, unstaffed but fully stocked, and Astrid follows. “Will Theo be driving separate then?”

“Yeah, he’ll be here right about when it starts. He has his evening class tonight.”

I pause, my hand reaching for a wine glass. Theo doesn’t have any night classes this semester. I’ve studied his schedule since stealing it two weeks ago. But I shouldn’t know that, so I say nothing.

What could he be out doing? Does Astrid really believe he has a night class? Either she is being lied to, or I am.

I made a mistake, allowing myself to develop a soft spot for Astrid. It made me play nice when I should have been more ruthless. I tried to make this easier on her. Convince her to leave so it wouldn’t hurt her as much. I have been stupid and weak, but no longer. I can play tough. I can play hardball.

I pour us both a glass of white wine and spin to face her, extending a glass. “To you.”

“Me? This is your night! We should be toasting to you!”

“This party wouldn’t be possible without you. I can’t thank you enough for offering your gallery after my venue fell through. You’re such a good friend.”

She places her hand on her chest, flattered and humble. We walk back to the center of the gallery so I can watch the teams of people bring my vision to life. “So, is everything still all sunshine and daisies in paradise?” I ask nonchalantly.

“Theo and me? Yeah, things are great. I feel like there is just a big weight lifted off us. A release of pressure, you know?”

I nod and study my wine glass. Have the seeds of doubt I planted died before ever sprouting? She eyes me. Ever-observant.

“What is it?” she asks.

“What? What is what?” I play dumb.

“You reacted a little weird just then.”

I make an innocent face, a dismissive but guilty smile. “Nothing . . . it’s nothing.”

She presses. "It's not. I saw it on your face. You're a terrible liar."

I want to laugh. But I don't. Because I am an incredible liar.

I sigh and chew my lip as I stare at her. So torn. "You know, I've taken a few of Theo's writing classes."

"Yes," she says, nodding.

"I went to his class last week, and there was just something he said . . ."

"What did he say?"

I play like I'm not sure if I should say it for a few more minutes. Make her plead with me before I tell her: "He made a comment about how the only thing he's ever wanted in life was to be a father." I blurt out the lie and give my best sorrowful and empathetic expression.

Astrid looks more confused than hurt at first. She couldn't believe he really wouldn't have any lingering feelings about giving up on being a father, could she? But then she shakes her head, and the pained expression I'd expected appears.

"I'm sure it's just lingering thoughts. It's a big thing to let go of. But he loves you. You know that. I'm sure it was nothing."

She shakes her head 'no' then 'yes.' Then verbalizes it. "No, yeah. I'm sure it's fine. I'll talk to him about it."

"Oh — please don't say I said anything. I don't want him to feel like he has to watch what he says in class."

"Yeah, no. You're right." She shakes her head, looking distracted.

"I'm sorry I said anything. Today is supposed to be a happy day. I'm sorry if I just ruined it."

She laughs, seeming to snap out of her daze. "Olive. It's your day. Come on." She loops her arm through mine. "Let's go check to see if the caterer is here."

The rest of the setup goes without a hitch. People begin showing up, and I soak in the 'oohs' and 'ahs' when they take in the art of Astrid's gallery, along with the ice sculptures and creative decor.

Theo finally arrives, and the sight of him sends goosebumps across my skin. He spots me right away and smiles, crossing the distance between us to hug me. My heart pounds in my chest. Astrid is on the other side of the room, but he didn't even look for her. He came straight to me.

"Olive, you look incredible." He holds my hand and spins me in a circle. My face heats under his stare and his compliment.

"Thank you. You look pretty incredible yourself." His fingers are still lightly touching mine, and I jokingly make him do the same spin I just did. He has to stoop down to go under my arm, and we laugh.

I let my eyes flit to the other side of the room and see Astrid headed toward us, her face set nearly in a scowl. Just behind her, standing in the group of women Astrid just departed, is Corrie, who stares openly in disgust at Theo and me. I really should have taken the opportunity that Theo gave me not to invite her.

"Darling," Astrid says. She wraps her hand around the back of Theo's neck as she pulls him in for a kiss. "I didn't see you come in."

"I had to tell the woman of the hour congratulations," he says. "You look stunning." He eyes her up and down, and I wonder which is better. Incredible or stunning.

I move around the room, smiling and chatting with guests, being the perfect hostess. But I hate leaving Astrid to talk to everyone else. She stands with Tessa and Corrie, who are surely filling her head with nonsense.

I'm still not sure what Tessa's issue truly is. But after seeing Corrie's house, I'm beginning to understand her and her motivations. Corrie doesn't like me because she's a broke social climber, nervous I will get in the way of her ensnaring her cash cow.

When I've spent a sufficient amount of time talking to other guests, I make my way back to Astrid.

"Hey, guys. Are you all having a good time?" I say to the group as I approach them.

"Of course we are," says Astrid, reaching out to squeeze my arm. The others nod and mutter words of agreement.

"I almost didn't come," Corrie says. "My house was robbed, and they took my poor Pascal."

I let my mouth fall open, pressing my hand to my lips. "Oh, how horrible. Is that your cat?"

She glares at me. "My bird. I told you about him at Jericho's when I saw you and Theo having lunch together, remember?" She looks at Astrid out of the corner of her eye. I do the same. But Astrid doesn't look surprised.

"Yes, yes. Sorry. I'm so sorry for you." I make an exaggerated frown to show her just how sorry. "How odd that they took your bird. I'm sure you have so many valuables in your house they could have taken."

"It is strange. I think it was a targeted attack." Corrie raises an eyebrow conspiratorially.

"Targeted at you or your bird?" I ask with a hint of mock in my voice. I want to expose her as the penniless leech she is, but I have to walk a fine line, so she doesn't figure out that I was the one in her house.

"Both," says Corrie.

"You do live in Meridian Hills. If I was a thief, I'd bet on finding lots of expensive things in a house out there." I take a sip of my drink. "Please, excuse me. I have to check the kitchen."

I saunter across the gallery and let myself into the stainless-steel kitchen in the back. I don't feel guilty for taking the bird. Pascal is safe and sound in my apartment right now. I'm actually getting used to having him around. If I can get him to stop making every terrifying noise he knows at the crack of dawn, we'd be in an even better place.

Despite the drama with Astrid's friends, I can't wipe the grin from my face. A few short months ago, I was a different person with a different life. I step back into the gallery and take in the room, letting myself really appreciate this experience. I am surrounded by interesting and successful people. I have the friends I've always wanted, and they're all here for me.

Most of them are acquaintances I met through Astrid, but that's no matter.

After making another round through the room and checking in the back to ensure we have enough stock of wine and food, I make my way to Astrid. Theo and Neil are at the bar, but my drink is full, so I have no excuse to go over to them instead.

Astrid's and Tessa's backs are to me. Corrie has joined another group of women. I open my mouth to say something but shut it when I hear my name.

"Something is off about Olive. I know you like her, but I just needed to say something," Tessa says.

"You're being ridiculous. She's a nice girl," Astrid says, defending me.

"She just came out of nowhere. And where are her friends? Her family? Her fucking publishing team? This is a party to celebrate finishing her book, but no one from her publishing company is here."

I glance behind me and see that Theo and Neil are on their way back. I have to interrupt them or else get caught eavesdropping right behind them.

"Hi, ladies," I say, trying to sound chipper and not like I just overheard Tessa talking about me.

They spin around, both of them having the decency to look guilty. Or maybe I'm seeing what I want to see.

The men join the group, and Astrid tells everyone how she's trying to get an exhibition in Paris. The conversation is a welcome shift because I'm so mad I don't trust myself to speak. I ease myself out of the group once more and make my way to the back of the gallery where the food is prepared and the drink trays restocked.

There is a random chair against the far wall, near the back entrance, and I beeline for it. My feet ache from the heels I stupidly wore for the first time tonight without breaking them in.

I collapse into the chair and sigh as my feet get a much-needed reprieve. Who does Tessa think she is? How dare she bad-mouth me to Astrid? She is the one who invited me into the group in the first place. Invited a stranger to her child's birthday party and now she thinks I shouldn't be trusted?

"Guests aren't supposed to be back here," says a deep voice. I look up to find a bald, boxy man dressed in a black uniform. Security.

"It's my event. I'm not a guest," I say with a little more bite to my tone than I intended. My anger is overflowing, taking anyone down unfortunate enough to be in the blast zone.

"Apologies." He nods his head and lifts a Styrofoam cup to his lips. "You don't seem to be having a good time."

"Not anymore, no." I hate the pout in my voice, but I can't help it. I'm so close to getting what I want. I can feel it. And now Tessa wants to get in the way.

The man takes another drink from his cup but doesn't respond. His silence is uncomfortable, and I try to fill it, though I don't know why.

"Women can be so catty," I say.

"Some can be, sure."

"I'm Olive." I don't know why I don't just go back to the party. I need a minute to cool down, so I don't do something out of anger that I'll regret.

"Hank," he says.

The name suits him. "Have you worked in security for a long time?"

He nods. "Used to work up in Michigan. Left a few months ago."

"Why did you move to Indy?"

"Just needed a change."

"You're a man of few words, Hank," I say, and he smirks in response. "Well, I guess I should get back to my guests."

"Take care."

I stand up and breathe deeply. I take a step, but Hank's voice stops me.

"If there's one thing I learned from my last job, it's that you should be careful who you trust. I don't know what's happening out there, but take care of yourself."

I nod once, pinching my eyebrows together in thought, before continuing back to the party. *I will take care of myself, Hank. You're cautioning the wrong person at this party.*

# CHAPTER TWENTY

*"The price of anything is the amount of life you exchange for it." — Henry David Thoreau*

After feeding Pascal, I get dressed and send a text to Astrid. Theo's classes have been canceled until next semester, so I have no excuse to see him other than through his wife. I'm still trying to brainstorm a way to get to Theo when I get a response from Astrid.

> *Sorry! I can't today. Tess and I are going to a pop-up bar in Lafayette.*

Another text comes through before I can respond.

> *Sorry for no invite. Tessa needed some bestie time without kids.*
>
> *—Of course! Have fun! Does Neil have the kids then?*
>
> *Neil is out of town for work.. Again! Kids are with grandma.*
>
> *—Gotchya. Well, have a blast (:*

My cheeks are burning. I know that Tessa must have specifically told Astrid she didn't want to invite me. She's becoming more and more of a problem, and I won't let her get between me and the Connors.

I have to think of a way to get rid of her. At the very least, I need her busy and distracted so I can have more time with Astrid without her stealing her away like a jealous high-school best friend.

I can't break into her house like Corrie's. Her whole house is wired with technology that I don't quite understand. I wouldn't have a chance against the cameras and alarm systems.

A chime from my phone breaks my thoughts. I pick it up and tap on the new Facebook message from Ethan. The message is the written version of things he said to me at the bar when we met. He really leans heavily on some misguided belief that tech knowledge is impressive to women.

But then, a lightbulb moment. I recall a memory from the birthday party. Tessa complained about the smart system Neil set up in the house.

I tap out a response to Ethan.

> *OMG no way! What are the chances? So, I actually just moved into an apartment that has this whole smart system. But I cannot figure it out for the life of me. The landlord isn't answering, and I think it's actually still set up for the people who lived here before me. Do you know if there is any way to override their stuff? Am I even asking this question right?! Haha*

Ethan is online, and the three dancing bubbles at the bottom of the message appear immediately.

> *It's almost like fate *winky face* I designed the app myself. I can help.*

I leap to my feet and do a little dance. A plan is coming together. Ethan tells me the app to install and to make sure my phone is on the same Wi-Fi as the smart system. I pretend to struggle with the Wi-Fi as I drive to Tessa's house.

I check Astrid's social media, and a boomerang of them cheering their drinks confirms they're still out of town. The house should be empty.

I park along the curb, just past Tessa's house. It should be close enough to connect to the Wi-Fi. My phone picks it up automatically from the birthday party. I message Ethan to walk me through the next steps.

He explains how to login as a system administrator. Something normal users wouldn't need to do, but the people who support the app use to fix problems when customers call in. I reset the password, and within minutes I am connected to everything in their house. The cameras, their washer and dryer, the thermostat, the oven, and even their robot vacuum.

I thank Ethan enthusiastically and reward him with praise and compliments. I close the Facebook app and look through the smart app. I could shut off the cameras and go inside if I wanted to. But I don't need to do all that.

I click on the oven and set the temperature as high as it goes. Tessa's storage habits have always been a hazard. A fire waiting to happen. Hopefully, everyone will stay gone long enough for their precious smart house to burn to the ground.

They might see my car on the cameras, but they won't be able to prove anything. At least I don't think. Before I close out of the app, I delete the saved camera footage and factory reset the entire system. I didn't even need Ethan to figure that part out. Google is just as smart.

I pull away from the curb casually as I delete the app from my phone.

* * *

The floor vibrates beneath me, and I latch onto Theo's arm. He holds me protectively, but the ground continues to shake. And buzz? It's dark. Theo is gone. I'm alone. It's so cold. I'm shivering. My legs are trapped in sheets. Bed sheets. I'm in my bed. I was dreaming. But the buzzing, the vibrating, is still there. My phone. Where the fuck is my phone?

The light from the screen is blinding. I have to squint to see Astrid's name. The incoming call goes away, presumably to voicemail, and my home screen appears. Four missed calls from Astrid. The time on the top of the screen says it's eight in the morning, but it feels so much earlier. I groan just as her name appears again.

"Hello?" I say into the phone, trying not to sound too annoyed.

"Olive," she chokes out. "I'm so sorry to wake you, but I could really use a friend right now."

What now?

"Yeah, of course. What's going on? Are you okay? Is Theo okay?" I push myself out of bed and walk to the bathroom, the phone still pressed to my ear. I flick on the light and squint at the harshness of it.

"We're okay. Just — can you come over? I'll have breakfast and coffee in case you haven't eaten yet."

"Sure . . . yeah, okay. Just give me a minute to get ready and I'll be on my way."

"Oh, don't bother getting ready. Really. I'm in pajamas and I have no interest in changing. Be a bum with me," she says.

I laugh, unsure what to make of all of this. "All right. I'll be on my way then."

"Thank you so much, Olive. I don't know what I'd do without you."

I brush my teeth, racking my brain for what the hell could be going on — why she's blowing up my phone and requesting I come over in pajamas at eight in the morning on a Wednesday. I will not leave my house in what I just wore to bed. A fluffy pair of purple pajama pants and a T-shirt from high school. Instead, I change into a pair of leggings and an oversized sweater, tying my hair back and putting on a baseball cap. I look myself over in the full-length mirror and decide it's good enough. I imagine Theo is at work, so I don't have to worry about impressing him.

I take yet another Uber, and this time I don't tip because these people are making a fortune off me. On the walk to the gate, I open my email on my phone to see one from the romance author I've been ghostwriting for. She still isn't ready for me to work on the second book. I have a feeling she ran out of money. Whatever the reason, I'm a little fucked. All the money I managed to save up was spent on my party. I stayed up all night trying to find another worthwhile writing gig with very little luck.

I peel my eyes from my phone and look up at the house through the iron gate, every bit as blown away as the first time. The gates are locked today. I assume they always are when they're not throwing a party. I press the buzzer, and a loud sound from the gates comes almost immediately as they swing open.

I walk up the driveway. It's a long way, but I take in everything on the walk up. I imagine it all as mine. How it will feel to drive through the gates in a red Porsche. How I'll have the house decorated for the fall. How it will feel to call this place my home.

Astrid swings the front door open before I can knock. Her pajamas are one step back from lingerie. Her hair is perfectly wavy. The only thing that makes her look like maybe she isn't modeling for an underwear catalog is her puffy red eyes and tear-streaked face.

"Thank you so much for coming," she says. She pulls me into a hug and wipes her nose with a tissue when she pulls away. "Come in. I have coffee in the kitchen."

I follow her into the house, blissfully warm compared to the crisp morning air. A cold front has moved in, making it finally feel like fall is here. There are clear glass coffee mugs set out on the counter and the delicious scent of expensive dark roast fills the air.

I walk over and take a mug, filling it with coffee before opening the fridge to search for creamer. I register my audacity, and I don't want to appear rude, but I can't help feel like this is already my home. It's really just a matter of time. So I make myself at home and take a seat at the breakfast table, and Astrid follows me.

"Now," I say. "Tell me what's going on." I take a sip of my coffee and can't help closing my eyes as the smooth liquid ecstasy slides down my throat.

"It's hard to explain. But basically, I thought we could be done. You know, pursuing having kids? But it turns out we can't just yet."

The coffee turns sour in my stomach. "What do you mean?"

She shakes her head, tears spilling over and cascading down. "It's this thing we agreed to be part of for a set amount of time."

"I'm not understanding," I say. "Like foster care or something?"

Astrid nods, eyes latching onto me before letting her face fall into her hands for a moment. Her shoulders shake, and I hesitate. I guess I should comfort her? Begrudgingly, I move to her side and wrap my arms around her shoulders. "It's okay. It's going to be okay." What I think is: *I can't catch a fucking break.*

When Astrid calms down, I move back to my seat. My coffee is probably cold, and it won't taste as good if I heat it up. I suppress a sigh and push it away from me. I'll make a fresh cup when I'm done figuring out what the hell is going on now.

"I'm sorry. You must think I'm such a mess," she says, wiping her nose again.

"Are you kidding me? You're far from a mess. One of the most put-together people I know." I'm a little annoyed at the truth of that statement. Despite the few times she's called me crying, she is more put together than I normally am, even in her weaker moments.

"We will still be done," she says. "I just thought it would be immediate."

"Do they have a kid you have to foster?"

"No."

"So . . . you just have to be available to be a foster parent for a certain amount of time?" I ask, trying to connect these scattered dots.

"Yes, exactly."

Footsteps sound in the hall outside the kitchen. "Astrid? Baby? You in here?" He rounds the corner before she can answer. "Oh, Olive. I'm sorry. I didn't know we had company."

My heart sinks. At the way he called her 'baby' and the way he referred to me as company. Astrid slides out of her chair and is in his arms in an instant. "Thanks for coming home," she says into his shoulder.

"Of course. Hey" — he holds her by her shoulders, arm-length away — "what do you think about taking a little time away? A vacation?"

"Oh, that sounds so nice. Can we really go? With everything—"

"Yes, we can," he says. Then he looks over Astrid's head. "Olive. Come with us. You could use a vacation too. Another way to celebrate your book."

I watch Astrid pull away from him a little to look up at him. Her back is to me, so I can't see her face, but her posture insinuates she's not happy about the invitation extended to me.

"Wow, that's so kind of you to invite me on your trip. I would love to come. You're right, I could definitely use a vacation after that book," I say before the offer can be rescinded.

Astrid turns to me with a wide smile. "Great! This is exactly what we need."

## CHAPTER TWENTY-ONE

*"How bold one gets when one is sure of being loved." — Sigmund Freud*

I don't know why I'm surprised when the Connors tell me they travel by private plane. I should have expected just that. My Uber drops me off at my apartment. It took a little convincing to get back to my place without them so I could pack. Astrid kept insisting the limo could take us to my place and I could pack while they waited.

I could tell Astrid was pushing harder than necessary, and I can only assume it's because Tessa put thoughts into her head.

I'm not prepared for a random vacation. Theo wants the location to be a surprise, so the only thing he told us is that it is a tropical climate and to bring bathing suits. The problem is, I only have the bathing suit I wore to Tessa's kid's birthday party.

There's also the problem of Pascal. I stick my finger in the cage's side and hesitantly pet his head. We're making progress. Quickly, I jog into the hall of the apartment building and tap on Logan's door, praying he's home.

"Just a sec!" he shouts from behind the door. I hear a crash and then the door swings open. "Hey. What's up?"

"I need you to take care of Pascal for a few days."

"Uh — sure."

"Great. Come get him and his stuff."

He follows me to my apartment, and I begin stacking his things near the door. "Let him out of his cage every day. He doesn't like to go far from his cage, but he likes the space."

Logan nods. "Is your sister not taking him back?"

I pause for a moment, remembering the bad lie that slipped out those weeks ago. "No. She's not."

I help him move Pascal and his things over to his apartment. He leads the way into the kitchen. The layout is the same as mine, but it has a much different feel. It's not the college frat boy dorm room I expected it to be, though still unmistakably a bachelor pad.

A large, framed photo hangs on the living room wall. It's a collage of photos. I step closer, curious for some unknown reason. I spot Logan in most of the pictures. He's with, I'm assuming, friends and family. Camping, hiking, snowboarding, and on a boat. "Well, aren't you the outdoorsman," I say.

"You should come camping with me sometime."

I look over and he's grinning, leaning against the counter.

"Not a chance in hell."

He shrugs, still smirking.

"I should be back in a few days, but I'll keep you updated."

"That means you have to give me your number."

I sigh dramatically and hold out my hand for his phone. After I save my contact information, I give him more instructions for taking care of Pascal, then run back to my apartment to grab my things and head out the door.

I take an hour to shop for my last-minute items and to get an Uber back to the Connors' house, where a limo is parked with the trunk open. A man who looks like a bodybuilder in a suit is standing beside it.

Astrid and Theo walk out the front door as I climb out of my car. She looks upset, and my pulse quickens. I took too long. She's changed her mind.

"Is everything okay?" I ask, hauling bags from the Uber.

"Olive, don't worry about the bags, they can get it," says Theo. The large man, and another I hadn't seen, walk over to the car and begin transferring my things to the limo.

Astrid runs to me, swinging her arms around my neck. "Poor Tessa. She came home yesterday to find her house on fire." Astrid sniffles. "I just called her to see if they could get away with us for a mini vacation and she told me her house is gone."

"How many times has Neil, and everyone else for that matter, told her to stop storing things in the oven?" says Theo.

Astrid lets go of me. "She wasn't even cooking anything yesterday. She has no idea how the oven got switched on. They think it might have been the cleaning lady. That she might have accidentally switched it on when cleaning it."

"Oh, that's terrible," I say. "Tell me no one was hurt."

Astrid shakes her head. "No. Thankfully, everyone was out. The fire department told her the cause was definitely the oven, but the house is too far gone to fix."

"So sad." I frown, moving closer to the limo, hoping to get us all going. I'm suddenly terrified that Astrid will want to cancel the trip to stay and help Tessa.

"Tell Tessa we'll be back next week to help with anything we can. If she needs anything, she or Neil can give us a call," Theo says. "Olive, do you have your passport?"

I nod, thankful I thought to get a new one a few weeks ago. He holds his hand out, and I pull it from my purse and hand it to him. He hands it, along with his and Astrid's, to the driver. He gestures for me to get into the limo, so I do.

I try to kick the third-wheel feeling. This will all be mine soon. He will be mine soon. When the limo pulls into the private airport, excitement bubbles in my stomach. I've only ever been on a plane once, and I was nine, so I hardly remember. The roided-out limo driver transports our bags from the trunk to the plane as we climb the steps to board.

Stepping into the plane is stepping into pure luxury. White carpet covers the floor, and plush beige leather seats are placed around small white marble tables that are bolted to the ground.

I follow Theo and Astrid to a back table in the center of four chairs. We all sit, and I'm about to marvel out loud about the plane, but a small woman approaches us from the front. "Mr. and Mrs. Connor. Ms. Tate. Can I get you a drink or anything to eat as we prepare for take-off?"

We all give her our drink orders and Theo asks for pretzels.

"This plane is incredible," I say. "So much better than first class." It sounds like a pretentious thing to say. Especially seeing as I've never flown in first class, but I don't want them to know that.

"It's the only way Theo will fly now," Astrid says. "But we invested in it because of all my trips selling and buying art for my gallery. It allows me to come and go at any hour without having to worry about finding a flight."

"That makes sense," I say. The woman is back with our drinks, and I thank her, lifting the glass to my lips.

* * *

We arrive in the Maldives nearly twenty-four hours later. Despite the next-level comfort provided by the plane, I'm eager to be back on the ground and out in the world. I had no idea where we were going. Theo wanted it to be a surprise for both me and Astrid. I didn't mentally prepare for a full day on a plane.

But the flight is over, and I'm hit with a dopamine rush when I step off the plane into sunshine. Summer is just ending back home, but somehow, it feels different from this. Maybe it's the palm trees. Or the fact that I can hear and smell the ocean.

A car waits for us about a hundred yards from the plane. As soon as we step onto the pavement, it drives closer and parks. The driver steps out. Another man who seems far too muscular to be a limo driver. He unloads our bags from the luggage compartment of the plane as we get into the car.

The house we're staying in is a giant white beach home. Theo rented it for the week. It has four bedrooms, and I wonder if they've invited anyone else. I kind of hope they did so someone can distract Astrid from time to time, but I'm sure they would have taken the plane here with us. The front door sees straight through the house. The living room, then the dining room on the right and the kitchen on the left. Then a wall of glass doors that fold like an accordion so that the whole back of the house opens to a wooden patio surrounded by sand. Farther down is the ocean.

The smell of salt and clean linen air fresheners hangs in the air. "Olive, pick any room you want," Theo says.

"Are there others joining us?" I ask.

He shakes his head. "I booked the place when I thought Neil and Tessa might join us, but we'll be alone."

"Still so sad about what happened. And that they can't be here."

"That's okay. It'll be nice with just us. A little more laid back. Tessa brings out my wild side," Astrid says, walking toward the right side of the house where two of the bedrooms are.

Will it seem weird if I choose the room next to theirs instead of on the other side of the house? I follow Astrid and see her leaning into a room from the hallway. She turns toward me. "The first pick is yours," she says. "Though they're all pretty much the same."

"Would you guys mind if I stayed in the room next to yours?" I ask. "I'm paranoid and would just sleep easier knowing you guys are close."

Astrid's brows knit in a compassionate expression. "Of course, Olive."

I smile gratefully. "I'll take this one then. If you guys like the other one?"

"Yeah, it's great. Like I said, they're all the same."

* * *

After unpacking, we all wind up on the back patio. Astrid is sitting on Theo's lap in a lounge chair. I try not to look over at them too often. We drink like we won't wake tomorrow, and I welcome the loss of my inhibitions. I feel lost and out of control. Every time I think I have a grasp, a plan, everything seems to change.

I keep thinking I waited too long to make a clear move. I've had so many opportunities, and I let each one slip by. Now they're cuddled up as though I'm not even here.

"Let's play a game," I say after the sun has disappeared behind the watery horizon.

"What kind of game?" Astrid asks.

I don't remember what happens next.

I fumble my way to my room, bumping into the walls and using them as support to guide me down the hall. I collapse into the bed, too tired to undress. Dipping in and out of consciousness, I have to take deep breaths to keep from hurling from the spinning sensation when I close my eyes.

Just as I'm starting to fade into sleep, a rhythmic bumping noise starts at the far wall. I try to sit up, but my body feels leaden. The bumping gets louder. Faster. Then Astrid's loud moans invade the room. My whole body tenses up. I hoped that being so close to them would ruin any attempts at them having sex, but I should have known better. Especially with how much we drank.

Astrid's whining gets louder each passing minute. I pull the pillow over my head to drown her out, but it doesn't work. My cruel mind summons images to match the noises, but all I can see is Theo positioned over Astrid's naked body.

"Stop." The word escapes my mouth as an elongated cry. Tears slip from my eyes, and I grip the pillow tighter over my ears. I just want them to stop.

My chest is tight with a mixture of emotions that I'm too drunk to rationalize or push down.

## CHAPTER TWENTY-TWO

*"He who learns but does not think, is lost! He who thinks but does not learn is in great danger." — Confucius*

I must've fallen asleep because light peeks through the blinds, reflecting off the water and becoming even brighter. It slips right between the bed and the pillow that still lies on top of my head. I push it off and assess the damage. Headache for sure. Little bit nauseous, but not too bad.

I stay still, listening for sounds in the house and not quite ready to move my body, knowing my hangover will only get worse once I do. There are noises coming from somewhere in the house. The kitchen?

Memories from last night buzz around in my head, and they're worse than the potential migraine I'll get from standing up, so I push myself out of bed and grasp the comforter when bile rises in my throat. I swallow it down and shuffle to the bathroom, unable to stand up straight.

I feel almost human again after a shower and force myself into the main living area of the house. It's empty now, but I smell coffee and follow the scent to where I find two empty coffee mugs. I fill one and walk toward the back of the house. Theo is sitting on the edge of the patio.

There isn't a single cloud in the sky, and it's already at least eighty degrees. Theo is shirtless, wearing only a pair of gray shorts.

"You're always the early bird," I say as I take a seat beside him.

He smiles, glancing over at me and then returning his gaze to the water. "Haven't missed a sunrise in at least ten years."

"Wow." He somehow keeps finding ways to be more beautiful to me. It's lovely and poetic that he never misses a sunrise. I want to see each sunrise with him. "Even when you stay up late and drink? I don't know how you do it."

"If I'm up late enough, I just stay up."

"You won't sleep at all?"

"Nah. It'll just throw off my sleep for the next day. Caffeine is my best friend on those days." He raises his cup with a crooked grin.

"So you haven't slept since the night on the plane?"

He nods. "I'll sleep tonight."

"Maybe. Maybe it'll be another all-night rager."

He laughs. "Astrid will be calmer today. The first night of a vacation is always exciting. And she'll be very hungover."

"What if I want to rage?"

"Then I'll have to suck it up. Gorgeous women shouldn't be made to rage alone."

"That's exactly what I wanted to hear."

We go into the house to refill our coffee just as Astrid makes an appearance in the land of the living. Her platinum blonde hair is tied at the nape of her neck and she's in a white sundress.

"I was going to make breakfast for us, but there aren't many ingredients to work with. I was waiting for you to wake up before I head into town in case you needed something," Theo says with a kiss on the side of her head.

"I don't need anything," she says. "Oh, maybe some more wine. I think we drank most of what we brought."

"Noted."

I set my cup on the counter, seeing a moment I don't want to slip away. "I actually need a few things. Would you mind if I came with you?"

"Olive, don't leave me!" Astrid says. "Write Theo a list and have mimosas with me on the beach."

My mouth opens, but no response comes.

"I'll be back in a flash. I'll pick up whatever you need," Theo says.

"Okay, yeah. Thanks," I say because arguing and insisting on going with him would just come off weird. I don't actually need anything, so I write 'gluten-free bread' and the ingredients for an old fashioned and hand the paper to him.

"Great. Be back in a few," he says, and he's out the door.

Astrid is at the counter pouring orange juice into large tumblers. "Okay, you grab a couple of towels and meet me down at the beach."

The sand is almost too hot to walk on. The soles of my feet burn, and I have to move quickly. The relief of wet sand near the shore is great. "The skin on my feet is going to peel off. Jesus," I say when I get to the chair Astrid brought down for me.

She laughs, her head thrown back. "Tell me about it. Next time we'll wear shoes." She hands me one of the tumblers she filled, and even though the thought of alcohol makes me want to puke, I take a small sip from the straw. She must see the face I make because she snorts and says, "Hair of the Dog. It's gross at first, but you'll feel like normal in just a few sips."

I make a face and take another sip.

"I still can't believe Tessa's house burned down. Have you talked to her lately?" Astrid says.

I still can't believe it actually worked.

"No, I haven't. Not since my party at your gallery. I'll have to text her when we go back to the house." I realize I haven't seen my phone this morning. I make a mental note to look for it later so I can check on Pascal.

"So what is Corrie's deal?" I ask.

"What do you mean?"

I shrug. "I don't know. She hangs around a lot. How did you guys become friends?"

Astrid stirs her drink by swirling it around. "We met when I was checking out another gallery downtown. She's an art dealer, you know. So we connected on that."

"I remember her trying to convince you to hire an art dealer," I say. "Isn't that what you do too?"

She nods. "Yes. But I do a lot of other jobs for the business too."

"Seems to me like she wants you to hire her for the job. There must be good money in it."

She tilts her head, considering it. "Yeah, I guess that makes sense. I usually go after more expensive art, so an art dealer would make a good commission. I obviously don't take commission from myself, so it saves me a lot of money."

I don't respond because she seems to have caught on to Corrie's motivations. It's quiet for a moment. The only sounds are the crashing waves as they rush over the sand and then pull back into the vast ocean over and over again.

"I wanted to ask, but I didn't want to be nosy . . ." Astrid says, apparently waiting for me to give her permission to be just that. I tell her to go ahead because now I'm curious enough to want to know what it is she's been wanting to ask me. "Your party for your book. None of your family or other friends showed."

Fucking Tessa. She put these thoughts in her head.

"It's complicated," I say. Which is true. "My family isn't very supportive. I haven't even spoken to any of them in months."

Also true. The whole truth is that there is no book to celebrate. The only novel I've finished in years is not my own. "Then my agent, who is a good friend of mine, was out of state visiting family, and my other friend actually went into labor the day before." Lies. Though I downloaded pictures of some random woman's baby on the internet to show people. "I'll have to show you the photos of her when we get back to the house. Such a cutie."

"I'm sorry they weren't able to make it to support you," she says.

"That's okay. I had you guys there."

"True. And we're most important anyway." She extends her cup to me, and I clink mine against it.

We make our way to the house to see if Theo is back yet. We find him in the kitchen making breakfast. The smell of sausage makes my stomach growl.

I excuse myself while he finishes cooking to look for my phone. I rifle through my purse and pour the contents onto the bed when I don't find it. What the hell did I do with it?

Lowering myself to the floor, I look under the bed. With a sigh, I sit up. I had to have put it somewhere stupid when I was drinking last night. It'll pop up, eventually.

I rejoin Theo and Astrid in the kitchen and eat breakfast.

* * *

I lie in bed, less drunk than the night before. Noise reverberates through the walls again, but this time, they're hushed voices. Angry sounding, though I can't make out the words. Their bedroom door slams, and I jump and sit up. Theo's back glows under the moonlight outside my window, moving toward the beach. I watch him until he disappears behind a hill of sand.

I pause just a minute to make sure Astrid isn't going after him. When there's no more movement coming from their room, I creep quietly out of my room and to the back door. The balls of my feet stick to the wood floor that squeaks as my weight shifts from one floorboard to another.

I empty my aching lungs when I click the door shut behind me. The sand is so much cooler than it was earlier today. It sends goosebumps across my skin when a warm breeze sweeps my hair back. I spot Theo's broad shoulders sitting just out of where the tide has come in, his knees bent and forearms resting on them. I plop down beside him.

"Sorry if we woke you," he says.

"You didn't."

"I don't really want to talk about it."

"I didn't come to talk about it."

He looks over at me, and the way the moonlight highlights his cheekbones, his shoulder muscles, makes my heart skip before pounding harder. "Then why'd you come?" His voice is low, and the vibrato of it sends tingles through my hands and low in my stomach. I won't miss this opportunity like I have all the rest.

"For a swim," I say. I stand up and pull the swimsuit cover over my head. My swimsuit is hanging in the shower back at the house, and I stand naked in the moonlight before walking to the water without looking back.

The water is colder than I thought it'd be, but I keep walking and suppress a sharp intake of air when a wave splashes up higher on my skin. I take a deep breath and dive under the surface. The shock of the cold makes me feel so awake and alive. The water slides across my bare skin, bringing every nerve ending, every pore, to attention.

When I come up for air, I dare to turn back toward the shore to see if Theo has taken the invitation. I brace myself, trying not to think about the embarrassment I'll feel if he's gone back to the house.

My heart sinks when my eyes fall on an empty beach. I jump as a mass breaks the surface of the water. As he stands up and waves push and pull, I see bare skin where his shorts would be. My stomach dips and twists as my eyes lock with his. He reaches me, and in one motion, one hand cradles the back of my head as the other wraps around my waist and pulls me into him, his mouth closing over mine.

We wade farther into the water, and I wrap my legs around his waist, pressing our naked bodies together. The warmth from him with the coldness of the ocean intensifies every feeling. His hand moves down to my back to hold me to him, as his other hand snakes around to cup my breast.

He walks us back to shore, and I hold myself close to him as he lowers me onto the sand. My mind races, having a hard time accepting the reality of finally getting what I've wanted. Part of it, anyway.

I watch his face, his eyes as he takes in my body. He loves me. He loves me. He loves me.

His eyes close, and my lower back grinds into the wet sand as we make love. I grab his back with sand-covered hands, wishing he'd open his eyes and look into mine.

When he's done, he rolls onto his side beside me, and I turn to face him.

"It's terrible of me to say this, but I've wanted to do that for a long time," he says.

His words have the same effect as his body, and I feel my whole body warm. "I've wanted you to do it for just as long."

He strokes my hair. We're wet and covered in sand, but I don't want to move, too afraid to break the spell and ruin this moment.

After a while, we make our way back to the ocean to wash off. He brushes the sand off my back, kissing me and groping me as he does. When we're clean, we put our clothes back on and sit on the beach.

"You were supposed to get some sleep tonight," I say, my head resting on his shoulder as we look out into the water.

"I'd trade sleep for what just happened anytime."

We sit there for a long time. So long that the sun starts to creep up into the sky. Theo holds me, and together we watch our first sunrise together. I wonder if he'll tell Astrid he's leaving her out here or wait until we get home.

# CHAPTER TWENTY-THREE

*"Always you came trustingly to all that is terrible. You wanted to caress every monster." — Friedrich Nietzsche*

We walk back up the beach to the house shortly after the sun rises. Astrid will be asleep. And Theo may be used to pulling all-nighters, but I am not. I go into my room and shower before going into the inside zipper of my suitcase to pull out the Edgar Allan Poe button Theo bought me all those months ago.

I look for my phone to set an alarm for a few hours but remember that I was never able to find it. I'll have to really look for it when I wake up more so I can check on Pascal. I climb into bed and fall asleep as I rub my thumb across the surface of the button, thinking of how I'll explain Pascal to Theo when I move both of us in with him.

Theo is gone when I wake up. It's late afternoon, and Astrid is at the kitchen table nibbling on a piece of toast. "Good morning," she says. "Hungry?"

"Starving."

I go to the fridge and stare into the white void like it's going to tell me how to behave with Astrid now that everything has changed. Because to her, nothing has changed.

I take an apple from the shelf and sit at the table.

"Long night? You slept forever." She leans to the side and folds her legs underneath her.

"Couldn't fall asleep. And I think all the time in the sun just caught up with me."

"You're not wanting to go home early, are you?" she asks.

"No, of course not." I scrunch my face in confusion. Why would she ask that?

"Good. I'm just having a nice time with you. Thank you for coming." She stares at the table like she's somewhere else now. I almost ask her what's wrong. But I have to stop thinking about Astrid's feelings. It's almost lost me my chance with Theo.

"Yeah. Thanks for inviting me. I'm sure a couple's getaway would have been nice."

"We're around each other a lot," she says before taking a sip of her coffee. "We work, but we still spend a lot of time alone. It's nice to have someone else on a trip with us to change things up."

I nod, though I don't really understand. Theo and I will be taking plenty of vacations together without the need to 'change things up.'

"Has your publisher told you a release date for your book yet?"

"No. Not yet."

"Hmm. They should really get on that. You've already turned in the final edits after all. What are they waiting for?"

"Probably just doing a last pass through the manuscript to make sure there aren't any last-minute things to change."

"Are you working on your next book?"

"A bit," I say. "It's hard to focus on a new story while still being involved in another. But now this one is complete, I'll be spending more time on it." It must be because of my love of fiction that I'm able to concoct these lies as I go. It's easy. I actually find myself believing them from time to time.

Astrid goes quiet again for a while, and the silence feels uncomfortable and tense, but I can't tell if I'm projecting or if it's coming from her. I'm about to go to the back patio when she speaks again.

"There are storms rolling in. The trip back Monday could be pretty dangerous. I could help you get back tonight if you'd like to leave early."

I'm not sure why, but her words feel ominous. Warning. She must have some idea what's happened. "I'd very much like to enjoy my last two days here."

Theo returns around dinnertime. It's a long time to be gone from your vacation house, and I wonder what he was doing. If maybe he needed time away to process last night. A sliver of doubt wiggles into my chest like a worm in a decaying ribcage. He and Astrid had been fighting. What if he regrets what happened? If he only slept with me because he was angry with Astrid?

*No.* I can't think that way. Even if this isn't the end-all like I truly believe it to be, I've made real progress with Theo on this trip. He's given into his feelings for me, and I can't discount that.

I'm sitting on the patio, taking in the last rays of sunlight before they disappear and I have to head back to the colder, and increasingly dark, Midwest. Theo and Astrid come out, a glass in Astrid's hand and two in Theo's. He hands me one.

I take it, grateful, and sip the chilled white wine. The tension between the three of us is thicker than the dense Indian Ocean air. Astrid sits half propped against the railing of the deck, and Theo takes a chair at the table across from me. While it's a relief that Theo and Astrid don't seem to have made up, I can't stand much more of the awkwardness.

We make small talk until Astrid stands and walks toward the back door. "I'm tired. I'm going to get an early night. Theo, will you come to bed with me?"

My cheeks burn, and I silently beg him to tell her no. But he stands up. "Yeah. Of course. Goodnight, Olive. See you in the morning."

They turn and disappear into the house just as my vision blurs with unshed tears. When they're gone, I can't decide what to do. Part of me wants to go to my room, listen for any clues as to what is happening. But part of me doesn't want to know. That part wants to protect my heart from utter disappointment and stay out on the deck all night.

Ultimately, I decide to go to bed. There is no sound coming from their room when I slip beneath the blankets. They must already be asleep. Which means they aren't arguing. But they're also not having make-up sex, so there is that.

When I wake up the next day, I walk out into the kitchen to find Theo sitting at the kitchen island, a cup of coffee in his hand. He hears me approach and turns to face me, a tired smile on his lips.

"How did you sleep?" he asks.

"Not great."

He nods knowingly. "Neither did I."

I cross the room to make myself a cup of coffee.

"I told Astrid about us," he says. I freeze. "She left."

I feel lightheaded. Did I hear him wrong? I had to have heard him wrong. "What do you mean?"

"She's gone. She took the plane back home late last night. It will be back for us tomorrow. She's left me, too."

My mouth falls open. It's happened. It has finally happened. But I don't yet know how Theo is feeling about this. His wife just left him. He could have told her about us because he felt guilty, and he needed to relieve his conscience.

"I'm so sorry," I say. I watch his face for clues. *Tell me what this means, Theo.*

He stands up, and I hold my breath. His hand reaches for mine, and our fingers intertwine. I can feel my heart in my temples. "We can be together now."

Gravity seems to give way. I feel as though I would float away if he let go of my hand. He is mine. Everything Astrid has is mine. I use my free hand to cup Theo's head and pull him in for a kiss.

"Let's enjoy our last day here," he says as he pulls me to the bedroom. The bedroom he shared with Astrid just last night.

Afterward, I lie on his bare chest, listening to his heart pound against my ear. What would he say if he knew how we *really* met? If he knew who I was before I became Olive. I don't think I'll ever tell him.

We make our way back to the kitchen at some point. My stomach growls loud enough for Theo to hear. He laughs. "I'll get started on breakfast."

I watch him from a stool at the kitchen island. I still can't believe this is happening, having pictured moments like this a million times. But I can't help thinking about Astrid. Her red, tear-streaked face the night she was fighting with Theo pops into my head. She must be devastated.

"Have you seen my phone?" I ask as Theo pushes eggs around in the pan.

"Your phone? No, I haven't."

Hopping down from my stool, I go to my room and start searching through my things. Clothes and blankets are everywhere. It has to be lost under the mess. That's what I get for being a slob.

"What's this?" I jump and spin around at Theo's voice.

"You scared me. What's what?"

He picks something up from the ground and my heart stops. "Oh," I choke out. "A button I found at the bookstore. It's funny, isn't it?"

"Yeah. It's cute." He looks up at me and smiles. "Breakfast is ready." He flips the button onto a pile of my clothes and leaves the room.

I force myself to take a shaky breath. He didn't remember it. His face showed no sign of recognition. I'm okay. Everything is okay.

I follow Theo out to the back patio where two plates of food wait. His expression is still pleasant. Not suspicious. Does he really not remember? How frequently does he buy gifts for strangers?

The sun is already becoming brutal, shining directly in my eyes. Using my hand as a shield, I squint to look at Theo.

"Thank you for breakfast. It's delicious."

"Of course. Did you find your phone?"

"No. I need to clean up my mess. I think it's lost in the clothes piles."

I think he smiles and nods. But I can't be sure. "What do you want to do on our last day in paradise?" I ask.

"I was thinking of taking a swim."

"Yeah, that sounds nice."

There is an awkwardness between us that wasn't there before. Is it because he *does* remember the button? Because we could not truly be ourselves with each other until now and we're still adjusting? I'm not sure.

Maybe I should ask him how he's feeling about Astrid. This is all so new. They may have been having problems for a while, but they've been together an entire decade, and he doesn't seem too upset. He's probably hiding it from me to protect my feelings.

"We can talk about Astrid if you'd like," I say. "I know this has to be difficult, even if it is what you want."

I want to be a supportive partner. Someone he can be honest with and open up to. So, I prepare myself to listen to him. To comfort him about the end of his marriage.

"I don't really want to talk about that now. I'd rather not spoil the end of our vacation."

"Sure. Okay."

I nibble at my lip. The awkwardness is temporary. We will fall into comfortability soon. The beginning is going to be the hardest part. Supporting him through a divorce. Moving Astrid out and me in. But in time, this will be our new normal.

We spend the afternoon by the beach, sipping cocktails and diving into waves. The alcohol lessens our awkwardness, and soon we are laughing as the water knocks us around. I lie on the sand, my muscles weak from swimming and vodka.

"Let's go back to the house for dinner," Theo says as he leans into me and presses his lips to mine. Butterflies dance in my stomach, and I let him take my hand and lead the way up the beach.

After dinner, we sit on the patio. The sun is gone, along with the abrasive heat. Theo brings out a pair of glasses filled with red wine.

"To a lovely vacation. May we readjust well to what waits for us back home."

We clink our glasses together and I take a sip.

Theo chugs his, and then eyes me with a flirtatious grin. "Oh, come on, you're not going soft on our last night here, are you?"

I give him a wink. "I wouldn't dream of it." I empty the glass in one long drink.

"That's what I'm talking about." He claps his hands.

I try to ignore the feeling in my gut that Theo is acting strangely. He is on the precipice of divorce from his college sweetheart. The woman he wanted to have children with. But maybe he's been ready to leave her for a long time. He did flirt with me as a barista at a café. It has been a long time coming. Or maybe the reality of it all just hasn't hit him yet.

I turn down a drink on the next round, but Theo brings one back for me anyway. I let it sit because the effects from what I've already had are intense. When I turn my head, the world takes a second longer to catch up.

When I try to make a joke about being a lightweight, the words come out a mess of smashed up things that don't make sense. I laugh, nervous. Embarrassed. I need to go to bed.

I move to stand, but my legs are noodles beneath me. I collapse to the wooden patio, and my heart begins to race madly. Oh my God. What's wrong with me? I haven't even drunk that much.

A blur of movement and sounds swirl in my peripheral like the beach waves on the shore last night, and then I see Theo's face. It's close to mine. My heart slows. He'll take care of me. My eyes close, and everything goes silent as I give into the darkness, knowing I'm safe.

* * *

My muscles ache like never before. And my chest is tight. Like I can't breathe. I can't open my eyes. I can't move. I focus on my breath. Dragging air in and pushing it out. Slowly and deeply. Why is it so hard to breathe? I wiggle my fingers and almost sob when I feel them rub against one another. I feel cramped. As I gain consciousness, I can feel that I'm curled into a ball. My legs ache like I've been this way for a while. I try hard to push them out, to extend and give my limbs a stretch. But nothing happens. When I push my body outwards, it's held in place. My arms are folded into my chest, and I work them up to my face, feeling around. It's only when I feel a flutter of my eyelashes that I realize my eyes are open. It's just too dark to see.

My heart explodes into a frenzied beat as my mind races with possibilities of what the fuck is happening.

A dream. I fell into somewhere strange when I was drunk. Hallucination. Someone broke into our beach house, and I've been kidnapped.

I strain to hear something. And that's when I get the bumping and moving sensation. Am I in a car? The bumps come quicker and quicker, and we're going so fast, too fast. And then it stops. Kind of. I feel the odd sensation of falling before it stops. Then once more. Then there is a mechanical sound right below me.

It's like my body realizes it before my mind. I scream. Panic claws through my chest, and I can't breathe.

Whether from fear or lack of oxygen, I feel myself start to lose consciousness as I try to figure out how the fuck I ended up in the luggage compartment of a plane.

# CHAPTER TWENTY-FOUR

*"There is a charm about the forbidden that makes it unspeakably desirable." — Mark Twain*

Orange and yellow bursts of light dance behind my eyelids. I'm no longer confined in whatever container I was being held in on the plane. I'm on something soft. A bed. Or a couch. I smell clean laundry, and it's oddly comforting. The air is warm, and I hear a faint buzzing. Then a crunching, and I tense in fear. The crunching continues. Then a rustling.

I dare to open my eyes, holding my breath as I do. I'm staring at a ceiling. White fan blades spinning so quickly they blur into one. Fear spreads through me like tiny spiders scurrying in my bones. Slowly, I turn my head to the left, the direction of the crunching.

There is another bed next to the one I'm lying in. Empty. And then there is a recliner chair. In it sits a girl. A woman? A bag of baby carrots on her lap. It's such an odd and misplaced sight that I almost laugh. But the terror and uncertainty keep me serious. The girl must sense my eyes on her. She turns, and our eyes meet. Her brows crease in pity, and she stands up.

Her movement shocks me into motion and I jolt upward, scooting back until my back meets resistance. The girl stops, her hands up in a placating gesture.

"I won't hurt you. It's okay. Well . . . it's not really. But at this specific moment, it's okay."

"Where am I?" My throat is dry. The words come out in a hoarse whisper.

"Tell me your name," she says, ignoring my question. She reminds me of fall with her willowy limbs and chestnut-colored hair. Her eyes are the color of tree bark.

"Olive," I say. "Where am I?"

The girl's face is awash in pity again. "In the basement of the Connors' house," she says soberly.

The girl goes blurry. My ears ring. I open my mouth, but I can't seem to find words.

"Wh—" I clear my throat. "Why? How?"

She inhales deeply, then sits on the edge of the bed, staring at the far wall. Her hair is long and brown. She's young, but I can't pinpoint her age. Why does she look so familiar? She still hasn't spoken, so I ask, "Who are you? What happened to you?"

Her eyes go glossy. "My name is Holly Fisher."

The name sounds familiar, but I don't know why.

"I was a freshman at Holloway. Professor Connor was my Intro to American Lit professor."

My blood turns to ice, and I suddenly realize where I know her from. The missing persons posters I've seen for months. Years? Around my old work. Around the university campus.

I launch off the bed. There is an open door to the left, and I fling myself through it to find myself in what looks like a mini apartment. A large, open-concept area with a kitchen, dining room, and living room area. There are two more doors. One a standard wooden one, and the other, large and imposing, that looks like it's made of steel.

I run for the metal door, assuming it's the one meant to keep me down here. There is no handle. Only a keyhole. I ram my shoulder against it, a sob or a scream working its way up my throat. Or maybe it's vomit. Pounding my fists against the door, I feel tears trailing down my face.

This isn't happening. This cannot be happening.

"There is no way out," Holly says from behind me.

I spin around, fear and anger bubbling in my gut. "You have to help me get out of here!"

"Help you? Do you think I'm down here because I want to be? There is no way out."

But there has to be. Because this isn't the way my life is supposed to go. I had a plan. My new life was at the tips of my fingers. I can still taste it. The expensive wine on Theo's lips. How has everything gone so horribly wrong so quickly?

I fix my eyes on Holly's. "Tell me everything you know."

# CHAPTER TWENTY-FIVE

*"You sensed that you should be following a different path, a more ambitious one, you felt that you were destined for other things but you had no idea how to achieve them and in your misery you began to hate everything around you." — Fyodor Dostoevsky*

Holly stands a few feet away from me, arms crossed.

"Tell me everything you know about what's going on. Tell me how you got here and what's happened since. I need to know everything."

"It won't make a difference." She turns and walks back to the bedroom I just ran from.

I wipe my face with the bathing suit cover I still wear from the vacation house. Goosebumps spread across my skin, and I shiver, though the room is perfectly warm.

I follow Holly and try to swallow down the massive lump in my throat. I need information.

When I enter the room, she hands me a pile of clothes. "Those will probably be more comfortable than what you have on."

I look down at the gray sweatpants and dingy white T-shirt in my hands. "Are these yours?"

"No." She collapses back into the armchair with her bag of baby carrots.

I cross the room and sit on the edge of the second bed, facing her. The urge to rip her hair out is so great that I have to clench my hands together to keep from reaching for the brown strands.

"I just woke up in a foreign place that you're telling me is the basement of my friends' house. You're the only person that can give me some answers and you're being very tight-lipped. What is fucking going on?" I keep my voice low and slow, trying to reason with this unreasonable woman.

She laughs humorlessly. "You think they're your friends?"

"That is beside the point!" I scream. No longer able to keep my cool.

She sets her bag of food on a small table beside her and shifts to face me. "Your friends are sick psychopaths. They kidnapped me. And you. And many, many others."

"Please, Holly. Don't leave me in the dark. Tell me what you know."

She chews the inside of her cheek and then takes a deep breath. "Theo Connor was one of my professors my freshman year." She rolls her eyes and laughs through her nose. "All the girls had little crushes on him. Myself included."

My jaw is clenched so hard my teeth feel like they'll shatter as I try to listen to the pointless parts of her story. I want to throttle her and make her tell me how she got here and what's happened since then.

"I didn't have his class second semester, but I went to him for help with my Shakespeare class. I was close to failing, and I'd lose my scholarship. He invited me to his house for dinner with his wife, and afterward he'd help me on my final paper."

She pauses, and her face hardens. Her eyes are glassy as she inhales slowly. When she exhales, she closes her eyes. Come on!

She finally opens her eyes, and the glassiness is gone. "I thought it would be fine. Safe. You know, since his wife would be there. I'm not stupid. I know to be wary of sketchy situations. But he was a trusted professor. He'd been helping me for a few weeks. And his wife would be there."

I nod, encouraging her to continue.

"She answered the door. Astrid. She took me to Theo's office and offered me a glass of wine. I was only eighteen, but I felt sophisticated and respected." She snorts and wipes her sleeve across her nose.

"I don't remember much after that. Just that I started feeling really tired. Then flashes of memory of Theo carrying me somewhere. I woke up down here sometime later."

My stomach churns as seemingly unconnected things start to align in my mind. I can't quite get myself to understand that Theo is connected to the missing student at his university.

"Why did they take you? What do they want from us?"

Her face crumples, and all at once, her tough exterior disintegrates. I can feel my heart in my throat, making it impossible to breathe.

"They're into some shady shit. I don't know exactly. But they want . . . they want babies." The last part comes out in a whisper, but I hear her loud and clear.

Even though I've heard her, I don't understand what she means. Babies? For what? What does that have to do with me?

She must see the confusion on my face because she leans over and lifts something from the side of the bed. A strap. I turn to look at the other bed and see the black straps attached to the corners. My stomach rolls.

"They want you, us, to get pregnant and have children. And when we do, they will take the baby. I don't know anything else."

My head spins, and I feel as though I've fallen into a weird alternate reality. Or a dream. None of this makes sense. Theo loves me. He was going to leave his wife for me.

I can't catch my breath. Leaping from the bed, I start pacing, looking around again. Trying to spot a way out. More than fear, I feel anger.

"How have you been here this long? Haven't you tried to get out?" I spit the words like fire from my mouth.

Holly's eyes narrow into slits. "Of course I have. But they're not stupid. They didn't start this shit on a whim. They've prepared and thought everything through. There is no way out."

"There has to be."

I continue looking around our twisted apartment, looking for anything that might help me. Holly watches me from the doorframe. I want to hit her. To tell her to help me, for fuck's sake. But after nearly an hour of scouring the place, I reluctantly come to the same conclusion. The only way in or out is through that giant metal door. And it's impenetrable.

I collapse to the floor, near hysterics. Why the hell do they want babies? The reality I'm in is so at odds with everything I've known for the past several months. My head aches trying to reconcile the two.

A sound like metal grinding against metal comes from the big door. I get to my feet and start moving toward Holly, but she's gone from the doorframe. Panicked and unsure what to do, I brace myself and watch Theo come through the door. Even after waking up this way and being told the things I've been told, my body relaxes when I see him. A sense of relief and love send me stepping toward him.

"Hi there, Olive." He pushes the door shut behind him. He carries a paper bag. He stops, a look on his face like he's remembering something. "You do prefer Olive, right? Not Laura?"

My blood freezes in my veins.

He smiles, devilishly handsome. Devastatingly gorgeous and equally dangerous. He continues to the small dining table, setting down the large paper bag. "I have to admit, you were an interesting one."

I don't like the way he refers to me in the past tense. As if I've already stopped existing. I take a step back.

"It was a bit of a challenge figuring out what was truth and what was fiction," he says, taking items out of the bag. A white-and-pink pill bottle. A notebook. A crayon. "Your intentions were pretty clear from the start. I don't know if you thought you were being subtle."

"Just as subtle as you were at the beach house," I say.

The sarcastic smile melts from his face and he glares at me murderously. In an instant he's moving toward me, and before I can flee, he's on me, pushing me into the wall, hand gripping my throat.

Fear chokes me more than his fingers do as he leans down and whispers into my ear, "You are nothing to me. Nothing about you is desirable. You are a disposable tool. When I'm done with you, you will be thrown away. Never allow yourself to think otherwise."

He releases me and goes back to the table as I slink to the ground, tears falling freely.

"Pay attention now. I have to run," he says. "I don't know how much Holly has told you, but these" — he slides the pill bottle across the table in my direction — "are your prenatal vitamins. It's best to take them after dinner and before bed. They tend to make the girls nauseous."

I'm already nauseous, and I bite back the bile that rises in my throat.

"This notebook has charts for your cycle. Fill out what you remember and make sure to start tracking everything. There are ovulation strips in the bathroom you're expected to use every day."

"You'll never get away with this," I say.

He smiles with almost a hint of pity in his eyes. "They all say that."

"I'll be reported missing. I disappeared while on vacation with you and your wife, you stupid fuck. They'll figure it out."

"Who, exactly, will figure it out?" He tilts his head. "Your family you haven't spoken to in months? Your publisher?" His smile widens, delighted to be revealing just how much he knows. "You don't have close family or friends. You don't have an employer. And we kindly gave your landlord notice that you won't be renewing your lease. No one will even begin to look for you for quite some time. By then" — he shrugs — "any trail will have already gone cold. If the police ever do get involved and happen to question us, we'll tell them what the rest of them will say. That you were a typical gold-digging social climber who moved on when she realized there was no place for her here."

I shake my head back and forth, and I can't stop. This can't be happening. Every piece of my reality is being shattered right in front of me, and my brain is not doing a great job at processing it all.

"I have to run. But make sure to take a peek at the other notebook. It has your exercise requirements in there, and that's where you'll mark off when you've done them each day."

He moves toward the door, and I watch him, trying to see how he opens it, but his body blocks my view. He turns just before shutting the door behind himself. "See you soon, Laura." He winks and shuts the door. I break into sobs.

## CHAPTER TWENTY-SIX

*"Thinking is difficult, that's why most judge."* — *Carl Jung*

I sit, catatonic, for a long time. The smell of food brings me back to my current nightmarish reality. I blink hard, trying to clear my vision. Holly is in the kitchen, jabbing her finger at the microwave with a plastic fork in her mouth.

She pivots and sees me staring at her. "I can heat yours up if you want."

I grimace. "I'm not really in the mood to eat."

"Doesn't matter." The microwave beeps, and she turns to take her food out. "You have to eat what they give you. Part of your nutrition plan." She uses the fork to point at the stack of notebooks on the table.

"And what happens if I decide not to follow the nutrition plan? Is he going to force feed me?"

I get to my feet, a white-hot rage bubbling up from the pit of my stomach, making my whole body warm.

"You sit down here like a good little girl and do everything they tell you to, and where has it gotten you?"

She takes another bite of her food, and I want to smack the chicken from her mouth. Throw her plate on the ground and scream in her face. How can she sit here so calmly? Her acceptance of her situation bothers me on such a deep level that I can't stop myself from yelling at her.

"You were a stupid college kid trying to snuggle up to a professor. For what? A good grade?" I jab a finger into my chest. "I don't deserve to be here. This isn't supposed to happen to me. I had a plan."

"And yet, here we both are," she says, her voice calm and even as I wipe spit from the corners of my mouth. Holly looks up at me. "Life doesn't owe you shit. My decisions landed me here. Same as you."

I roll my eyes and laugh angrily, wiping my tears with the palm of my hand. I turn and go to the bedroom before I'm unable to stop myself from attacking her.

Grabbing the remote from the top of the television, I flip through the channels, hoping to find the news. After a minute, I find a local channel. They're talking about a tropical storm down south. I sit on the floor against the foot of the bed and watch for any mention of me.

But Theo was right. My family won't worry when they don't hear from me. I haven't spoken to any of them in months. I have no job that might alert the authorities if I didn't show up. Just an email in my inbox for a writing gig that will go ignored.

I think about Logan and feel a small flicker of hope. He is expecting me to come back. Though, if Theo has my phone and has already taken care of my apartment, I'm sure he will come up with something to take care of Logan too.

I find myself reliving every single moment of my life since I first saw Theo in Café Rêvasser. It feels like an entire lifetime ago. And it was, when I really think about it.

I relive all the moments I spent with Astrid. They were trying to have a baby. To adopt or something like that? But then, that's not exactly what she said, is it? It's what she let me believe, but it isn't what she said. How did she word it?

She wanted to be done 'pursuing children.'

I think about the times both Astrid and Theo asked about my relationship with my family, and I told them we didn't talk. I think about Astrid questioning my lack of friends at my party and how I thought it was Tessa that put doubts about me in her mind.

But all along, they were trying to figure out if I was a good kidnapping candidate, and I gave the interview of my fucking life.

* * *

I must've dozed off. I wake up to the sound of humming in the other room. I scramble up and move to the doorframe. Peeking around the corner, I watch Holly. She's making food again. I don't recognize the song, and I wish she would stop. Her cheerfulness in a situation like this is sickening.

She opens a cabinet and pours varying pills into her palm before popping them into her mouth and swallowing them down with water.

I stomp out of the room. "Why do you take the pills they give you? Flush them down the toilet or something."

Holly nods at the corner of the room. I turn and see a camera fastened to the ceiling.

"There are three cameras in plain sight, but I'm pretty sure they have more hidden," she says before taking a bite of what looks like ground beef.

I charge the camera, reaching up to rip it down, but it's just out of reach. I go back to the table and drag the empty chair over to the wall.

"What are you doing?" Holly says, fear clear in her voice. Pathetic. "Olive, stop. Don't do that."

I stand on the chair and yank at the camera until it comes free from the wall, almost knocking me down. I step down from the chair with the remnants of the camera in my hands and beam at the broken electronic pieces.

"Where are the others?"

She shakes her head. "You're going to get both of us in trouble."

"Do you want to stay in here forever? Die here? We have to do something."

"No. But this isn't going to get us out."

"Sitting there eating their prepared food and taking their prescribed vitamins isn't going to get you out either."

"He's going to see that the camera is out, and he's going to come down here, pissed off, and we're both going to pay."

"If we take out all the cameras, we can prepare without him seeing us. Attack him."

"Were you not listening to me? They have cameras hidden. He probably already knows the camera is out and is on his way here. So now you think you're going to tear down the rest of the cameras, find all the hidden cameras I haven't found in the years I've been down here, and then prepare to overtake him?"

I clench my jaw, staring at the wall behind her.

"You're making up a plan as you go, and you're going to get us both killed."

I open my mouth to argue, but the words disappear along with the crazed anger. She's right. I'm being irrational and sloppy. Theo and Astrid have clearly thought through their prisoners trying to escape. Any obvious way of getting out would have been considered and planned for.

I am a planner. Calculating. I have to approach this the same way.

I nod. "Okay." Walking back to the table, my chair in tow, I sit down. Holly is visibly shaken. The image of Theo grabbing me by the neck earlier comes to mind, and I wonder if he's ever attacked her. If he'll really hurt me.

"Eat your dinner and take your vitamins. He'll only be angrier if he gets here and you haven't."

I roll my eyes. I admit I need to think out my escape better, but I'm not taking prenatal vitamins and eating their shit food. I've gotten good at being hungry. And with a solid plan and a little luck, I'll be out of here by the time the hunger gets to be too much.

Holly shakes her head, still shaky from my outburst. Her fear is contagious, and the more nervous she is, the more I start to worry about the consequences of what I've done.

The anticipation is the worst. Time drags on as I watch the big metal door from the corner of my eye. When Holly prepares for bed, I follow her to the bedroom and begrudgingly accept the used clothes she offered me earlier.

The door opens in the middle of the night. The prison apartment is completely dark. I heard Holly get out of bed an hour ago, but she didn't leave the room. So I moved to the floor, pushing myself into the corner next to the twin bed meant to be mine.

I strain my ears, trying to hear any sound coming from the other room, but there is only complete silence and the sound of my wild heart.

Suddenly, the darkness disappears, and I am blinded by bright light. A piercing, high-pitched sound blasts through the room and my hands fly to my ears. I try to open my eyes, terrified of the sudden loss of my hearing and sight. Tears well in my eyes. I don't know if I'm crying or if they're just watering from the light.

It takes too long for my eyes to adjust, and I don't see Theo until he's pulling me from the ground by my hair.

## CHAPTER TWENTY-SEVEN

*"Friendship is unnecessary, like philosophy, like art . . . It has no survival value; rather it is one of those things which give value to survival."*
*— C.S. Lewis*

I only see flashes of his face as I'm thrashed around the room. It hurts to open my eyes for more than a second. I feel like I'm blinking in reverse. I can't hear anything but the deafening screech.

I smack into a wall face first. I have to choose between using my hands to brace myself against whatever is in front of me and covering my ears. I can't make a decision, so I switch between the two and always seem to be covering my ears when I'm thrown toward a solid object.

My face burns and throbs. My heart hammers furiously against my chest. Theo's face blurs in front of me again. He's wearing sunglasses. Without thinking, I reach for them. They don't come right off. They're holding to his head. A strap? Like goggles. But I don't let go. I rip at them until they come loose.

His hands release me, and I fall to the ground, scrambling backward. I lost the goggles, but within seconds, the assault on my senses stops. My ears are ringing, and I wipe at my eyes, seeing spots. The lights are the normal room lights. I'm disoriented, and my heart still hammers away as I try to take in my surroundings.

Again, Theo is on me before I can orient myself.

"You disobey my instructions. You destroy my property," Theo says between gritted teeth. He rears his hand back and slaps me, hard, across the face. "This can all go fairly easily for you if you let it, Laura. Or it can be an incredible nightmare every single day. I can go either way."

His fingers press into my jaw so hard I feel like it'll pop right off my face. I push against him, but he doesn't budge. An image of his muscular back and arms on the beach flashes in my mind. Just a night ago, I gripped him in pleasure. I never could have imagined how drastically it all would change.

He throws me to the ground and backs away, breathing hard. "Are you going to cooperate, or are you going to make the rest of your life a living nightmare?"

I stare at him through blurry eyes, and unable to stop it, I break into sobs. Theo watches me cry, arms crossed over his chest.

This cannot be the rest of my life. I don't deserve this. I am supposed to be sipping wine with my husband in front of a fireplace. Discussing literature and art and the way the world works. I am meant to be enjoying cocktails in fine dresses with brilliant company. But honestly, right now I'd take my small, crappy apartment and beat-up Honda. I'd give anything to be going to work at Café Rêvasser in the morning.

"I'll give you some time to decide. Get back into the bedroom so I can fix the camera you ripped off the wall like the insolent ape you are."

When I remain still, he takes a step toward me, which spurs me into movement, afraid of another lashing. I stumble to the bedroom, where I spot Holly in the corner by her bed with her head down and arms folded over her head in a defensive position. I go back to the corner Theo dragged me from and collapse, hearing the bedroom door shut and then lock.

Adrenaline is the only thing keeping me awake. After some time, my pulse slows, moving closer to a normal rate. My eyes grow heavy as the adrenaline fades. I hear the metal door open and then close.

My whole body aches. I tenderly press my fingertips to my cheek and wince. Inhaling a shaky breath, I push myself up from the floor. My knees tremble, almost giving out beneath me.

I clamber my way to the bathroom, shutting my eyes to the florescent light that floods the room when I flip the switch. My head throbs so much that my vision blurs. I've never so much as been in a grade-school fight. This is a pain I've never experienced.

When I'm able to open my eyes, my stomach turns at the sight of my reflection. A gash across my cheek bleeds down onto my neck. My right eye is swollen and a sickening shade of purple. Which explains why I can't see very well. My throat burns, and my scalp is sore.

My muscles feel weak, and I worry I won't be able to get back to bed. I start toward the bedroom, gritting my teeth with every painful step.

Holly is in bed, hidden beneath blankets when I return. I shut off the light and climb into bed, wincing when my head hits the pillow. My mind and body are utterly exhausted. The thought that I may have a concussion and probably shouldn't sleep crosses my mind just as I fall unconscious.

* * *

Holly nudges me awake. My right eye refuses to open.

"What do you want?" I ask. I'm irritated with her, though I can't articulate exactly why.

"Put this on your face. And you need to clean the cut on your face."

I grab what she holds out to me. A bag of frozen peas. My breath catches when the cold surface connects with my face, and I suck in air through my teeth.

It takes me several minutes to get out of bed. Holly sits at the table, poking at her food with a fork. "I told you not to do that," she mumbles.

"Well, don't look so fucking heartbroken. He didn't touch you."

She huffs out air and shakes her head. "Has anyone ever told you that you're really self-centered?"

Yes.

"No. Because I'm not. Nothing happened to you. Why are you crying?"

"I'm not crying, first of all."

"Might as well be," I say, taking a seat across from her. I feel like a teenager bickering with this woman I barely know.

"Second of all," she says, her voice rising. "You had no regard for me or what would happen to me if you did something stupid."

"Nothing happened to you!"

Holly leaps to her feet, pushing her chair back with a loud screech that sends my headache into a frenzy.

"Have you noticed there are two beds in that room?" She jabs her finger over my shoulder. "It's not a new addition, Olive. Someone else used to be here, and she's not anymore. Theo took her, and she never came back."

She sniffs and wipes her nose with the side of her hand. "The lights and noise that happened last night? The last time it happened was the night he took Celia." Her words break off in a sob. "I thought he was going to take me last night."

I don't know what to say. Mostly because everything I want to say wouldn't come off well. I get she was afraid she was going to be taken away, but she wasn't. Instead, I was attacked. Yet she's yelling at me like she was the one hurt.

I don't say any of this. Instead, I lay my head on another bag of frozen vegetables and pray the headache goes away soon.

Holly and I barely speak all day. It isn't until she slams a bottle of pills on the table beside my head that I sit up. It's a bottle of painkillers.

I look up at her, mouth gaping. "I've been sitting here in pain for hours and you just now let me know you have painkillers?"

She shrugs. "You said you weren't taking their pills."

"What—" I start to shout but have to stop when the effort sends stabbing pains through my skull. "What is wrong with you?" I ask in a softer, but still bitter, tone.

She doesn't respond. Instead, she walks past me, and I hear the television click on in the bedroom. I'm fuming. Of all the people to get held captive with, I had to get her.

My stomach rumbles, making me feel nauseous and lightheaded. It's been too long since I've eaten anything. I can't even remember the last time I had water.

Cautiously, I move to the sink. I don't want to consume anything here, but not doing so is a drawn-out suicide, which I'm not ready to do just yet. I find a glass and fill it with water, sipping it slowly.

I open the fridge and the cabinets and scan the contents. There are food containers stacked in the fridge in sets of three. Breakfast, lunch, and dinner. I look around the kitchen and realize for the first time that there isn't a stove. Just the fridge and microwave.

In one of the cabinets I find a container of crackers. I take them and my water to the bedroom and sit in bed with my back propped up with a pillow against the wall.

Holly glances at me as I get situated, but she says nothing and doesn't offer to help me. She's watching some show from the early 2000s. I can tell by the low-rise jeans and cropped shirts. I wonder if there are any books here. Holly watches a lot of television, but so far, I haven't seen so much as a magazine, let alone a novel.

I open my mouth to ask her, but press my lips back together. We're not off to a good start. As much as I don't like Holly, I can't get out of here without her help. And she will not help me as things stand right now. I need her on my side.

"What is this show called?" I ask.

She stares at me for a moment, then turns her eyes back to the television. "*Gilmore Girls.*"

I know I've heard the name before, but I've never seen it. I nibble on my crackers and watch the screen, trying to discern what's happening.

"Why does she talk so quickly? I don't know what she's talking about half the time."

Holly grins. "It's her character. It's a lot of 80s rock and pop culture references."

The channel is having a marathon of the show, and we watch several episodes together, me asking questions along the way. Holly answers them happily, and it's the first time she hasn't been tight-lipped or borderline hostile toward me.

I want to ask questions about Theo and Astrid. About what she knows and what happened before I got here. I want to come up with a plan and start preparing to get out. Every part of me itches to move. It feels like Savasana all over again.

# CHAPTER TWENTY-EIGHT

*"Hope is the thing with feathers / That perches in the soul / And sings the tune without the words / And never stops at all." — Emily Dickinson*

The next day, I do all the things I am supposed to do. I eat the designated breakfast, take the vitamins, and even do what I can of the prescribed workout until my head swims and I have to sit down.

In the afternoon, I take a bath. Allowing myself to strip down and sit in a tub of water is difficult, least of all because of the injuries. I find myself tensing up all day, watching the door. Waiting for him to come back.

I use a wet wash rag to dab at my broken face, crying out when I hit a particularly sensitive spot. When the cleaning is done, I try to force myself to relax into the hot water, if only for a minute. I wonder if Pascal is okay and hope Logan is taking care of him. I hope Theo and Astrid don't find him and take my bird back to Corrie.

Holly gives me another set of used clothes I now know to have belonged to Celia. But I'm sure they belonged to someone else before her. I sit at the dining room table in a dead girl's clothes and eat lunch.

"How often do they come down here?" I ask hesitantly.

Holly sits across from me, a forkful of broccoli halfway to her mouth. She puts the vegetables in her mouth, and her teeth scrape the plastic fork as she pulls it out.

"She doesn't come down often. Only when Theo can't, for some reason or another. It's usually him. He comes twice a month most of the time. Extra only when he's putting someone else down here or taking them out."

She takes another bite of broccoli, like she's talking about how often she sees her grandparents on the weekends instead of how often she sees her kidnapper.

I want to ask more questions, but I'm afraid to push my luck with her. Holly finishes eating, washes her food container, and goes to the bedroom. I know she's going to turn on something to watch and I'm not in the mood to watch television, but I follow her anyway.

"I'm surprised they let you have a TV." I climb into the bed and sit cross-legged against the wall.

"There wasn't one when I got here. I earned it with six months of perfect behavior," she says.

I nod, picking at my fingernails. "What other privileges have you earned?" I try to keep any trace of sarcasm or judgment from my voice, but it isn't easy.

"Food from my favorite restaurant every once in a while. Crab cakes from Jericho's. Mmm!"

She does a chef's kiss, and I try not to puke, remembering the restaurant Theo took me to for lunch. He ordered that exact dish to go. And then I remember Corrie's comment that she thought Astrid was allergic to shellfish.

"I went there with him," I say, almost in a whisper because my throat is so constricted.

Holly is quiet for a moment. I think I may have put her off again and I'm about to give up for the night and roll over when she speaks. "Is there anyone who will look for you? I heard Theo say there was no one. Was he right?"

"I don't know," I say honestly. "I'm sure the debt collectors will keep looking for me." I laugh lightly. "But I don't think my family or anyone else will do much when they don't hear from me."

"Well," she says. "It's more than I had."

I think about that for a moment. "You haven't asked about anything going on outside of here. Don't you have family?"

She shakes her head. "My mom died when I was eight. Breast cancer. My dad got sick when I was in high school. He died my freshman year of college. I was an only child, and so were my parents, so I was alone when he passed."

My chest is tight with emotion. I feel uncharacteristically bad for her. My family means close to nothing to me. And as terrible as it sounds, losing them would not have been much of a loss. But I can feel her pain from across the room, though she isn't even crying.

"People are still talking about you. A girl from your school. A classmate. Maybe she was your roommate? I don't know. She puts up posters all over the city. Updates them with new pictures every few months."

"Hmm. Well, I'll be damned." The words are light, but I can hear the strain in her voice. "If it's my roommate, her name is Malica." She pauses, then laughs. "Actually, it's definitely Malica. My dad used to say this thing, 'never met a stranger.' I didn't understand the phrase until I met her. She's never met a stranger. The moment she meets someone, she cares about them like they're her best friend since childhood." She smiles, and her eyes go glassy.

I smile too. It sounds nice. Foreign, but nice. The idea of caring so deeply for anyone.

"She would meet someone new and within five minutes know more about them than their closest friends," Holly says, laughing. "I remember the day I moved in, she stopped unpacking her own things to help me unpack mine, and the second question out of her mouth was 'what's your relationship with your parents like?'"

I watch Holly reminisce, telling the story with a far-off look in her eyes like she's back in her dorm room.

"I thought she was a psych major for sure. But she wasn't. Business management, of all things."

She goes quiet, seeming to keep the rest of the memory to herself. In the quiet, I think about my own friendships. My lack of them. Astrid and Tessa were the closest things I had to real friends in a very long time, and we can see where that got me.

But before now . . . before I woke up in a basement prison, I was actively trying to convince Astrid that I was her friend, and I have no idea what her relationship with her parents was like. I don't even know if her parents are still alive.

I try to swallow down the self-consciousness. The idea that I don't even know how to pretend to be a good friend. The fact that it kind of bothers me.

"Can you do me a favor?" Holly asks after a long while.

"Sure," I say, my eyes getting heavy with sleep.

"If you do get out . . ." She trails off. Clears her throat. "If you get out and I don't. I have two children . . . that they took. A boy and a girl. I don't know where they took them. And I know it's a big ask because they would have obviously covered their tracks . . . but would you try to find them?"

I can't swallow behind the lump in my throat.

"I'll probably be dead and won't know if you do or don't. But just tell me you will."

"I will," I say. "I promise."

## CHAPTER TWENTY-NINE

*"People with a grudge against the world are always dangerous. They seem to think life owes them something." — Agatha Christie*

I convince Holly to move the television set into the living room. It felt more depressing somehow to sit in the bedroom all day, and there isn't much to do other than binge TV shows. It helps keep your mind busy, too. Which is important down here.

When I asked her if there were any books, her face fell, and she shook her head. She tried to explain that she felt her love of literature connected her to Theo, and after being kidnapped, raped, and having her children stolen from her, she denounced her love of books and, therefore, her connection to Theo.

I don't understand it. Even psychopaths have interests, and you're bound to have something in common with a few of them. It doesn't mean you should stop liking what you like. Unless you like eating human flesh or unlawfully holding someone in a basement against their will. In that case . . .

But I nod sympathetically. I'm learning that empathy is something I can practice. Like yoga and running, it all sucks and feels entirely unnatural, painful even, in the beginning. But it gets easier.

Holly has been tense all morning. She fills a cup of water and sets it on the counter. When she leans over to grab her vitamin bottles, she knocks into the cup, and it tips over onto the floor. She jumps back, and I get to my feet, looking for a towel to help her. She pulls her foot back and kicks the empty plastic cup across the room and lets out a frustrated shout.

"Okay, what is wrong with you today? You're all worked up," I say, tossing the towel onto the puddle of water on the floor and using my foot to move it around.

"He's coming tonight," she says, staring at the floor.

"How do you know?" My heart falls into my stomach. I haven't seen him since he bashed my face in. A week ago, now. I can finally open my right eye, though the entire side of my face is still a terrible green color that makes me look sick. The cut on my cheek still pops open and bleeds from time to time, but it's getting better.

"It's time . . . you know." She nods downward. I look down, not understanding for a second. And then I get it. It's time for Theo to try to get her pregnant.

My hand goes to my mouth. Holly moves around me, getting on her hands and knees to finish cleaning up the spilled water. When she's done, she walks to the couch and sits down, turning the television on with the remote.

I sit on the other end and stare at the screen. "How does it work?" I ask. "What happens?"

"Now that there are two of us down here again, he'll make you wait out here. He'll go into the bathroom. Do his thing. Then he'll come into the bedroom, lock the door, and start the . . . process."

"The process?"

"Don't make me detail the whole thing," she says. "He gets off, puts it in a glorified turkey baster, and puts it into me."

I wince. "I'm sorry." I shake my head. This is so fucked up. The whole thing. "They're his own kids. What does he do with them?"

Holly doesn't respond right away. Her knees are pulled to her chest with her arms, hugging them close. "I have no clue. I can only pray they're okay."

The implications aren't good. But I don't say that.

"What did you name them?" I ask. "You must've named them," I say gently when she doesn't answer.

"Amber and Jasper," she says, eyes wide, staring at her lap.

"They're good names. How'd you decide on them?"

"Amber was my mom's name. Jasper was my dad's." Her face crumples, and I immediately feel guilty. But I press on because I can't do this without her help, and I know that the prospect of seeing her babies and making sure they're safe is the only thing that will get her to help me.

I move closer and reach for her hands. She pulls them away, but I grab them and pull her to me, despite her resistance. "They need you, Holly. Amber and Jasper need you."

She's openly sobbing now. Her whole body shakes, and I feel sick with sadness and guilt. "I can't help them. I can't get out of here."

She sounds so young, and the child I hear in her voice breaks my heart in a way I didn't think was possible. I hug her, and she lets me. "We have to try. Holly. Listen to me. We're going to die when they decide they're done with us. Or we die getting the fuck out of here. We have to try. You have to try for Amber and Jasper."

She trembles in silence for a moment. I hold my breath, waiting for her to say something. And then she does.

"Okay," she whispers. "Okay. Let's try."

We don't know if the cameras have volume. Holly doesn't think they do, but we can't be sure, and there is no time to figure it out because it has to happen tonight. I can't let this happen to Holly one more time.

Channel five news tells us it's September 13th. A Tuesday. Which means that Theo is in class at 8:00 a.m. until 3:00 p.m. with a break at noon. I'm thankful for the hours I spent memorizing Theo's stolen schedule.

It's ten in the morning now, so we have two hours to prepare until Theo will have his phone. There are a lot of variables we can't account for. Whether the cameras have volume is one. If they record, allowing him to rewind and watch what we've been up to. And Astrid.

It should be safe to assume that Astrid has access to the cameras. She knows what's happening. She is part of it. But she's less involved. She doesn't come down here, so maybe she doesn't look at the cameras either. There is a lot that can go wrong. But we don't have time to figure out every kink in the plan. We have to act.

"We have to find anything we can use as weapons. Anything sharp or heavy," I say.

We both scan our surroundings from where we stand in the living room and dining room area. Holly bites her thumbnail, looking nervous already.

"There's nothing. We use plastic forks, for crying out loud."

"There is something. There is always something."

I turn slowly, willing something to pop out at me. I walk to the bathroom, an idea starting to form. The tank lid from the toilet is heavy in my hands. But it's light enough for me to swing. I bring it to the dining room.

Holly has a chair tipped over when I enter the room. "We can break off the legs. Maybe get lucky that some of them will splinter on the ends, so we have a sharp edge."

"That's smart. I'll help you."

We break apart the chairs in silence. I watch Holly out of the corner of my eye, worried she's going to talk herself out of our plan.

Twenty minutes till noon, we do our best to hide the preparations we've made and sit on the couch, staring at the television.

My heart is pounding out of my chest as I try to casually watch more *Gilmore Girls* reruns. We have to sit here for an hour before we can finish preparing. My jaw is clenched, and my shoulders are tensed. All I can think about is Theo seeing everything we just did and bursting through the door any minute.

When one o'clock finally hits, I get to my feet, ready to keep preparing. I look over at Holly, hoping the downtime didn't make her change her mind.

"What if he uses the panic thing again? The lights and noise," she says.

"I was thinking about that. I have an idea. The cotton swabs in the pill bottles. We'll put them in our ears."

"And the lights?"

"Do you have any sheer fabric? Like thin shirts?"

She thinks for a second. "Not really."

"My bathing suit cover. The one I was in when they put me in here. It's a thinner white material I think might work," I say, not fully convinced. I scan the room, looking for something else. "Can we cover the lights?"

Holly looks around.

"Is it the normal lights that go brighter or separate lights that turn on?" I ask.

"I don't see any other lights," she says.

She walks to the bedroom, gathering all the clothes from the dresser. She brings them out in armfuls.

"Okay. Let's do it. Let's get the fuck out of here," Holly says, looking more alive than ever. Her newfound courage gives me hope.

We use tape Holly earned to hang pictures because Theo would never allow nails. We tape shirts and blankets over the lights. It means we'll be in near darkness until he comes, but that's okay.

"I think we should take out the cameras," I say and hand Holly another piece of tape.

She shakes her head. "If the cameras are down, he's going to come down here on guard and ready. If we leave them up, he won't, and we'll have the element of surprise."

"Unless he just looks at the cameras and is like 'Oh. How weird. Why are there shirts taped over the lights? And why are the girls standing beside the door with broken chair legs?' He's going to know either way. We get the element of surprise when he can't see what to expect."

She chews her lip, considering my point. "What about the hidden cameras? I've never been able to find them."

"Why do you think there are hidden cameras?"

"Theo told me there were."

I roll my eyes. "He was lying. Making you think he could always see you, even from places you weren't aware of."

I watch her face as she thinks about the possibility that he's been lying all this time. Just to mess with her head even more. I can see when she decides it's true. Her jaw squares and her eyes go hard.

"Okay," she says finally. "Let's do it. When we're done with everything else. Because it will alert him. That I know for sure."

"How?"

"Celia broke all the cameras once. When I first got there. After he finished punishing her, he took out his phone and showed her the alert. Called her an 'imbecile'."

I set the back of the toilet against the wall where I'll be hiding and waiting. Holly has the air freshener spray from the bathroom to blind him. But chances are that he'll have the goggles on. Which is why I plan to smack him in the head with the tank lid. We have an extra blanket to throw over him, as well as the wood pieces from the broken dining room chairs.

They thought through a lot. There isn't much to work with, but I'd chew the wooden chairs into spikes if I had to. There are a few items that are heavy, like the television, for instance. But they're too heavy. I can't lift them, let alone throw them with enough force to injure Theo. The tank lid will be tough enough to swing.

When we are as prepared as we can be, we pull the cameras down. I stand on the dining room table and use all my weight to pull them from their ceiling brackets.

Then we wait in silence. Hearts pounding, cotton in our ears. My hands are shaking and sweating so badly that I'm afraid the toilet lid will slip right from them. I'm around the corner from the door, in the kitchen. We flipped the couch over and angled it toward the door. I thought it might look like someone was using it to hide behind. But Holly is right against the wall by the door. I can't see her, but I strain my ears against the cotton, waiting, waiting.

After a while, I opt to take one of the cotton balls out of my ear so I can better hear my surroundings. Holly hasn't said a word, and the irrational thought that she's fallen asleep keeps nagging at my brain. I'm about to call out to her when I hear metal against metal. The key in the lock.

All at once, my heart jumps to my throat. Adrenaline makes my fingers tingle, and I brace myself to jump into action. More afraid than I've ever been. I don't know if I should push the cotton into my ear or wait. I need to hear what's happening.

It must be a few seconds, but it feels too long for the commotion to start. I'm panicked. I pick up the toilet lid as quietly as I can. Before I have my grip on it, the room erupts into a screaming sound. I drop the porcelain lid and it lands on my foot. I shout in pain, but it's drowned out by the noise. I shove the cotton into my ear. It doesn't block the sound out, but it muffles it just enough that I'm not disoriented. Covering the lights worked. The room is still cast in darkness.

I heave the lid back up to my lap and then onto my shoulder. I turn the corner and see Holly and Theo embraced in a struggle. As I rush forward, fueled by pulsing adrenaline and fear, I notice he still has the goggles on. He can't be able to see with the amount of light they're designed to block out. I move as fast as I can but let the lid to the toilet slide down my body and onto the floor. It's too heavy to swing accurately when he and Holly are tangled together this way.

I grab one of the wooden chair legs and jab it into Theo's back. He somehow grips the chair leg and rips it from my hands. I jump into the tangle, reaching for Theo's hair and gripping my fingers into it. I fumble for his ears, trying to rip out the earplugs. My fingers scrape across something in his ear, and I claw at it, my nails catching skin.

I hit and bite and kick. He's on the ground. I look up, in search of the toilet lid, but I see the door to the room is open. I shout to Holly, but I know she can't hear me. I grab her arm, but Theo is getting back up, and she jumps onto him again. I move for the door, trying to get her attention as I go, but she isn't looking at me. I can't risk wasting any more time.

I can't breathe as I cross the threshold of the door. I scan the room frantically and see a staircase. I stumble to it as quickly as my shaky legs will move. As I reach the first step, I look back, hoping to see Holly behind me. But there is no one there. I tell myself she's coming. That she's going to run out any second and that I need to make sure we can get out the rest of the way. Neither of us knows what is outside this room.

I scramble up the stairs, and I'm met by another door. Another steel one. With another keyhole. I push against it, hoping against all odds that it opens. But of course it doesn't. I want to scream. And I do. A screech of frustration lashes through my lips as I descend the stairs.

I hold my breath as I slowly enter the room again. Theo must have the keys on him. Hopefully, Holly has him knocked out. But when I enter the room, my worst fears are realized.

Holly lies in a heap at Theo's feet. He stands over her, breathing hard as he reels his foot back and kicks her sickeningly hard in the head. She doesn't react. He pulls his phone from his pocket, and the assaulting sound stops.

Instinct kicks in. Fight or flight, and I have nowhere to run. I spring onto his back, trying to get my arm around his neck, though I haven't the faintest clue how to choke someone out.

He flings me to the floor as though I'm an annoying child and not a woman desperate for her life. My heart is in my throat as he closes the space between us. His hair is sweaty and pulled in every direction. Blood trickles from his ear, and his eyes look crazed.

He reaches down for me, and I scream out as I kick up at him. My foot catches his face with a gross but satisfying crunch. Theo stumbles back, his hands covering his face. I spin, crawling away toward the porcelain tank lid. I grip it and pull myself up.

My skin tingles with the expectation of his hands at any second, but when I spin around, he's gone.

No. No-no-no-no.

I run toward the door. It's shut. He's gone.

I collapse to the floor in angry and utterly hopeless sobs. That was my chance. My one chance. He'll never let his guard down again.

Through my tears, I see the outline of Holly's crumpled body. Fear shoots through every nerve. I crawl to her, rolling her onto her back. Her face is bloody and swollen. Vomit rises in my throat, but I swallow it down. Carefully, I push her hair away from her face and pull her head onto my lap.

"Holly. Can you hear me? Please wake up. Holly, wake up. Please." I plead with her through tears. I put my shaking fingers under her nose, feeling for a breath, but I can't tell.

My ears are ringing from the room alarm. I take the cotton out and rub the heels of my hands against my ears, trying to get it to stop.

The ringing finally dissipates, and suddenly everything is quiet. Too quiet. No sound of breath or life comes from Holly. My chest is tight with grief and guilt. I left her with him. I ran for myself and let her die.

# CHAPTER THIRTY

*"Never cut what you can untie." — Robert Frost*

Holly's body is starting to smell. I've started dabbing toothpaste around my nostrils to block out some of the scent, but it's making my skin raw.

It's been days since we tried to escape. Since Holly died. The day after it happened, I cleaned off her face, brushed her hair, and moved her into the bedroom on her bed. I closed the door and stuffed a towel under it, but the smell is seeping through.

I can't bring myself to go into the bedroom anymore. Even just to grab a change of clothes. I can't see her lifeless, rotting body. Knowing it was all my fault. It was my idea to try to escape. And I left her to take Theo on alone. I ran and left her behind and now she's dead.

I'm thinking that Theo is leaving me down here to die a slow and agonizing death. I ran out of food yesterday. The day we tried to get out was also the day our fridge was restocked, so we had little left, and like an idiot, I didn't ration it. It wasn't until today that I considered he might be leaving me down here to starve to death.

I haven't attempted to shower or clean myself up. I glanced in the mirror once, when I was getting the toothpaste for the smell. My hair was matted and sticking up, with my mousy brown roots emerging from my scalp. My face was bruised with traces of blood. I don't know if it's mine or not. I don't care.

I numbingly wander the house like I haunt it, and sometimes I wonder if I died that night too and now my spirit is stuck here. I even went as far as to walk into the wall to see if I could pass through it. I didn't.

I make trips to the sink often, drinking as much water as I can. Even in a numb trance, my will to survive is automatic.

My period comes and goes. I feel something for the first time in days. Weeks? Relief. Dread. It's around day eighteen when Holly starts talking to me through the bedroom door. I only realize I must be hallucinating when my mom's voice starts chiming in when Holly's goes quiet.

They both call me evil. Holly tells me she's dead because of me. She whispers her children's names on repeat when I try to sleep.

Amber. Jasper. Amber. Jasper. Amber. Jasper.

My mother tells me I've always been selfish. I tell her she's a terrible mother. That she never saw me. Never saw anyone but herself. And that she only ever saw people in relation to herself. She laughs and tells me I'm just like her, and I cry, finally admitting that I am. Mad at myself for becoming the person I hate most in the world.

But I never meant to be selfish. No one looked out for me. There was no one who had my best interest in mind, so I had to be that for myself. I wonder if my mother felt that no one cared about her. If that's why she always seemed to put herself first. Even to the detriment of everyone else.

Holly won't stop crying. "Stop!" she screams. "Look. Listen."

I plug my ears, but she won't shut up.

"Pay attention!"

"See her. See them. See."

I don't know what she wants me to see. Or who? No one is here. No one but me. I am dying alone. My only company, the ghost of a girl I got killed, and my fucking mother.

Astrid wipes my face with a cold cloth. I thank her. Tell her I'm sorry. Tell her I hate her.

She says she hates me too.

I sleep.

* * *

The pain in my head wakes me. It takes a few minutes for all my senses to catch up. For me to realize I'm lying in the bed. My heart leaps from my chest. Why am I in here? I jolt up and look over at Holly's bed. She's gone.

Panic claws from everywhere inside of me, and I feel like I've lost her all over again. He took her away. Took her from me like he's taken everything from me. I cry, sobs shaking me to my core.

I crawl out of the bed, weak and limp from lack of food and my inability to stop crying. "Where is she?" I scream as I make my way to the bedroom door. "What did you do with her, you bastard!"

I push the door open and stumble forward. I freeze when I see Astrid sitting at the dining room table.

## CHAPTER THIRTY-ONE

*"The human face is, after all, nothing more nor less than a mask."* — *Agatha Christie*

She sits at the dining table, facing the door I just stumbled from, hair pin straight and make-up impeccable. I take a step forward, my mouth hanging open with words I haven't yet found. Her eyes go to the table. To her right. I follow her gaze and see the shiny black pistol she's clearly notifying me of.

"Sit," she says, nodding to the chair across from her.

I shuffle forward. The apartment has been cleaned. The television put back into the bedroom. A piece of toast sits in front of the empty chair and my mouth waters. I sit and start eating it immediately. Shame pouring over me at the vast difference between us since the last time I saw her.

"Eat slowly. You'll make yourself sick."

I do as she says, chewing less frantically.

"I think it's time we talk."

I swallow the chewed-up toast. "What did you do with Holly?"

"The same thing we do with all the girls when they're no longer of use to us." Her voice is cool and even.

"Which is?" Mine is not.

She tilts her head to the side. "What does it matter to you? We still have much use for you, Olive. You won't meet your end for a bit."

The use of my new name throws me. She knows who I am. Why is she using Olive? "I just want to know what happened to her."

She grins, but her gaze falls to her nails, dismissive. "We usually like to take younger women. They're useful for longer. But how could we pass you up when you just threw yourself in our laps?"

I nod, staring at my hands. "That's what I get for trying to take what wasn't mine."

"You're damn right," she says, her voice taking on some heat. I look up and meet her eyes. "You vapid, foolish whore. How stupid of you to think you could come between Theo and me."

I raise my eyebrows and blow out air from my cheeks. "Well, I never could have guessed the level of fucking crazy that bonded the two of you. Admittedly, I was in over my head."

She shakes her head with a small laugh. "Ever the witty one. Even in a hopeless position."

I try not to show a reaction. I feel hopeless. The fire in my gut that drives me to wanting to escape feels like it's been snuffed out. Holly and my mother's voices echo in my mind. I laugh to myself. My mother berating me on death's door makes perfect sense.

"I'm glad you still have your sense of humor," Astrid says. "Holly never did have one."

My face burns as I slowly raise my eyes to meet hers. "Don't talk about her."

A perfect eyebrow arches up. "If I didn't know any better, I'd think you were friends. But I do know better. You're not capable of making friendships, are you?"

"I considered you a friend," I say, my voice quiet.

Astrid laughs. "God. I can see why you're alone in life." She leans forward. "Not that it matters now. But I'm feeling generous, and so here's a helpful tip. You don't try to sleep with your friends' husbands."

"Try? It was barely a challenge."

Her face falls. And at once, I know.

"You didn't know." I don't smirk, even though I want to. Gloating will only piss her off. And probably make her doubt me.

"You're a liar."

"I wondered why he bothered. If he was just going to stuff me into a damn cargo box, why bother sleeping with me and making me think we were going to be together?" I study her face as I talk.

She doesn't respond. She must've suspected, then. Because her denial is half-hearted, and I can see in her face that she believes me.

She shakes her head, though I haven't said anything else. "He wouldn't."

"He did. Twice."

"No. He wouldn't. Theo loves me. We've been through too much." Her expression changes to one of decidedness. I have a feeling the idea of Theo cheating on her is something that needs to fester. I need to leave it alone for a while.

"Why did you leave that night?" I ask.

She takes a deep breath. Clenches her jaw. "I didn't want to be part of it. Of taking you."

I shake my head. "You were still part of it, Astrid." When she doesn't respond, I change the subject. "Why are you here? Why now?"

"We couldn't let you die. We already lost Holly, and I didn't want to have to take another girl."

I nod. "Why not Theo, then?"

"Don't worry about it. I need to get going, but I need to change your bandages."

She gets up, grabbing the gun from the table, and goes to the counter where a first aid kit sits. She brings it over and motions for me to turn toward her. I let her clean the wounds on my face and replace the bandage on my cheek.

"I restocked the fridge," she says, standing and collecting her things. "If you step out of line again, and I mean so much as a missed vitamin, I will leave you down here to starve to death." With that, she turns and leaves.

I go to the kitchen, dying for another piece of toast. I nibble it and force myself to wait a few hours to eat again so I don't get sick.

When I eventually convince myself to go back into the bedroom, I turn the television on to stave off the silence. I lie in bed on my side, facing Holly's bed. Tears fall across my nose and onto the pillow.

I can't stay in here. I can't fall asleep staring at a dead girl's bed. My head spins when I get to my feet, but I keep moving. I drag the pillow and blanket to the couch and lie down there.

For the first time, I contemplate the reality of being here for the rest of my life. And how long the rest of my life might be, now that I'm only going to live for as long as I can have children. I remember hearing about women having children in their forties. So at best, I have ten years.

I must've slept for a long time because sleep now evades me like the stray cats I used to try coaxing into my house when I was younger. Every time it gets close, it sprints off again for seemingly no reason.

I can't seem to quiet my mind. I'll never see the outdoors again. I'll see nothing but this dungeon apartment for the rest of my life. I'll see no one besides Astrid and Theo. I'll never finish my book. I'll never be an author. I'll never go to another party or wear another pretty dress. I won't be at my sister's wedding.

*You're doing it again.*

Holly's voice plays in my head. I huff and roll to my other side.

*Pay attention. Stop thinking about yourself.*

*Fine.*

I think about seeing Astrid today. About how she didn't know about Theo sleeping with me and leading me to believe we were going to be together. I think about that second to last day at the vacation house. Sitting at the table with Astrid when I thought I'd won. What had she said? She had told me the trip back the next day would be dangerous. That she'd help me leave early if I wanted.

She was giving me a chance to get out. I thought it was because she knew I'd won Theo over and she wanted me to leave. But it wasn't that. She didn't want to take me. She said earlier the only reason she didn't let me die is because she didn't want to take another girl.

I remember farther back. The arguments she and Theo were getting into. She wanted to stop trying to have a baby. Theo didn't. They were never talking about conceiving their own child. They were talking about this. Astrid wanted to stop. She wanted out.

That's something I can work with. A spark of hope ignites in my gut. But why should I get out of this when I'm the reason Holly will never see freedom? All the people I have wronged in my life. It's a long list. I don't deserve to go free. What's happening is the consequences for everything I've done.

I list names in my head. Everyone I've ever been cruel to. Stolen from. Plotted against. My parents, my sisters, Ethan, Donna, Jackson, Tessa, Astrid, Corrie. I finally doze off when I go back to elementary school and start listing the names of kids I was mean to.

# CHAPTER THIRTY-TWO

*"I am out with lanterns looking for myself." — Emily Dickinson*

I could barely sleep last night and instead spent the time pacing the apartment. Maybe I deserve this for the things I've done, but maybe I can get a second chance. I can be a different person if I get out of here. And most importantly, I can find Holly's children. I made her a promise. I've already let her die. I can't sit back and give up, leaving her children to the monsters that took them. The monsters that created them. They should know about their mother.

I have to convince Astrid to let me go. It's my best chance. She wanted out. She didn't want to keep doing this. And she already tried to give me a way out. This woman. The woman I lied to, manipulated, scammed, stole from, is my only shot. My only chance is making her realize that this isn't the life she wants. And that Theo is keeping her in it.

But what if that was the only time Astrid came down here? What if Theo returns from now on? What if neither of them comes for weeks? My stomach is in knots as I watch the door, willing Astrid to walk through it. When I can't take the anticipation any longer, I force myself to the bathroom.

I absolutely reek, and I really don't know if my hair can be salvaged. I fill the tub with hot water and gently lower myself into it. Careful not to get my head bandages wet, I wash the best I can.

I'm tipping my head back at an awful angle, trying to get the soapy strands into the water without soaking my bandage when I catch sight of a figure in the doorway.

I scream and slide back, knocking my head against the wall of the shower. My eyes close against my will as pain shoots through my skull.

"Careful," says Astrid. "You're going to knock open the wound again. Here. Let me help."

I peel my eyes open to watch her lower herself onto the ground next to the tub. "It's fine. I got it," I say, trying to cover my body with my arms.

"Oh relax. But I do have my gun, so don't get any stupid ideas. Now lean back. Lay your head in my hand."

I do as she says, reminding myself that she doesn't want me dead and probably won't push my head under the water. It's an oddly tender and intimate moment, letting her cradle my broken head and wash my hair. I watch her face as she focuses on my head. I could be seeing what I want to see. I have a habit of that, but she looks sad.

I wonder if she misses having a friend. Even a bad one like me. She pulls me forward, allowing me to sit up. "All done," she says. "I'll wait for you out there."

Without a change of clothes, I wrap a towel around my body and go to the dining room.

"Where are your clothes?" she says.

"All the clothes are in the bedroom. I don't want to go in there. I don't want to wear dead girls' clothes."

Almost imperceptibly, Astrid flinches. "I'll bring you clothes."

I nod, tears blurring my vision. "Thanks."

She clears her throat and pushes the bottles of vitamins toward me. "Take these, please."

I unscrew each lid and swallow them, looking into her eyes and trying to see how I could have missed the monster in her. How I could have been so foolish as to think that I was the predator in this relationship.

She is less angry and combative than she was yesterday. Maybe I should plead with her. Beg her to let me go. But maybe that will pull her defenses back up and cause me to lose any possibility in the future to get through to her. It's hard to know.

"Did you get your Paris show?" I ask hesitantly.

Her eyes lock with mine for just a second before she looks away. "I did."

"How did it go?"

"It sold out," she says. I can hear the pride she tries to hide.

I smile widely. "I knew it would. Congratulations."

"Thank you." A small smile traces her lips as she looks down at the vitamin bottles.

"When is your next show?" I ask when Astrid makes no move to leave, even though I've taken the pills already.

"I'm going to have another here in my gallery. The artist from Nigeria that I've been trying to work with for years finally responded to my requests and he's going to feature three pieces in a February show."

"That's incredible," I say.

She nods. "Thank you."

We sit in silence, awkward and loaded with things each of us is too afraid to say.

"I have to go," she says, getting to her feet.

I stand too.

"I'll bring you some clothes later today."

"Okay. Thanks." I shift uncomfortably, unsure what to do or what I'll do with my day when she's gone.

I find myself searching for something to say so that she'll stay a little longer. I don't want to be alone. She looks like she wants to say something too, but she doesn't. She moves to the door and lets herself out.

The loneliness is instant, and it is crushing. Trying to distract myself, I attempt to brush out my hair. I have to remove the bandages from around my head, and after a few minutes of painful tugging on the tangled mess with the brush, I feel warm liquid trickle down my neck.

The sensation sends icy panic through my limbs, and I scramble to the bathroom to press a towel to my head and wait for the bleeding to stop. When it finally does, I maneuver the bandage back into place.

I have nothing to fill the time. The television was moved back into the bedroom, and I won't go back in there. There are no books. Nothing.

I long to write. The desire is like an ache in my bones. All afternoon, ideas and lines of a potential story have been filling my thoughts. I consider using the crayon and notebook meant for tracking my cycle, vitamins, and exercise, but decide against it. I don't want to make Astrid or Theo angry and risk giving them a reason to let me die down here.

Maybe I can ask Astrid for another notebook to write in. It's a good idea, I think. How she responds will tell me how she's feeling toward me. If there truly is any warmth toward me left in her.

* * *

Astrid enters the room with a shopping bag. She's breathless with pink cheeks, and I can feel the cold air that still clings to her coat.

"I got you something," she says.

"Yeah?"

She pulls things out of the bag. Clothes. She lays them out on the table one by one. Soft cashmere, jeans, silk pajamas. I run my fingers across the fabric, afraid I'm dreaming. "You got these for me?"

She nods. "Do you like them?"

"I love them." I smile, still in disbelief. "Thank you, Astrid."

"You're welcome."

Something like guilt rises in my gut and my smile slips from my lips. I let my hand fall from the fabric. Astrid watches me with a curious expression, but she says nothing.

"I know I'm in no position to ask for anything," I say. She looks at me, eyebrow arched. "But I was wondering . . . if I could have a notebook and a pencil or something to write with."

I don't meet her eyes. I'm afraid to see a look of cruel amusement or disgusted disbelief.

"I know you've already given me so much with the clothes, and I really am so grateful," I rush to say, not wanting her to think I'm being unappreciative.

"I'll think about it," she says simply. I look up.

"Really?"

"I didn't say 'yes.' I'll think about it."

I nod. "Okay. Thank you. For considering it, I mean."

She gathers herself, ready to leave once again. But she stops, staring at the closed bedroom door.

"You'll need to go back to the bedroom at some point, Olive."

My eyes fall to my feet.

"I can do what I can to make it easier. I can remove the old clothes. Change out the bedding. Make it look different within reason. But you'll have to go back, eventually."

"Okay," I say, the word sounding coarse.

She nods once more and leaves me again. When she's gone, I try on the clothes. The feel of the fabric on my skin is an odd sensation. Its luxury is so at odds with everything else. I want to enjoy it. The way I would have before. But I can't. It feels wrong, and nauseating, and like a betrayal to Holly somehow.

But I can't stay in a towel forever, so I change into a loungewear set and simmer in the self-hatred. I wonder if Astrid will actually bring me a notebook. She didn't shut me down, which is a good sign. The clothes are a good sign too.

I've seen the clothes the other girls have been provided over the years. Old, worn, and stained. I know these gifts must reflect at least a small favor over them. It doesn't make me feel good. Just hopeful that I might be able to reason with her.

# CHAPTER THIRTY-THREE

*"Illusion is the first of all pleasures." — Voltaire*

The sound of the door wakes me. I sit up too quickly, and my vision darkens. Each time the door opens, I am afraid Theo will step through. But it's Astrid. And then, to my surprise, two men follow her, carrying bags, mattresses, and a number of other things my brain can't quite comprehend through the fear and the innate reflex to escape, to get help.

"Don't," Astrid warns. "They work for us. They can't help you."

I deflate back into the couch, still unable to take my wide eyes off the large men carrying things in and out of the bedroom. Astrid sits beside me.

"How?" I whisper.

"Money will get you anything you need," she says simply.

The men move efficiently, carrying things from the bedroom and from the basement prison. The door opens wider when they carry the old mattresses out and I see another man standing guard just within the stairway.

When they're done redoing the bedroom, the men leave. Astrid hangs behind for a moment, staring past me like she's somewhere else. "You'll have to sleep in the bedroom again."

"Okay." I'm in a daze and I can't quite bring myself back to the present.

Astrid leaves, and when the lock clicks into place, I wander toward the bedroom, still in a haze. She kept her word. It looks nothing like before. The furniture is even rearranged to give it the feel of a completely different room. I still don't like the idea of sleeping in here, but I don't like the idea of any of this. And I don't have a choice.

When the time comes to sleep in the room, I do my best to pretend I'm somewhere else, but every time I close my eyes, my mind rearranges the room back to what it was. In the blackness of my mind, I see Holly lying in her bed. Too stiff to be sleeping.

At some point, I doze off and wake up to the sound of a drill. I shoot out of bed and creep to the door to look out, but the door is locked. I sit on the edge of the bed and wait until I'm allowed out.

When the door clicks, I stand quickly and walk out into the main living area. In the corner, a typewriter sits on a desk. I look over at Astrid, who is standing by the table, my eyes wide in disbelief.

"The desk and the typewriter are bolted down. There are several reams of paper in the drawer."

"Thank you," I say, my eyes blurring with tears. I move toward her without thinking, my arms extending to hug her. She steps back and I stop. "I'm sorry." I shake my head at my stupidness. "Thank you."

"You're welcome. This doesn't have to be torturous. I've shown you kindness and good faith. Please don't make me regret it."

I shake my head. "I won't."

She nods, grinning. "Do you like it?"

"I love it," I say as I run my fingers along the keys.

"Good. It wasn't as easy to find as you'd think."

She sits at the dining room table, and I follow, sitting across from her. The handgun she is usually sporting is missing.

She slides the bottles of vitamins across to me.

"What are you planning to write?" she asks.

"I'm not entirely sure yet. I've been getting story ideas."

"So, the writing wasn't a lie?" Her eyes bore into mine. It's a very strange dynamic we have. Both having lied and betrayed each other.

I decide to be honest. Because what do I have to lose? "I lied about the publisher. About finishing my book. But I am a writer."

"Fair enough," she says.

I swallow my last vitamin. "Have fun writing today," she says. She leaves, and I approach the typewriter with awe and excitement. I've always wanted to write on a typewriter. But the one I found in a thrift store was broken, and the ones online were always too expensive, and I couldn't justify it when I had a perfectly good laptop to write on.

I spend the afternoon typing. Just a stream of consciousness, brainstorming a story idea. When I finally break to use the bathroom, I realize several hours have passed. I heat my food and scarf it down. I have to eat dinner in an hour and have only just now eaten my lunch. I hope they don't notice I've accidentally gone off my eating schedule.

I do my exercises, eat my dinner, though my stomach is so full it feels like it might explode, and then I go back to the typewriter.

When my eyes feel heavy, I change and go to bed. I stare at the ceiling, thinking. Plotting.

The story is all I can think about. I spend hours thinking about what I'll write tomorrow before I finally fall asleep. It distracts me from my reality in just the way I thought it would.

## CHAPTER THIRTY-FOUR

*"We are rarely proud when we are alone."* — *Voltaire*

I write about a lonely girl. A girl with no friends, no family. A girl who cannot seem to find her place in the world. A girl who wants so desperately to belong, she does the only thing she can think of to achieve it. She mimics someone else's life that looks like the one she might want. She becomes obsessed with the idea of inhabiting this life of friends, family, purpose, and wealth. But she becomes trapped by the very people she strove to be like. She is forced into solitude, alone again. Forced to sit with her thoughts, her regrets, her insecurities. With nothing else to do, she dissects her life. Her choices. Her mind. When she finally comes to terms with herself and her failures and shortcomings, she's able to see the world as it is, instead of through the skewed lens of an envious and prideful girl. And only then is she able to concoct a plan of escape.

I write my story. And by writing my story, I'm able to see how the story will end. I'm able to see the things I missed. My flaws and shortcomings. But more importantly, I'm able to see Astrid's and Theo's weaknesses.

The door clinks, and I jump, spinning to watch her step through.

"Can you give me a hand with these?" she asks, her attention on the bags in her hands. "I got you something . . . some things . . . but they're really freaking heavy. I need to stop skipping yoga."

I rush over and grab a few bags from her. "What on earth did you get?" I peek inside the bags as I carry them over to the table.

"Books! Lots of books."

I smile, feeling grateful and sick all at once. I take a few from one of the bags. "Wow. You did a great job picking them out. My favorites, and some I've been wanting to read."

She smiles a closed-mouth, telling smile. I know what she's going to say before she says it. "I had Theo write a list of books he'd think you'd like."

I try not to react, studying the book covers.

"How's the writing going?" Astrid asks, quickly changing the subject.

"Really good. I can't even tell you how good it's been for my mental health," I say with a laugh.

It feels strange, pretending like this is a normal situation. We both dance around it, somehow. I'm nervous about causing an upset to our dynamic. We've come a long way from that first reunion only a week ago. But it has to be done.

I've written the end of my story. It's twisted and sick, and now it has to be put into motion.

The speed with which she has warmed to me tells me she feels guilty for what she's doing. Not to mention all the other signs she's given me that she doesn't want to do this.

She married Theo in college because she was pregnant. She was brought into this sick family business. And while she's sick enough to have gone along with it, I'm more confident now that she is the chink in the armor.

"I didn't want to ask, but I can't stop thinking about it," I say. Astrid faces me, a curious expression. "My fertile window starts today. Should I be expecting Theo down here soon?"

Her face pinches, but I can't place the emotion. "Yes. He's out of town today, but he will be home tomorrow."

I nod. "Oh, okay."

She's quiet. I've shattered our fragile illusion.

My vision blurs with building tears, and before I can stop them, they're streaming down my face. I look up at Astrid, hoping my expression conveys everything I'm feeling. Her face pulls down, a mixture of sadness and guilt.

"Astrid, please let me go," I say through my ever-constricting throat.

"I can't." The words are a whisper. An apology.

I nod. "You can. You can let me out. Let me go."

She shakes her head. "Theo would kill me. And he'd just find you again. And . . ." She trails off.

"And what?"

She bites her lip, not wanting to say it, but after a moment, she does. "We need you."

I want to scream, but I fight the urge. She's my only hope. My only hope. "You're selling them, right? The babies."

She flinches. And it angers me in a way I can't control. "Don't shy away from the reality of what you're doing. You are kidnapping women. Raping them. Stealing their babies and selling them." My gums ache with the force of my jaw clenching.

Astrid wipes at her eyes but stands up a little taller. "Yeah. Yes. That's what we're doing. I know it's wrong. I know it makes me disgusting and monstrous. But you don't understand the whole story. We didn't just wake up one day and say 'Hey, babe. You feel like maybe storing some women in our basement, getting them pregnant, and selling babies on the black market?' It didn't go like that, Olive."

"It doesn't matter how it went. You're doing it," I say, my voice returning to a normal volume.

"Only a little while longer."

"You know that's a lie," I say as Astrid shakes her head. "It's a lie, Astrid. You know it's a lie. He already lied about it once."

"No. He didn't lie. He wanted to quit too. But we can't yet. Theo says if we can ramp up our sales for the next few years, then we can get out after that."

My stomach turns. The way she uses 'sales' like she's talking about selling cars instead of babies. I'm also struck by the implication that if they're getting 'out' in a few years, then I only have a few years left to live if I don't get out of here.

"How are you going to 'ramp up your sales' with only me?" I ask, the beginning of understanding taking place.

Astrid is quiet, and I have to press her. "Astrid?"

"You might have a roommate soon," she says finally.

A lump forms in my throat. She won't meet my eyes. "I thought you didn't want to take another girl," I say softly, trying to keep any trace of accusation or judgment from my voice. I see her tear up.

"You cannot tell me you guys are hurting for money this badly. I've seen the pieces you sell through your gallery. I looked at the prices on your website. And you're booking more and more shows."

She laughs bitterly. "The website? You really are a lousy stalker, Olive."

I don't know what that is supposed to mean.

She tilts her head. "Did you bother to look up any of the artists? The pieces? See why they are so expensive?"

"I couldn't find anything on a lot of them. Not everyone puts their life online."

"These people sell their art to make a living. You'd be able to find something," she snaps.

I'm not sure why she's gotten so agitated all of a sudden. I wait for her to continue, unsure how to do so myself.

"That's how they find us. The people who buy the babies. They're paying for a child, not an oil painting."

I wince and shake my head. "I thought . . ." I trail off because it doesn't matter what I thought.

"You think selling art and a salary from a state university could afford all of what we have? The house. The clothes. The cars. The furniture. The art. The vacations."

"Theo's family. His family money. I thought that's why you have so much money."

"It is." Her face twists into disgust and anger. "Welcome to the Connor family business."

I stop breathing.

"So do you see how it's a little more complicated than you're making it?"

"It doesn't have to be complicated for you. You know this is wrong. You don't have to take part in it." I swallow thick saliva pooling in my mouth, afraid to say the next part. "You can leave him, Astrid. You can turn them in."

Her eyebrows knit together. "I love him, Olive. He's my soulmate."

"Astrid . . . at what cost? What you're doing . . . it's evil."

She stares past me, eyes unfocused. Then she turns and heads for the door.

"Astrid, wait!"

She stops.

"You're selling your soul for a man you love. But he doesn't love you the same way."

"What the hell are you talking about? Theo loves me."

"Then why did he sleep with me on the beach?" I ask, my tone compassionate and careful.

Her eyes well up again. "He said you were lying. Trying to turn me against him to save yourself."

I shake my head slowly. "We had sex. Down on the beach. The night before you left. I initiated it. I stripped down and walked into the water. But he followed me in. And carried me out . . ." I don't say the rest. She knows the rest. In her heart, she knows. "The next day, he said you left because he'd told you about us. He said we could be together now. We slept together again that morning. We spent the day holding hands and kissing, Astrid."

"Watch the cameras," I say when she moves for the door again. "Watch the cameras on the day he comes down here."

## CHAPTER THIRTY-FIVE

*"We are more often frightened than hurt; and we suffer more from imagination than from reality." — Seneca*

It's just after two in the afternoon when Theo comes through the door. Seeing him again is surreal. From a distance, you can't see any sign of the fight a few weeks ago. But as he approaches me, I see a small red scar on the side of his face. Likely from a set of fingernails.

"Miss me?" he says.

"Oddly enough, I did."

He smirks like he doesn't believe me. Holly told me how it would go. How he'd strap me to the bed before going to the bathroom. How he'd sit in the room for thirty minutes after the insemination before untying me and leaving.

But that's not how it will go today.

I've seduced Theo before. I know I can do it again. Well, I hope I can.

"Go to the bedroom," he says.

I stand from the couch and walk to the bedroom. Astrid's little shopping spree provided me with the thin white nightgown I'm wearing that barely covers anything. I lie on the bed. As he moves to tie my leg, I arch my back and peel the nightgown over my head. He pulls the knot tight, then stops, eyes raking over my body.

For a long moment, nothing happens. I replay the words he spat at me the first day he brought me here. *Nothing about you is desirable.* Maybe I'm being stupid. This will not work. I am an idiot, and I've probably ruined any chance I had of getting free.

But then I watch as he unbuckles his pants. I fight back the nauseous feeling and try my best to look into this. To look seductive. He pulls his phone from his pocket and taps at the screen a few times. He sets it face-down on the dresser before continuing to undress.

I want to say something to coax him further, but I'm afraid any sound will end the spell he's under and he'll get a hold of himself and stop. And I need him to keep going. I need Astrid to see the man she loves enough to sell her soul for does not love her. Only himself.

Thoughts are flying through my mind a million miles per minute. Theo climbs onto the bed, holding himself over me. I rise up to kiss his shoulder. When he doesn't stop me, I move to his neck.

Theo grabs at me. His mouth finds my ear. "I turned off the camera so we can be alone," he says as he nibbles my earlobe.

I try not to panic. I have to assume that Astrid has the same control of the cameras. If he turned it off from his phone, Astrid should be able to turn it back on. I told her to watch the cameras, and I know she will. She's too uncertain not to.

Neither of us hear her come into the room.

"I hate you!" Astrid screams from the doorway. A visceral scream.

Theo flies off me like I've just emitted a thousand volts of electricity. And I feel like I could in this moment. I scoot myself up to the top of the bed against the wall.

Theo grabs the blanket from the bed to cover himself, and I am left exposed. I search half-heartedly for the nightgown I discarded, but my attention is on Astrid.

She stands rigid, face wet with tears and red from either crying or her anger or both. She points a pistol, the one she used to keep me in line for days, right at Theo.

"Baby. Put the gun down. What are you doing?" His words are calm and even.

"What am I doing? What are you doing?" she says, near hysterics.

"I'm doing what we have to do, baby."

"This isn't how you're supposed to do it!" She jabs the gun at him, and he flinches. "Why are you doing this?" Astrid's voice is so filled with pain that I want to cry. But then I remind myself that I'm tied to a bed, and she helped put me here.

"I tried to do it the right way, and it just wasn't working. I had to do what needed to be done. I need you to put the gun down and be rational."

Astrid's eyes go wide. "Rational?"

"She's been filling your head with lies, Astrid. I told you not to come down here every day. She's a manipulator. She's turned you against me. You can see that, can't you?"

She looks at me. I say nothing. She knows the truth.

Theo continues his pleas as he steps around the side of the bed and toward Astrid. "She lied and manipulated her way into your life with the goal of taking everything away from you. You can't believe anything she says."

I watch as Astrid turns the gun toward me.

It feels like a good time to break my silence. "I don't have to say anything. Astrid, you're not blind. Use your own eyes."

Theo jumps in. "She's not tied down. I wasn't forcing myself on her. This is just another one of her manipulations. I'm ashamed to admit that I'm not immune to her lies either."

My mouth hangs open in bewilderment. I raise my left leg as far as I can to indicate that I am *kind of* tied down. "You know the truth, Astrid. I told you to watch the cameras. You know he's lying to you. He's the manipulator. He doesn't love you, Astrid. Not like you love him."

Her knees buckle, and she slinks to the ground in a mess of sobs.

No, no, no, no. Get up!

Theo moves toward her. It's over. It's all over. I lost my chance.

Astrid sits up, and as Theo reaches her, she fires. We all jump. But then Theo falls. The room feels like it's spinning, and I sit motionless in shock as Astrid screams. She crawls to Theo, and they disappear behind the foot of the bed. I bend forward to untie my ankle, and scoot off the side of the bed hesitantly. My ears are ringing, but I can still hear Astrid's screams.

Theo lies on his back, bleeding from his chest. It's less blood than I imagined would come from a shot to the chest. Astrid is by his side, her face pressed to him. Theo is grasping his chest in one hand, and his other cups Astrid's head.

I climb back over the bed, not wanting to walk past them. I pull on a pair of sweatpants I left in the corner of the room. Theo is lying in front of the dresser. Blocking his discarded jeans that hold the keys to the door and his cell phone. The gun is behind Astrid. I have to move for something. I can't keep wasting time.

I take a step. Theo coughs.

"Don't let her get away," he says, breathless.

Astrid turns toward me, and I freeze, eyes wide. Theo's bloody handprint contrasts against her pale face.

"His cell phone is on the dresser. The keys should be in his front jeans pocket. Call an ambulance before you leave. Please."

I nod. And then move so fast that I keep fumbling with the pocket. My hands shake with adrenaline and fear. Like if I'm not fast enough, she will change her mind, or Theo will summon the strength to get up and stop me himself.

My fingers slide against the metal of a key in his pocket, and I grab it. I snatch the phone from the dresser and run to the door. As it clicks open, I remember the last time I walked through this door. I remember Holly and how I basically left her for dead. I start to run through the door but stop.

I run back to the table with the bolted down typewriter and grab my manuscripts from the drawer. Then I run up the stairs and let myself out the top door.

The house is quiet and dark. I walk farther into the house as I tap on Theo's cell phone screen. It's locked, but I hit the button for an emergency call. I give the police the address I memorized, thinking one day it would be my own. I tell them to send the police. That my name is Olive Tate and I've been kidnapped. I tell them to send an ambulance because a man has been shot. They ask me to stay on the phone, but I end the call.

Something . . . some feeling, sends me back down the stairs to the prison I just escaped. I descend the stairs, and the hair on my arms rises in the pure silence. I push through the fear because there is no time to waste. Astrid sits with her back against the dresser, Theo's lifeless hand gripped in hers. She stares blankly at the wall across from her.

I hurry to her side and drop next to her. She doesn't move or acknowledge me. I take her free hand in mine. She blinks.

"Astrid. The police are on their way."

"He's dead," she says. Her voice is like gravel.

"I know." I gently turn her head to look at me. "Astrid. The police are on their way. You need to leave. Take whatever money you can get, take the plane and leave. You can still get away. You can start over."

She turns her head, staring at the wall once again.

"Astrid!" I raise my voice. Urgency making me anxious. I don't know why I suddenly feel the pressing need to get Astrid out of here. She is guilty. Just as guilty as Theo. But this has ended so many lives already. The girls that came before. Holly. Theo.

Theo is dead. Someone has paid for these terrible sins.

"You have to go." I pull her arm, but she yanks her hand away from me.

"I'm not leaving him."

"You have to leave him." A sob escapes my mouth. "Please, Astrid. They'll arrest you."

"I have to pay for what I've done. It's only right."

"Theo paid. The price has been paid. Just go."

"His family," she says, and I understand. "You should go." She looks at me once again. "I'm sorry, Olive. I'm so sorry."

I sit back beside her, leaning my head against her shoulder. "I'm sorry, too."

# CHAPTER THIRTY-SIX

*"In everybody's life there are hidden chapters which they hope may never be known." — Agatha Christie*

Astrid hasn't spoken a word since she was arrested in her and Theo's basement four weeks ago. I've begged the police to let me talk to her, but they've refused until now. A detective called my phone an hour ago and asked me to come to Heinz Psychiatric Hospital. And now I sit, waiting, in the lobby on the second floor.

"Ms. Tate?" A tall man stands at the edge of the waiting area. "You can come with me."

I stand and walk toward him. "Before you talk to Mrs. Connor, we need to speak with you."

I spent days in the hospital for no real reason other than the police wanted to keep questioning me, and they did it under the guise of wanting to keep me for observation. But the truth is, any wounds I'd received had already been treated and were mostly healed. I was well fed, hydrated, and exercised regularly. I was healthier than I'd ever been.

I told them everything I knew. I told them about Theo's family being involved and how they've been doing this a long time.

The details of the case have been held closely under wraps. The press has been told a slightly different story. That the woman they were holding against her will attacked both Astrid and Theo, killing them both. And that the woman succumbed to her wounds before the ambulance reached the house.

The story is being temporarily altered as they work to arrest the Connor family. They think it will keep them from going into hiding and trying to keep Astrid and me quiet. I've been staying in a safe house, waiting for Astrid to talk so that I can be released.

"We're trying to learn the names of the women they took before. And what's been done with their bodies. We'd also like to know how many children were born and sold. To whom. How. And who else is involved. Anything you can get her to tell you would be a great help."

I nod. "I'll do what I can." I try to hide my frustration. This is what I've been wanting to ask her, but they refused to let me. I made a promise to Holly. To my friend. I need to find her children.

Astrid sits tall in her chair when I walk in. Her eyes meet mine and she smiles. A happy and surprised look on her face.

"Hi there, babe," I say. She's dressed in a gray sweater and sweatpants. Her hair is flat, and her skin is dull. "You look like shit."

She laughs. "Gray never was my color." Her voice is hoarse from the disuse.

I sit down across from her, getting straight to the point. "You have to talk, Astrid. It's why you stayed."

She takes a deep breath. "I know."

"Then why haven't you?"

"I don't know," she says. "I want to help. I want to do whatever I can to make any bit of this better. But every time they ask me, I freeze." Her eyes go watery.

"Tell me. Just talk with me."

She nods, taking a shaking breath.

"Holly's children," I say. "A boy and a girl. Where are they?" I'll ask the other questions the police want to know. I'll ask everything. But I need to know this first.

"Theo has a computer. It has everything. The names of every woman. Every child born. The details of the . . . of the sale."

"The police went through every computer at the house. They didn't find anything."

She shakes her head. "It's in a compartment in the stairway. Between the steel doors. The back of the top step pulls out."

I swallow hard and nod, knowing the police will be on their way there.

"But, Olive . . . The children are sold to all kinds of people. We — we don't know what happens to them once they're gone."

My stomach rolls. "Okay."

"Where are the bodies of the girls?" I ask.

Astrid hangs her head, crying openly now. I give her a minute to collect herself. Eventually, she picks her head up. "They were all cremated."

My heart sinks. No remains for their families to bury.

"They're in the vases," she says, her voice so quiet I almost don't hear her.

"What?"

"They're in the vases. In Theo's study."

It takes all my strength to hold the rising vomit from coming out as I remember the decorative vases on the shelves in his study. The ones he brought back from his travels. The ones I touched.

* * *

There is a sea of people standing in front of me. All eyes glued to me. My heart pounds, but I stand tall. I spin the bottom of my hair between my fingers. My publicist begged me to dye it dark. He said I needed to separate myself from Astrid. Look as different from her as possible. But I couldn't do it.

I decided to also keep my name as Olive. It's difficult to articulate why, though I've tried my best to do just that. To explain that I was reborn in the basement of the man I thought I loved and a woman I tried to take everything from. I could never be Laura again. And while I hate who I became when I took on my new persona, I have to live with that. I can't let myself forget how far I was willing to fall.

Plus, changing my name a second time would be a bit overkill.

I stare down at the podium, my book lying on the wooden surface. Husband Theft and Black-Market Babies: A Memoir. The title is horrid and makes light of a disgusting thing, but I like it. Because it's the way I'm learning to deal with the not-so-great things in my life. Humor instead of envy so intense it rots my insides.

A woman in the center of the crowd raises her hand. A boy with pockmarked cheeks squeezes through the crowd to hand her the microphone.

"Was it hard to cast yourself in such a negative light and let the world read it? Did you ever want to make yourself more of the traditional victim and hero?"

"I'd spent my life believing I was a victim and a hero. Both without cause. It was hard to write the truth, sure. Being so honest with oneself is always hard. Especially if you've been as wicked as I have been. But it felt like I was setting myself free. Telling the truth was like shedding that skin. It allowed me to change. To grow."

Another hand goes up, and I wait for the microphone to get to them. "How many of the children have they found? Are they still looking for them?"

Sadness and joy battle in my chest. "They've found nearly all of them. And yes, the authorities are still searching for the few that remain."

The computer that Astrid told me about kept a record of every woman they held captive and every child they birthed.

Up until Holly, that is. Holly is listed in the records, but her children are not. The police argued that maybe she didn't actually have any. That she made them up. But I know it isn't true.

It's the one thing Astrid refuses to speak about. She won't tell me who took Holly's babies. But she helped the police to arrest several of Theo's family members and the guards that helped them. She signed over any right to contest the custody of the children. It was an unusual situation, since they are all Theo's children. Astrid is still in the mental hospital, and it's where she will serve her twenty-five-to-life sentence. Money talks.

And speaking of money, Astrid liquidated everything she and Theo owned. She paid sizable sums to each of the women's families. And a large sum to me. I considered not taking it. It was something I felt like I should have wanted to turn down. But none of the other families turned the money down, and so I accepted it as well. I used it to pay off my debts and buy a house in Monticello, near my family. I put the rest in investment funds, and now I'm able to live off the dividends and spend my time writing my books.

Nearly everything has been put right. As right as something such as this can be put, anyway. But my promise to Holly still rings in my ears.

I step down from the podium, grateful to be done with this event. I spot Logan in the back and smile, making my way to him. But as I'm almost through the crowd of people, I see a familiar face about to exit the bookstore. Tessa.

I hold up a finger, signaling Logan to wait a minute, and run after Tessa's retreating form. I'd been hoping she would show. I pull an envelope from my jacket and grab her arm.

"Tessa. Hey, wait."

She spins, pulling her arm away from me, then looking apologetic for the reflex. "Sorry. I . . . oh, God. I came to say sorry. For the things I said about you. For what Astrid and Theo did. We had no idea."

"It's okay," I say, interrupting her flustered words. "You couldn't have known about them. And you were right about me. You were being a good friend."

Neil approaches from behind Tessa, holding their young daughter, Leah. I hand Tessa the envelope and hug her quickly before she can push me away. When I let her go and step back, I see her eyes are shiny with tears. They look like glass, an almost clear blue.

"Ice cream, Dada?" Leah says shyly.

I smile at the small girl. She's looking at me, lips turning up in a bashful grin, and I am struck with an overwhelming sense of familiarity. I've seen Leah before, but never paid her close attention. But there is something about her eyes. The shade of brown like the trunks of trees.

I look at Neil. At his eyes. Blue as the cloudless sky overhead.

Tearing my eyes from the girl, I jog back over to Logan. My heart exploding behind my ribcage, I glance back to watch Tessa open the envelope. Inside she will find $1,107. She probably still has no idea that I'd taken it from her. It's the least of what I took from her. She also does not know that I burned her house to the ground.

I couldn't be that honest in my memoir.

Logan takes my hand and leads me to his car. "Ready?"

"As ready as I'll ever be," I say. "You fed Pascal before you left, right?" Another part of my story I didn't admit to in my memoir.

"Duh," he says, squeezing my hand.

"Just a second." I pull my phone from my pocket. I pull up Tessa's Instagram and zoom in on a picture of her family. The two young children, less than a year apart. The boy has the same eyes as the little girl. The same eyes as their mother.

I screenshot the picture and send it to the detective on the Connor case. My phone lights up almost immediately, and I answer it, my heart in my throat.

"The last two kids. Holly's babies. That's them. Tessa and Neil Sigurdsson have them. It's why Astrid won't tell us. Tessa is her best friend." The words come out rushed, and the detective asks me to slow down. I can feel Logan's worried stare on the side of my face.

The detective hangs up with a promise to secure the children and perform DNA tests. I understand the legal need for the tests, but it is unnecessary for my own knowledge. And I understand why Astrid wouldn't tell me or the police about them. Holly is gone. And she had no family left. There will be no one to take the children home, so why not let them stay with the people they know to be their parents?

The idea tugs at my conscience. At my skewed idea of right and wrong. But I know Holly wouldn't want her babies to grow up with people like them. People who would buy children through sketchy sources. People who probably knew, at least a little bit, that something wrong was taking place.

Logan drives us toward Wolcott. We're having dinner with my family tonight, and I'm a ball of nerves. I try to focus on what is ahead of me and trust the police to do their job. I've seen my family only once since I got out of the basement. I was apologetic for the way I had been. My sisters were skeptical, but my parents were tearful and happy I'd survived the ordeal.

I have a lot of amends to make. It's not exactly the life I'd wanted badly enough to lie, cheat, and steal for. It's better. I've removed myself from the people I feel so desperate to be like. I try to stay in my own lane now. And be grateful I didn't end up like every other woman who was dragged down to that basement prison.

**THE END**

## ACKNOWLEDGMENTS

This trope, the 'I want her life' trope, is one of my favorites to read. And it was so much fun to write. I am *thrilled* (pun intended) to have a book of my own in this niche sub-genre. I hope you had just as much fun reading it as I did writing it.

Let's get to the 'thank yous.'

First and foremost, thank you to YOU. Thank you for taking a chance on my book. For spending your valuable time and money on reading this story. It honestly means the world to me. I don't think I'll ever get used to this. To my words and stories being read by people all over the world. This is my dream come true, and it wouldn't be if it wasn't for you. From the bottom of my heart, *thank you.*

Thank you to my friends and family who continue to support me and make me feel like a rock star for making up stories for a living. Thank you for trying not to judge me for the messed-up stuff in my brain. I love you all.

A special thank-you to Venissa Ivasiecko and Kelli Patrick. The best book club in the entire world. (Yes, it's a club. We have shirts. It's official.) I will be forever grateful that we all showed up to that bizarre book club meeting because it brought us together and introduced me to two of the best people I know. Thank you for hyping me up and making me feel like I know what I'm doing. Thank you for reading this story and helping me to make it better. Thank you for all the Mighty Mick's chats about books and life. I am so grateful for your friendship.

Last, but never least. Thank you to my incredible husband, Ryan. For making me feel like I could achieve this crazy dream. For every long talk about stories and what makes them good. For all the work you do to support us. For all the extra work you do to help me with my books. For being the best dad and partner I ever could have dreamed of. I love you.

# THE JOFFE BOOKS STORY

We began in 2014 when Jasper agreed to publish his mum's much-rejected romance novel and it became a bestseller.

Since then we've grown into the largest independent publisher in the UK. We're extremely proud to publish some of the very best writers in the world, including Joy Ellis, Faith Martin, Caro Ramsay, Helen Forrester, Simon Brett and Robert Goddard. Everyone at Joffe Books loves reading and we never forget that it all begins with the magic of an author telling a story.

We are proud to publish talented first-time authors, as well as established writers whose books we love introducing to a new generation of readers.

We won Trade Publisher of the Year at the Independent Publishing Awards in 2023 and Best Publisher Award in 2024 at the People's Book Prize. We have been shortlisted for Independent Publisher of the Year at the British Book Awards for the last five years, and were shortlisted for the Diversity and Inclusivity Award at the 2022 Independent Publishing Awards. In 2023 we were shortlisted for Publisher of the Year at the RNA Industry Awards, and in 2024 we were shortlisted at the CWA Daggers for the Best Crime and Mystery Publisher.

We built this company with your help, and we love to hear from you, so please email us about absolutely anything bookish at feedback@joffebooks.com.

If you want to receive free books every Friday and hear about all our new releases, join our mailing list here: www.joffebooks.com/freebooks.

And when you tell your friends about us, just remember: it's pronounced Joffe as in coffee or toffee!

Made in United States
Cleveland, OH
29 April 2025

16532118R00152